Emily Virginia Mason

The Southern poems of the war

Emily Virginia Mason

The Southern poems of the war

ISBN/EAN: 9783743303386

Manufactured in Europe, USA, Canada, Australia, Japa

Cover: Foto ©Andreas Hilbeck / pixelio.de

Manufactured and distributed by brebook publishing software
(www.brebook.com)

Emily Virginia Mason

The Southern poems of the war

THE

SOUTHERN

Poems of the War.

Collected and Arranged by

MISS EMILY V. MASON.

BALTIMORE:

JOHN MURPHY & CO., PUBLISHERS,

182 BALTIMORE STREET.

1867.

THESE POEMS,

THE OFFSPRING OF SOUTHERN HEARTS,

SUNG BY SOUTHERN FIRESIDES, AND SOUTHERN CAMP FIRES,

ARE AFFECTIONATELY INSCRIBED

To the Southern Soldiers,

BY ONE WHO ADMIRED THEIR HEROISM, SYMPATHIZED WITH

THEIR SUCCESSES, MOURNED THEIR SUFFERINGS,

AND SHARED THEIR PRIVATIONS.

" No marble slab or graven stone
    Their gallant deeds to tell;
No monument to mark the spot
    Where they with glory fell:
Their names shall yet a herald find
    In every tongue of fame,
When valley, stream, and minstrel voice,
    Shall ring with their acclaim."

PREFACE.

In the beginning of the war I conceived the design of collecting and preserving the various War Poems, which (born of the excited state of the public mind,) then inundated our newspapers. For a time, I carried out this intention, but a very busy life soon obliged me to relinquish it; so that I am indebted to the kindness of friends for most of the later Poems in this collection.

Travelling since the war through many portions of the South, I have heard every where the wish expressed, that these Poems should be collected and published in a form so cheap as to be accessible to all. This desire I have endeavored to fulfil.

Besides a "Memorial" volume, to preserve these "songs," expressive of the hopes and triumphs and sorrows of a "lost cause," I have another design—*to aid by its sale the Education of the Daughters of our desolate land; to fit a certain number for Teachers*, that they may take to their homes and spread amongst the different Southern States the knowledge of those accomplishments which else may be denied them.

I appeal to all good people to aid me in this effort to provide for the women of the South, (the future mothers of the country,) the timely boon of education. Many of these children are the orphans of soldiers, from whom they have inherited nothing but an honorable name, and the last hours of more than one of whom I was enabled to soothe by the promise that I would do something for the little ones they left behind them. That promise, I trust, this humble effort may enable me in part to redeem.

Emily V. Mason.

1*

CONTENTS.

(7)

PAGE

SOUTHERN POEMS OF THE WAR.

—•••—

"THE SOUTHERN CROSS."

BY ST. GEORGE TUCKER, VA.

Oh! say can you see, through the gloom and the storm,
More bright for the darkness, that pure constellation?
Like the symbol of love and redemption its form,
As it points to the haven of hope for the nation.
How radiant each star, as the beacon afar,
Giving promise of peace, or assurance in war!
'Tis the Cross of the South, which shall ever remain
To light us to freedom and glory again!

How peaceful and blest was America's soil
'Till betrayed by the guile of the Puritan demon,
Which lurks under Virtue and springs from its coil
To fasten its fangs in the life-blood of freemen.
Then boldly appeal to each heart that can feel,
And crush the foul viper 'neath Liberty's heel!
And the Cross of the South shall in triumph remain
To light us to freedom and glory again!

'Tis the emblem of peace, 'tis the day-star of hope,
Like the sacred *Labarum* that guided the Roman;
From the shore of the Gulf to the Delaware's slope,
'Tis the trust of the free and the terror of foemen.

2

Fling its folds to the air, while we boldly declare
The rights we demand or the deeds that we dare !
While the Cross of the South shall in triumph remain
To light us to freedom and glory again !

And if peace should be hopeless and justice denied,
And war's bloody vulture should flap its black pinions,
Then gladly to arms ! while we hurl in our pride,
Defiance to tyrants and death to their minions !
With our front in the field, swearing never to yield,
Or return like the Spartan in death on our shield !
And the Cross of the South shall triumphantly wave
As the Flag of the free or the pall of the brave !

ADDRESS TO PRESIDENT DAVIS.

BY MRS. F. K. BLUNT.

In the name of God!—Amen!
  Stand for the Southern rights!
Over ye, Southern men,
  The God of Battles fights!
Fling the invaders far,
  Hurl back their work of woe,
The voice is the voice of a brother,
  But the hand is the hand of the foe.
They come with a trampling army,
  Invading our native sod;
Stand, Southrons! fight and conquer,
  In the name of the mighty God.

They are singing our song of triumph
  Which was made to set us free,
While they are breaking away the heart-strings
  Of our Nation's harmony.
Sadly it floated from us,
  Sighing o'er land and wave,
Till mute in the lips of the poet,
  It sleeps in his silent grave.
Spirit and song departed,
  Minstrel and minstrelsy,
We mourn thee, heavy hearted,
  But we will, we shall be free!

They are waving our flag above us,
  With a despot's tyrant will,
With our blood have they stained our colors,
  And call them holy still.
With tearful eyes, but steady hands,
  We'll tear its stripes apart,
And fling them, like broken fetters,
  That may not bind the heart.
But we'll save our stars of glory
  In the might of the sacred sign,
Of Him who hath freed forever
  Our Southern Cross to shine.

Stand, Southrons! Stand and conquer!
  Solemn, and strong, and sure,
The strife shall not be longer
  Than God shall bid endure.
By the life that only yesterday
  Came with the infant's breath,
By the feet which ere the morn
  May tread the soldier's death,
By the blood which cries to heaven
  Crimson on our sod,
Stand, Southrons! Stand and conquer!
  In the name of the mighty God!

SOUTHERN CHANT OF DEFIANCE.

BY MRS. C. A. WARFIELD, KY.

You can never win them back;
　　Never, never;
Tho' they perish on the track
　　Of your endeavor:
Tho' their curses strew the earth
That smiled upon their birth,
And tho' blood pollute each hearth
　　Stone forever!

They have risen to a man--
　　Stern and fearless.
Of your curses and your ban
　　They are careless.　　.
Every hand is on its knife;
Every gun is primed for strife;
Every palm contains a life—
　　High and peerless!

You have no such blood as theirs,
　　For the shedding:
In the veins of cavaliers
　　Was its heading.
You have no such stately men
In your abolition den,
Marching on through foe and fen,
　　Nothing dreading!

2*

They may fall beneath the fire ·
    Of your legions,
Paid with gold for murderous hire—
    Bought allegiance;
But for every drop you shed,
You shall have a mound of dead,
So that vultures may be fed
    In all your regions.

But the battle to the strong
    Is not given,
While the Judge of right and wrong
    Sits in Heaven!
And the God of David still
Guides the pebble with his will.
There are giants yet to kill—
    Wrongs unshriven!

WRITTEN BEFORE THE SECESSION OF VA.

BY MRS. REBECCA TABB, OF GLOUCESTER, VA.

"It is given unto women to weep; to men to remember."

[*Motley's Dutch Republic.*

Weep! yes, we *will* weep; but not from coward fears,
Poor woman! what has *she* to give her country save her
    tears?
Were we men we would remember the lessons we were
    taught
How our fathers fought for freedom. Was the boon too
    dearly bought?

We'd remember how the glory is passing from our State,
Nor blind our eyes with weeping and wildly mourn her
    fate;
We'd remember how our fathers had won immortal fame,
And prove that *we* were worthy to bear a patriot's
    name.

We'd remember how to battle for our country and her
    right,
Nor veil our heads in darkness, and wail Virginia's
    night;

We'd remember we have children—how can they dare
    forget?
Is it ease that thus beguiles you? You *cannot fear* their
    threat?

Weep, daughters of Virginia! Weep for her old renown,
Weep, that our glorious mother has lost her ancient
    crown;
But e'en amid our tears, *this* we'll remember well,
'Twas the treason of her children by which Virginia fell!

Your mothers and your sisters, your wives and daughters
    weep,
Can you remember, men, how swords from scabbards
    leap?
Have you forgot your *honor* that you meekly bear their
    sneers?
But surely you'll remember *now*, when you see our bitter
    tears.

Alas! that we should weep, save with a woman's pride,
That those we loved had battled for their country ere
    they died.
We'd not forget *them* in their graves, but tell with swell-
    ing heart,
How Virginia's sons could bleed and die, but not with
    honor part.

THE FALL OF FORT SUMTER, APRIL, 1861.

BY A. L. D., RALEIGH, N. C.

'Twas in the early morning, all Charleston lay asleep,
While yet the purple darkness was resting on the deep.
In the middle of the channel Fort Sumter stood afar,
Above it waved the banner which yet bore every star.
Outside the bar, at sunset, seven steamers we could see,
We knew they brought the slaves of slaves who would
    coerce the free.
At midnight came the order, that when the day should
    break,
The guns from out our batteries must then their chal-
    lenge speak.
O, how anxiously we waited for the dawning of the day !
There was little sleeping all that night in the forts of
    Charleston Bay.
All night along the sea-shore, and up the shelving
    strand,
Like the ghosts of our old heroes, did the curling sea-
    mist stand.
They saw their children watching there, as they had
    watched before,
When a British fleet had crossed the bar and threatened
    Charleston shore.
But when the first loud gun announced the dawning of
    the day,
The mists they broke, and lingering, slowly rolled away.
When the first red streak upon the East, told of the
    rising sun,

'Twas then the cannonading from the batteries begun.
All day the cannon thundered along the curving shore,
All day the sea resounded with Sumter's steady roar.
When the land-breeze from the city brought the noon-
    chimes clear and strong,
We saw the starry flag no more, which had floated there
    so long;
For while the fight was raging, we'd seen that banner
    fall,
A round shot cut the staff in twain, and tore it from
    the wall.
But when they raised no other, our General sent them
    one,
For they'd kept the lost one bravely, as true men should
    have done.
The fleet turned slowly southward, we saw the last ship
    go,
We had saved old Carolina from the insults of the foe;
O, we were very thankful when we lay down to rest,
And saw the darkness fall again upon the harbour's
    breast.
For now above Fort Sumter floats a banner yet unknown,
Upon it are but seven stars, where thirty-two had shone.

A CRY TO ARMS.

Ho! woodsmen of the mountain side!
   Ho! dwellers in the vales!
Ho! ye, that by the chafing tide
   Have roughened in the gales!
Leave barn and byre, leave kin and cot,
   Lay by the bloodless spade;
Let desk, and case, and counters rot,
   And burn your books of trade!

The despot roves your fairest lands
   And till he flies, or fears,
Your fields must grow but armed bands—
   Your sheaves be sheaves of spears!
Give up to mildew and to rust
   The useless tools of gain,—
And feed your country's sacred dust
   With floods of crimson rain!

Come with the weapons at your call—
   With musket, pike, or knife,—
He wields the deadliest blade of all
   Who lightest holds his life.
The arm that drives its unbought blows,
   With all a patriot's scorn,
Might brain a tyrant with a rose,
   Or stab him with a thorn!

Does any falter?   Let him turn
  To some brave maiden's eyes,
'And catch the holy fires that burn
  In those sublunar skies,
Oh! could you like your women feel,
  And in their spirit march,
A day might see your lines of steel
  Beneath the victor's arch!

What hope, O God! would not grow warm
  When thoughts like these give cheer?
The lily calmly braves the storm—
  And shall the palm-tree fear?
No! rather let its branches court
  The blast that sweeps the plain;
And from the lily's regal port
  Learn how to breast the rain.

Ho! woodsmen of the mountain side!
  Ho! dwellers in the vales!
Ho! ye that by the roaring tide,
  Have roughened in the gales!
Come! flocking gayly to the fight,
  From forest, hill, and lake,—
We battle for our country's right,
  And for the lily's sake!

POEM ON THE DEATH OF "JACKSON."

Killed by a New York Zouave in Alexandria, Va., May 24, 1861.

Not where the battle red
Covers with fame the dead,—
Not where the trumpet calls
Vengeance for each that falls,—
Not with his comrades dear,
Not there—he fell not there.

He grasps no brother's hand,
He sees no patriot band;
Daring alone the foe
He strikes—then waits the blow,
Counting his life not dear,
His was no heart to fear!

Shout! Shout, his deed of glory!
Tell it in song and story;
Tell it where soldiers brave
Rush fearless to their grave;
Tell it—a magic spell—
In that great deed shall dwell.

Yes! he hath won a name
Deathless for aye to fame;
Our flag baptized in blood,
Always, as with a flood,
Shall sweep the tyrant band
Whose feet pollute our land.

3

Then, freemen, raise the cry,
As freemen live or die!
Arm! arm you for the fight!
His banner in your sight;
And this your battle-cry,
"Jackson and victory!"

DEAD JACKSON.

A chaplet! as ye pause ye brave
Beside the broad Potomac's wave;
A wreath! above dead Jackson's grave!

Against a hundred thousand—ONE
Whose dauntless manhood held alone
Virginia's threshold, and his own!

Hath vengeance tarried? Swifter, none
Since midnight lightning flashed upon
The sword of God and Gideon.

Hath God forgotten? *Who* hath led
Your legions to this narrow bed?
Whose very name recalls the dead?

A Jackson! Let your banners fly
And forward with the battle cry
Of *Jackson*, and of *liberty!*

RALLYING SONG OF THE VIRGINIANS.

BY SUSAN ARCHER TALLY.

———

"Scots wha hae wi' Wallace bled."

———

Now rouse ye, gallant comrades all,
   And ready stand, in war's array,—
Virginia sounds her battle call,
   And gladly we obey.
Our hands upon our trusty swords,
   Our hearts with courage beating high,—
We'll fight as once our father's fought,
   To conquer or to die !

Adieu, awhile to loving eyes,
   And lips that breathe our names in prayer ;
To them our holiest thoughts be given,
   For them our swords we bare !
Yet linger not when honor calls,
   Nor breathe one sad, regretful sigh,—
Defying fate, for love we'll live,
   Or for our country die !

No tyrant hand shall ever dare
   Our sacred Southern homes despoil,
No tyrant foot shall e'er invade
   Our free Virginia soil.
Lo ! from her lofty mountain peaks,
   To plains that skirt the Southern seas,

We fling her banner to the winds,
　Her motto on the breeze!

We hear the roll of stormy drums,
　We hear the trumpet's call afar!
Now forward, gallant comrades all,
　To swell the ranks of war;
Uplift on high our battle cry,
　Where fiercest rolls the bloody fight;
" *Virginia! for the Southern cause,*
　And God defend the right!"

1861.

Virginia's sons are mustering, from every hill and dale,
The sound of fife and drum is borne upon the rising gale,
Virginia's voice is ringing out, in accents loud and clear,
" Come home, my wand'ring children, thy mother needs
　　ye here!"

She is watching still and waiting for a lost but loved
　　one, *
So long the heir of glory bright, her brave and valiant
　　son;
O, how his mother's heart doth yearn to welcome him
　　once more,
With open arms and loud huzzas to her sweet Southern
　　shore.

* Scott.

Come, come from every valley, from mountain and from
      plain,
From every far-off country, to your boyhood's home
      again.
With hearts so firm and fearless, we'll strike hard for
      the right,
For no one but a dastard slave would shrink from such ·
      a fight.

Unfurl her banner, let it float far out upon the air,
Shout forth your triumph, far and wide, and let the
      tyrants hear.
Still let your motto be, my boys, with neither fear nor
      hate,
"*Sic semper tyrannis*," "God and our native State."

1776—1861.

Air—Bruce's Address.

Sons of the South! from hill and dale,
From mountain top, and lowly vale, ·
Arouse ye now! 'tis Freedom's wail—
      To arms! to arms! she cries.

Strike! for freedom in the dust;
Strike! to crush proud mammon's lust,
Strike! remembering *God is just!*
      Thus a freeman dies.

3*

Southrons! who with Beauregard,
Day and night, keep watch and ward,
Southrons! whom the angels guard,
  Strike for Liberty!

Smite the motley hireling throng,
Smite! as Heaven smites the wrong,
Smite!—they fly before the strong
  In God and Liberty!

By your hearth-stones, by your dead,
By all the fields where patriots bled,
A freeman's home or gory bed
  Let the alternate be.

Weeping wives and mothers here,
Sisters, daughters, dear ones near—
Seas of blood for every tear,
  God and Liberty!

Louder swells the battle-cry,
Flaming sword and flashing eye
Light the field where freemen die!
  Death or Liberty!

Backward roll your poisonous waves,
Infidel and ruffian slaves!
'Tis Heaven's own wrath your blindness braves,
  God and Liberty!

II.—SEVENTY-SIX AND SIXTY-ONE.

Ye spirits of the glorious dead !
 Ye watchers in the sky !
Who sought the patriot's crimson bed
 With holy trust and high—
Come lend your inspiration now,
 Come fire each Southern son,
Who nobly fights for freemen's rights,
 And shouts for sixty-one.

Come teach them how on hill, in glade,
 Quick leaping from your side,
The lightning flash of sabres made
 A red and flowing tide ;
How well ye fought, how bravely fell,
 Beneath our burning sun,
And let the lyre, in strains of fire,
 So speak of sixty-one.

There's many a grave in all the land,
 And many a crucifix,
Which tells how that heroic band
 Stood firm in seventy-six.
Ye heroes of the deathless past,
 Your glorious race is run,
But from your dust springs freemen's trust,
 And blows for sixty-one.

We build our altars where you lie,
　On many a verdant sod,
With sabres pointing to the sky
　And sanctified of God—
The smoke shall rise from every pile,
　Till freedom's fight is done,
And every voice throughout the South,
　Shall shout for sixty-one.

BY ALBERT PIKE, OF ARKANSAS.

Yes, call us rebels! 'tis the name
　Our patriot fathers bore,
And by such deeds we'll hallow it,
　As they have done before.
At Lexington and Baltimore,
　Was poured the holy chrism,
For freedom marks her sons with blood,
　In sign of their baptism.

Rebels, in proud and bold protest,
　Against a power unreal;
A unity which every quest
　Proves false as 'tis ideal.
A brotherhood, whose ties are chains,
　Which crushes what it holds,
Like fabled Laocoon of old,
　Within the serpent's folds.

Rebels, against the malice vast,
  Malice that nought disarms,
Which fills the quiet of our homes
  With vague and dread alarms,
Against th' invaders' daring feet,
  Against the tide of wrong,
Which has been borne, in silence borne,
  But borne perchance too long.

We would be cowards, did we crouch
  Beneath the lifted hand,
Whose very wave, ye seem to think,
  Will chill us where we stand.
Yes, call us rebels! 'tis a name
  Which speaks of other days,
Of gallant deeds, and gallant men,
  And wins them to their ways.

Fair was the edifice they raised,
  Uplifting to the skies;
A mighty Samson 'neath its dome
  In grand quiescence lies.
Dare not to touch his noble limb,
  With thong or chain to bind,
Lest ruin crush both you and him,
  This Samson is not blind!

          N. O. Picayune, May, 1861.

BY REV. MR. GARESCHE, OF ST. LOUIS.

Rebels! 'Tis a holy name,
  The name our fathers bore,
When battling in the cause of right
Against the tyrant in his might,
  In the dark days of yore.

Rebels! 'Tis our family name,
  Our father—Washington—
Was the arch-rebel in the fight,
And gave the name to us—a right
  Of father unto son.

Rebels! 'Tis our given name,
  Our mother, Liberty,
Received the title with her fame,
In days of grief, of fear and shame
  When at her breast were we.

Rebels! 'Tis our sealed name!
  A baptism of blood!
The war—aye, the din of strife—
The fearful contest, life for life,
  The mingled crimson flood.

Rebels! 'Tis a patriot name!
  In struggles it was given,
We bore it then when tyrants raved,
And through their curses 'twas engraved
  On the Doomsday book of Heaven!

Rebels! 'Tis our fighting name,
  For peace rules o'er the land,
Until they speak of craven woe,
Until our rights receive a blow,
  From foe's or brother's hand!

Rebels! 'Tis our dying name,
  For although life is dear,
Yet freemen born and freemen bred,
We'd rather sleep as freemen dead
  Than live in slavish fear.

Then, call us Rebels if you will,
  We glory in the name;
For bending under unjust laws,
And swearing faith to unjust cause,
  We count a greater shame.

HYMN.—GOD SAVE THE SOUTH.

BY GEORGE H. MILES, OF FREDERICK COUNTY, MD.

God save the South!
God save the South!
Her altars and firesides,
    God save the South!
Now that the war is nigh,
Now that we arm to die,
Chaunting our battle-cry,
    " Freedom or death!"

God be our shield,
At home or afield,
Stretch thine arm over us,
    Strengthen and save!
What though they're three to one,
Forward, each sire and son,
Strike, till the war is won,
    Strike to the grave!

God make the right
Stronger than might!
Millions would trample us
    Down in their pride.
Lay *Thou* their legions low,
Roll back the ruthless foe,
Let the proud spoiler know
    God's on our side.

Hear Honor's call,
Summoning all,
Summoning all of us
   Unto the strife.
Sons of the South, awake !
Strike till the brand shall break,
Strike for dear honor's sake,
   Freedom and life.

Rebels before
Our fathers of yore !
Rebels ! the righteous name
   Washington bore.
Why, then, be ours the same,
The name that he snatched from shame,
Making it first in fame,
   Foremost in war !

War to the hilt !
Theirs be the guilt
Who fetter the freeman
   To ransom the slave.
Up, then, and undismayed
Sheathe not the battle blade,
Till the last foe is laid
   Low in the grave.

God save the South !
God save the South !
Dry the dim eyes that now
   Follow our path.

4

Still let the light feet rove
Safe through the orange grove,
Still keep the land we love
  Safe from thy wrath.

God save the South!
God save the South!
Her altars and firesides,
  God save the South!
For the great war is nigh,
And we will win or die,
Chaunting our battle-cry,
  "Freedom or death!"

ANTHEM OF THE CONFEDERATE STATES.

O God! our only King,
To Thee our hearts we bring,
Now hear us while we sing,
    God bless our land.

With all Thy bounty yields,
Crown Thou her harvest fields,
And when the sword she wields,
    Strengthen her hand.

O'er every enemy
Give her the victory,
Thou mad'st her—keep her free,
    God bless our land.

May Justice, Truth and Love,
In all her councils move,
That in all good she prove
  First of all lands.

Pattern of Excellence,
Bulwark of Innocence,
Freedom's secure defence,
  God bless our land.

Thou, in the days of old,
Our fathers did'st uphold
When they for right made bold,
  Unsheathed the sword.

We for the Liberty,
Which we received from Thee,
Now meet the enemy,
  Help us, O Lord.

Thou art the God of might,
God of the Truth and Light,
'Tis in their cause we fight,
  Be Thou our aid.

Strike with us 'gainst the foe;
Cause his swift overthrow,
That all the earth may know
  Thou art our aid.

GOD SAVE THE SOUTH.

BY R. AGNEW, OF NEWBERN.

Wake every minstrel's strain,
Ring o'er each Southern plain,
   " God save the South !"
Still let this noble band,
Joined now in heart and hand,
Fight for our sunny land—
   Land of the South !

Armed in such sacred cause,
We court no vain applause,
   Our swords are free.
No spot of wrong or shame
Rests on our banner's name,
Flung forth in Freedom's name,
   O'er land and sea.

Then let the invader come ;
Soon shall the beat of drum
   Rally us all.
Forth from our homes we go,
Death ! death ! to every foe !
Lay each invader low—
   God save us all !

Sound, then, with loud acclaim,
Davis ! our Chief's great name,
   God save him long !

May the Almighty power,
Blessings upon him shower,
And still from hour to hour,
    Shield him from wrong!

Then, 'mid the cannon's roar,
Let us sing evermore,—
    God save the South!
Ours is the soul to dare,
See! our good swords are bare!
We will be free, we *swear!*
    God save the South!

December, 1861.

HURRAH!

BY A MISSISSIPPIAN.

Hurrah! for the Southern Confederate States,
    With her banner of white, red and blue;
Hurrah! for her daughters, the fairest on earth,
    And her sons, ever loyal and true.

Hurrah! and hurrah! for her brave volunteers,
    Enlisted for freedom or death;
Hurrah! for Jeff. Davis, Commander-in-Chief,
    And three cheers for the Palmetto wreath!

Hurrah! for each heart that is right in the cause,
   That cause we'll protect with our lives;
Hurrah! for the first one that dies on the field,
   And hurrah! for each one who survives!

Hurrah! for the South, shout hurrah and hurrah!
   O'er her soil shall no tyrants have sway,—
In peace and in war, we will ever be found
   "Invincible," now and for aye.

Mobile Register, 1861.

THE SHIP OF STATE.

BY MRS. C. A. WARFIELD.

A good ship o'er a stormy sea,
   Before the gale is driving,—
The billows leap against her prow,
   With more than demon striving.
The lurid lightning half illumes
   The sun-deserted heavens,
And shines upon her pennon proud,
   Her sails and cordage riven.

Her decks are thronged with storm-beat men,
   A crowd of eager faces,
Where desperate hope and suffering stern,
   Have left their iron traces.

But not a sign of craven fear
    Proclaims one base emotion,
In souls that grapple with their doom,
    And dread not wind nor ocean.

Clear rings a voice above the throng,
    So sweet that all may hear it,
'Tis from the helmsman, slight and pale,
    With the look of a ruling spirit.
He hath dropped his mantle on the deck,
    His brow is bare and gleaming,
And he stands before them like those shapes
    That Jacob saw in dreaming.

" Come weal, come woe, I share your fate,
    " No human power can part us,
" And while we bend to his behest,
    " Our God can ne'er desert us.
" Why heed the rest? let tempest rage,
    " And sun refuse its shining,
" We know *one* hand is over all,
    " And clouds have their silver lining.

" Then cast away to the foaming deep
    " Our treasures prized and golden,
" Lighten the good ship on her way,
    " And her course will yet be holden.
" And see afar the Southern star
    " Gleams through the rifted heaven,
" Till seas o'erwhelm I'll hold this helm
    " While by the gale we are driven."

And still across that stormy sea,
  The noble ship is driving,
But the frantic waves shall drop to rest,
  Vain is their demon striving.
And far above her shattered sails,
  The Cross and Star are flying,
'Tis a crew that looks to God alone,
  The elements defying.

THE SOUTHRON'S WAR SONG.

BY J. A. WAGNER.

Arise! arise! with main and might,
  Sons of the sunny clime!
Gird on the sword; the sacred fight
  The holy hour doth chime.
Arise! the hostile host draws nigh,
  In thundering array;
Arise! ye brave! let cowards fly—
  The hero bides the fray.

Strike hard, strike hard, ye noble band,
  Strike hard, with arm of fire!
Strike hard, for God and fatherland,
  For mother, wife and sire!
Let thunders roar, the lightning flash,
  Bold Southrons! never fear
The bay'net's point, the sabre's clash!
  True Southrons do and dare!

Bright flowers spring from the hero's grave,
  The craven knows no rest,—
Thrice cursed the traitor and the knave,
  The hero thrice is blessed.
Then let each noble Southron stand
  With bold and manly eye;
We'll do for God and fatherland!
  We'll do, we'll do or die!

Charleston Courier, June 11th, 1861.

4*

"ON TO RICHMOND."

(*After Southey's March to Moscow.*)

BY JNO. R. THOMPSON.

Major-General Scott
An order had got
To push on the column to Richmond,—
For loudly went forth,
From all parts of the North,
The cry that an end of the war must be made
In time for the regular yearly fall trade.
Mr. Greely spoke freely about the delay,
The Yankees "to hum" were all hot for the fray;
The chivalrous gray
Declared they were slow,
And therefore the order
To march from the border,
And make an excursion to Richmond.

Major-General Scott
Most likely was not
Very loth to obey this instruction, I wot;
In his private opinion
The ancient Dominion
Deserved to be pillaged—her sons to be shot;
And the reason is easily noted:
Though this part of the earth   .
Had given him birth,

And medals and swords,
Inscribed with fine words,
It never for Winfield had voted.
Besides, you must know that our first of commanders
Had sworn quite as hard as the army in Flanders,
With his finest of armies and proudest of navies,
To wreak his old grudge against Jefferson Davis.
Then, " Forward the column," he said to McDowell;
And the Zouaves, with a shout,
Most fiercely cried out,
To Richmond or h–ll, (I omit here the vowel,)
And Winfield, he ordered his carriage and four,
A dashing turn-out, to be brought to the door,
For a pleasant excursion to Richmond.

Major-General Scott
Had there on the spot
A splendid array
To plunder and slay ;
In the camp he might boast
Such a numerous host
As he never had yet
On the battle-field set ;
Every class and condition of Northern society
Were in for the trip—a most varied variety ;
In the camp he might hear every lingo in vogue,
" The sweet German accent, the rich Irish brogue,"
The beautiful boy
From the banks of the Shannon,
Was there to employ
His excellent cannon,

And beside the long files of dragoons and artillery,
The Zouaves and Hussars,
All the children of Mars,
There were barbers and cooks,
And writers of books,
The *chef de cuisine*, with his French bill of fare,
And artists to dress the young officers' hair,
And the scribblers all ready at once to prepare
An eloquent story
Of conquest and glory,
And servants with numberless baskets of Sillery.
Though Wilson, the Senator, followed the train,
At a distance quite safe, to " conduct the *champagne ;*"
While the fields were so green, and the sky was so blue,
There was certainly nothing more pleasant to do,
On this pleasant excursion to Richmond.

In Congress, the talk, as I said, was of action,
To crush out at once the traitorous faction.
In the press and the mess
They would hear nothing less,
Than to make the advance, spite of rhyme or of reason,
And at once put an end to the insolent treason.
There was Greely,
And Ely,
The blood-thirsty Grow,
And Hickman (the rowdy, not Hickman the beau,)
And that terrible Baker,
Who would seize on the South—every acre,
And Webb, who would drive us all into the Gulf, or
Some nameless locality smelling of sulphur.

And with all this bold crew
Nothing would do
While the fields were so green, and the sky was so blue,
But to march on directly, to Richmond.

Then the gallant McDowell
Drove madly the rowel
Of spur that had never been "won" by him,
In the flank of his steed,
To accomplish a deed
Such as never before had been done by him.
And the battery called Sherman's,
Was wheeled into line,
While the beer-drinking Germans
From Neckar and Rhine,
With Minnie and Yager,
Came on with a swagger,
Full of fury and lager.
(The day and the pageant were equally fine,)
Oh, the fields were so green and the sky was so blue,
Indeed, 'twas a spectacle pleasant to view
As the column pushed onward to Richmond.

Ere the march was begun,
In spirit of fun
General Scott, in a speech,
Said this army should teach
The Southrons the lesson the laws to obey,
And just before dusk of the third or fourth day
Should joyfully march into Richmond.

He spoke of their drill,
Of their courage and skill,
And declared that the ladies of Richmond would rave
O'er such matchless perfections, and gracefully wave,
In rapture, their delicate kerchiefs in air,
At their morning parades on the Capitol Square.

But alack! and alas!
Mark what soon came to pass,
When this army, in spite of his flatteries,
Amid war's loudest thunder
Did most stupidly blunder
Upon those accursed "masked batteries."
There Beauregard came,
Like a tempest of flame,
To consume them in wrath,
On their perilous path;
And Johnston bore down in a whirlwind to sweep
Their ranks from the field,
Where their doom had been sealed,
As the storm rushes over the face of the deep;
While swift on the centre our President pressed,
And the foe might descry,
In the glance of his eye,
The light that once blazed upon Diomed's crest.
McDowell! McDowell! weep, weep for the day,
When the Southrons ye met in their battle array;
To your confident hosts, with its bullets and steel,
'Tw— orse than Culloden to luckless Lochiel!
Oh! the Generals were green, and old Scott is now blue,
And a terrible business, McDowell, to you,
Was that pleasant excursion to Richmond.

ᐧBATTLE EVE.

I see the broad red setting sun
　　Sink slowly down the sky,—
I see, amid the cloud-built tents,
　　His blood-stained standard fly,
And meek, meanwhile, the pallid moon
　　Looks from her place on high.

O, setting sun, awhile delay !
　　Linger on sea and shore,—
For thousand eyes now gaze on thee
　　That shall not see thee more ;
A thousand hearts beat proudly now,
　　Whose race like thine is o'er !

O, ghastly moon ! thy pallid ray
　　On paler brows shall lie !
On many a torn and bleeding heart,
　　On many a glazing eye ;
And breaking hearts shall live to mourn
　　For whom 'twere bliss to die.

MANASSAS.

BY MRS. C. A. WARFIELD, JULY, 1861.

They have met at last, as storm-clouds
    Meet in heaven,
And the Northmen, back and bleeding
    Have been driven·;
And their thunder has been stilled,
And their leaders crushed or killed,
And their ranks with terror thrilled,
    Rent and riven.

Like the leaves of Vallambrosa
    They are lying,
In the midnight and the moonlight,
    Dead or dying;
Like those leaves before the gale,
Fled their legions—wild and pale—
While the host that made them quail
    Stood defying!

When in the morning sunlight
    Flags were flaunted,
And " Vengeance on the Rebels"
    Proudly vaunted,
They little dreamed that night
Would close upon their flight,
And the victor of the fight
    Stand undaunted.

But peace to those who perished
  In our passes,
Light be the earth above them,
  Green the grasses.
Long shall Northmen rue the day,
When in battle's wild affray,
They met the South's array
  At Manassas.

"OUR LEFT."

From dawn to dark they stood,
 That long midsummer's day !
While fierce and fast
The battle-blast
 Swept rank on rank away !

From dawn to dark, they fought
 With legions swept and cleft,
While black and wide
The battle tide
 Poured ever on our "Left !"

They closed each ghastly gap !
 They dressed each shattered rank,
They knew full well
That Freedom fell
 With that exhausted flank !

"Oh! for a thousand men,
  Like these that melt away!"
And down they came,
With steel and flame,
  Four thousand to the fray!

They left the laggard train,
  The panting steam might stay;
And down they came,
With steel and flame,
  - Head-foremost to the fray!

Right through the blackest cloud
  Their lightning path they cleft!
Freedom and Fame,
With triumph came
  To our immortal Left.

Ye! of your living, sure!
  Ye! of your dead, bereft!.
Honor the brave
Who died to save
  Your all, upon our Left.

THE BATTLE OF MANASSAS.

BY MRS. CLARKE, WIFE OF COL. CLARKE, 14TH REG. N. CAROLINA.

DEDICATED TO GEN. BEAUREGARD, C. S. A.

"Now glory to the Lord of Hosts!" oh, bless and praise
    His name,
That He hath battled in our cause, and brought our foes
    to shame;
And honor to our Beauregard, who conquered in His
    might,
And for our children's children won, Manassas' bloody
    fight.
Oh, let our thankful prayers ascend, our joyous praise
    resound,
For·God—the God of victory, our untried flag hath
    crowned!

They brought a mighty army, to crush us with a blow,
And in their pride they laughed to scorn the men they
    did not know;
Fair women came to triumph, with the heroes of the day,
When "the boasting Southern rebels" should be scat-
    tered in dismay.
And for their conquering Generals, a lordly feast they
    spread,
But the wine in which we pledged them, was all of ruby
    red!

The feast was like Belshazzar's—in terror and dismay,
Before our conquering heroes, their armies fled away.
God had weighed them in the balance, and His hand
    upon the wall,
At the taking of Fort Sumter, had fore-doomed them to
    their fall.
But they would not heed the warning, and scoffed in
    unbelief,
Till their scorn was changed to wailing, and their laugh-
    ter into grief!

All day the fight was raging, and amid the cannon's
    peal,
Rang the cracking of our rifles, and the clashing of our
    steel;
But above the din of battle, our shout of triumph rose,
As we charged upon their batteries, and turned them on
    our foes.
We staid not for our fallen, and we thought not of our
    dead,
Until the day was ours, and the routed foe had fled.

But once our spirits faltered—Bee and Bartow both
    were down,
And our gallant Colonel Hampton lay wounded on the
    ground;
But Beauregard, God bless him! led the Legion in his
    stead,
And Johnston seized the colors, and waved them o'er
    his head!

E'en a coward must have followed, when such heroes
　　led the way,
And no dastard blood was flowing in Southern veins
　　that day !

But every arm was strengthened, and every heart was
　　stirred,
When shouts of "Davis! Davis!" along our lines were
　　heard.
As he rode into the battle the joyful news flew fast—
And the dying raised their voices and cheered him as he
　　passed.
Oh! with such glorious leaders, in Cabinet and field,
The gallant Southern chivalry will die, but never yield !

But from the wings of victory, the shafts of death were
　　sped,
And our pride is dashed with sorrow when we count our
　　noble dead;
Though in our hearts they're living—and our children
　　we will tell
How gloriously our Fisher and our gallant Johnson fell ;
And the name of each we'll cherish as an honor to his
　　State,
And teach our sons to envy, and, if need be, meet their
　　fate.

"Then glory to the Lord of Hosts!" oh, bless and praise
　　his name,
For he hath battled in our ·cause, and brought our foes
　　to shame.

And honor to our Beauregard, who conquered in His
    might,
And for our children's children, won Manassas' bloody
    fight.
Oh! let our grateful prayers ascend, our joyous praise
    resound,
For God—the God of victory our untried flag hath
    crowned!

VIRGINIA'S JEWELS.

BY MISS REBECCA POWELL, OF VIRGINIA.

"These are my jewels," said a Roman dame,
Long years ago;—Virginia says the same,
And proudly shows the sons, who at her call
Have gathered swift from cottage and from hall,
And stand beneath our skies, a noble band,
Ready to perish for their own native land.

"These are my jewels,"—ne'er was matron's brow
More richly gemmed than is Virginia's now;
Diamond and ruby pale before the light
Of souls inspired by the sense of right;
Of hearts with feeling and with virtue fraught,
Eyes lit with truth and shadowed deep with thought.

Not on her brow alone these jewels rest,
Some richer still are garnered in her breast;

Oh, with what mingled love, and grief, and pride,
She points to those who for her sake have died!
How tenderly she clasps them to her heart,
Ne'er from her fond embrace again to part.

Oh, Martyrs of Manassas! ye whose names,
Though writ in light are still more love's than fame's.
Long shall Virginia's sons and daughters tell,
How nobly on that bloody day ye fell,
And at a priceless cost redeemed our land,
From the fell grasp of the invader's hand.

Sons of Virginia, falter not,—to you
The loved, the tried, the trusted and the true,
Her hearths, her homes, her sacred honor—all
For which men live,—in whose defense they fall—
Your mother gives, be faithful to the trust,
For, lo! your brothers' blood calls from the dust.

Be strong, courageous, steadfast, trust in God,
Humbly submissive to His chastening rod,
Christ's faithful soldiers on the tented field,
In Him your trust, His providence your shield,
So shall God's blessing to our arms be given,
And peace on angels' wings descend from Heaven.

MARYLAND!

BY JAMES R. RANDALL.

The despot's heel is on thy shore,
  Maryland!
His torch is at thy temple door,
  Maryland!
Avenge the patriotic gore
That flecked the streets of Baltimore,
And be the battle-queen of yore,
  Maryland! My Maryland!

Hark to thy wand'ring son's appeal,
  Maryland!
My mother State! to thee I kneel,
  Maryland!
For life and death, for woe and weal,
Thy peerless chivalry reveal,
And gird thy beauteous limbs with steel,
  Maryland! My Maryland!

Thou wilt not cower in the dust,
  Maryland!
Thy beaming sword shall never rust,
  Maryland!
Remember Carroll's sacred trust;
Remember Howard's warlike thrust,
·And all thy slumberers with the Just,
  Maryland! My Maryland!

Come! 'tis the red dawn of the day,
    Maryland!
Come! with thy panoplied array,
    Maryland!
With Ringgold's spirit for the fray,
With Watson's blood, at Monterey,
With fearless Lowe, and dashing May,
    Maryland! My Maryland!

Dear mother, burst the Tyrant's chain,
    Maryland!
Virginia should not call in vain,
    Maryland!
SHE meets her sisters on the plain,
"*Sic Semper*"—'tis the proud refrain,
That baffles minions back amain,
    Maryland! My Maryland!

Come! for thy shield is bright and strong,
    Maryland!
Come! for thy dalliance does thee wrong,
    Maryland!
Come! to thine own heroic throng,
That stalks with Liberty along,
And ring thy dauntless slogan song,
    Maryland! My Maryland!

I see the blush upon thy cheek,
    Maryland!
For thou wast ever bravely meek,
    Maryland!

5

But lo! there surges forth a shriek
From hill to hill, from creek to creek—
Potomac calls to Chesapeake,
      Maryland!   My Maryland!

Thou wilt not yield the Vandal toll,
      Maryland!
Thou wilt not crook to his control,
      Maryland!
Better the fire upon thee roll,
Better the shot—the blade—the bowl—
Than crucifixion of the soul,
      Maryland!   My Maryland!

I hear the distant thunder hum,
      Maryland!
The Old Line bugle, fife and drum,
      Maryland!
She is not dead, nor deaf, nor dumb;
Huzza! she spurns the Northern scum!
Shè breathes—she burns! she'll come! she'll
      come!
      Maryland!   My Maryland!   .

CHARGE OF THE NIGHT BRIGADE.

At three o'clock, three o'clock,
Three o'clock, onward,
All in the silent streets—
    Strode the twelve hundred!
Forward, the Night Brigade!
"March to Kane's house!" he said.
On through the silent streets
    Strode the twelve hundred!

" Forward! the Night Brigade!"
Was there a man dismayed?
Not though the Yankees knew
    Some one had blundered;
Theirs, not to make reply,
Theirs, but to go and try
To catch one man on the sly,
    Gallant twelve hundred!

Houses to right of them,
Houses to left of them;
Some were "to let" of them,
    While the men wondered,
Whether, if shot and shell,
From the roofs of them fell,
Some would not go to —— well
Where there'd be hot work a spell,
    For the twelve hundred.

Flashed all their bayonets bare,
Flash'd in the gas-lit air,
Whom did they hope to scare,
Marching at dead of night?

    All the town slumbered,
Plunged in the depths of sleep,
None did a vigil keep;
All the poor pelicans
Grabbed ere they had a peep,
Overpowered—outnumbered.
Straight up St. Pauls street
Strode the twelve hundred.

Houses to right of them,
Houses to left of them,
Law books in some of them,
    Still they marched onward—
Straight to the house of Kane;
Straight on, the way was plain,
Seized him, with might and main,
As if "the mark of Cain"
Was on him—so back again
    Strode the twelve hundred!

When can their glory fade?
Oh! the wild charge they made,
    All the town wondered!
Honor the charge they made?
No, sir! for I'm afraid
They can't *prove* the charge they made.
    "Took in"—twelve hundred!

BALTIMORE, *July 13th,* 1861.

"THERE'S LIFE IN THE OLD LAND YET."

BY F. K. HOWARD.

Though the soil of old Maryland echoes the tread
　　Of an insolent soldiery now,
And a lurid glare reddens the sky overhead
　　From the camp-fires' lighted below ;
Though from mountain to shore the hoarse cannon roar,
　　And from border to border are sentinels set,
Whose bayonets shine in unbroken line,
　　There is life in the Old Land yet !

Though by treacherous hearts and unloyal hands,
　　Betrayed and disabled to-day,
And deserted at need by her sons, she stands
　　Confronting an armèd array :
Though tyrannous might hath o'erborne the right,
　　Hath discrowned and despoiled her, and men forget
As they bow the knee, that they once were free—
　　There's life in the Old Land yet !

But though patient and mute, she is still undismay'd,
　　Though passive, she is not subdued,
Though she shrinks from unsheathing her trusty blade
　　In a fratricidal feud,
Not long will she kneel, when oppression's heel,
　　On her neck, is by Monarch or President set,
And the blood even now, is mantling her brow,
　　For there's life in the Old Land yet !

She remembers with pride, what her children have done
    In the perilous days of yore;
And will never relinquish the rights which they won,
    Or disgrace the flag they bore.
Then let those beware, who boastfully swear
    They will conquer her now, for their vaunt will be
        met,
And the Maryland men, shall be heard of again—
    For there's life in the Old Land yet!

July 14th, 1866.

"INDEPENDENCE DAY."

Oh, Freedom is a blessed thing!
    And men have marched in stricken fields,
And fought, and bled, to nobly grasp
    The glorious fruits that freedom yields.
Then let the banner flout the air,
    The fairest once of freedom's types—
The stars are fading one by one—
    What matter? We have still the stripes!
        Oh! happy men of Maryland,
    Remember! we have still the stripes!

Why heed the cannon in your streets,
    The bayonets that block your way?
Rejoice, for you were freemen once,
    And this is, "Independence Day."

Then let the banner flout the air,
  The fairest once of freedom's types—
The stars are fading one by one—
    What matter? We have still the stripes!
      Oh! happy men of Maryland,
  Remember! we have still the stripes!

ARE WE FREE?

BY JAMES R. BREWER.

Are we free? go ask the question
  In the cells of Lafayette,
Ask it of your chain-girt brothers,
  Shut within its parapet;
Ask it of the silent journals,
  Crushed beneath an iron hand;
Ask it of the mighty armies
  Quartered on a groaning land.
To them let the question be,
Friends and brothers! are we free?

Ask it of the helpless women,
  Shut within a prison's grate;
Ask it of the weeping loved ones,
  Mourning o'er their wretched fate;
Ask it of the homes deserted,
  And the hearths made desolate;

Ask it of the freeman punished
.Who rebukes fanatic hate.
Speak kindly, lest a taunt they see
In the question, are we free?

Ask it of a helpless people
  Bending to a tyrant's throne;
Ask it of a State dismantled,
  And her sons' indignant groan;
Ask it of the wreck of freedom,
  Torn and strewn on every hand;
Ask it of your State dishonored,
  Prostrate, helpless Maryland;
Without a taunt of mockery,
Ask her, if we still are free?

Hear the answer from the towers,
  In the clank of rusty chains,
And the press in silence shows us
  Where the unchécked despot reigns;
See it in the homes deserted,
  And the hearths made desolate;
Hear it from the exiled freeman
  Fleeing from his native State;
And the blushing answer 'll be,
Maryland's no longer free!

Hear it in the wail of women,
  From the mouldy dungeon's gloom;
Hear it in the sobs of children,
  Weeping for their mothers' doom;.

Hear it in the shrieks of maidens
    Torn from friends' and brothers' care—
Hear it in their screams of·terror,
    See it in their wild despair—
Answered in their piercing cries,
Seen in tearful, pleading eyes.

Hear it in the taunts of cowards,
    Who accept dishonor's stains;
Hear it in the sullen clanking
    Of a State's ignoble chains;
And from Freedom's weeping goddess,
    Fleeing from her children's graves,
Comes a mother's sobbing answer,
    " Power binds my children slaves !"
Whilst groans proclaim from hill to sea,
" Maryland was, but is not free !"

ANNAPOLIS, *Oct.* 22, 1861.

5*

THE KENTUCKY PARTIZAN.

BY PAUL H. HAYNE, OF SOUTH CAROLINA.

I.

Hath the wily Swamp Fox
  Come again to earth?
Hath the soul of Sumpter
  Owned a second birth?
From the Western hill-slopes
  Starts a hero-form,
Stalwart, like the oak tree,
  Tameless, like the storm!
His an eye of lightning!
  His a heart of steel!
Flashing deadly vengeance,
  Thrilled with fiery zeal;
Hound him down, ye minions,
  Seize him if ye can;
But wo betide the hireling knave
That meets him, man to man!

II.

Well done! gallant *Morgan!*
  Strike with might and main,
Till the fair field redden
  With a gory rain;
Smite them by the roadside,
  Smite them in the wood,

By the lonely valley,
   And the purpling flood;
'Neath the mystic starlight,
   'Neath the glare of day,
Harrass, sting, affright them,
   Scatter them, and slay.
Beard, who durst, our Chieftain!
   Bind him—if you can—
But wo betide the Hessian thief
Who meets him, man to man!

III.

There's a lurid purpose
   Brooding in his breast,
Born of solemn passion
   And a deep unrest,
For our ruined homesteads,
   And our ravaged land,
For our women outraged
   By the dastard hand.
For our thousand sorrows,
   And our untold shame,
For our blighted harvests,
   For our towns of flame—
He has sworn (and recks not
   Who may cross his path,)
That the foe shall feel him
   In his fervid wrath—
That, while will and spirit
   Hold one spark of life,

Blood shall stain his broad-sword,
　　Blood shall wet his knife.
On! ye Hessian horsemen!
　　Crush him—if ye can!
But wo betide your staunchest slave
Who meets him, man to man!

IV. •

'Tis no time for pleasure!
　　Doff the silken vest!
Up, my men! and follow
　　Marion of the West!
Strike with him for freedom;
　　Strike with main and might,
'Neath the noon of splendor,
　　'Neath the gloom of night.
Strike by rock and roadside,
　　Strike in wold and wood,
By the shadowy valley,
　　By the purpling flood.
On! where Morgan's war-horse
　　Thunders in the van,
God! who would not gladly die
　　Beside that glorious man!

JOHN MORGAN's credentials—
The very essentials
To honor and glory, you know,
Were not signed at West P——,
So consequently,
His promotion has been rather slow.

"Why, d——n it," says Pat,
As he stamps on his hat,
"Does shape-skins make soldiers—indade!
On the temple of Fame
They ne'er scratched a P——'s name
Till Morgan first taught 'em to *raid!*"

THE TOAST OF MORGAN'S MEN.

BY CAPT. THORPE, OF KY.

Unclaimed by the land that bore us,
Lost in the land we find,
The brave have gone before us,
Cowards are left behind!
Then stand to your glasses, steady,
Here's a health to those we prize,
Here's a toast to the dead already,
And here's to the next who dies.

LOUISIANA.

Ho! Louisiana!
    There is no clime like thine,
Land of the broad savanna,
    Land of the citron vine;
Land of the monarch river,
    Of lake and prairie plain,
Our free-born home forever,
    A beauteous, bright domain.

Above, the deep blue heaven,
    Looks down with laughing eyes,
And breezes mildly driven,
    Float o'er thy sunny skies.
Around, rich fields extending,
    Are clothed in emerald green,
And birds their music blending,
    On every bough are seen.

With orange blossoms laden,
    Or golden fruit, each bower
Reveals the dark-eyed maiden,
    Herself a fairer flower.
The sunny Creole beauty,
    With voice of song and mirth,
And true to love and duty,
    The houri of the earth.

Ho! Louisiana!
  Home of the brave and free,
Thy fertile, broad savanna
  Goes smiling to the sea;
Where princely wealth inherit,
  And generous thoughts expand
The chivalric high spirits,
  The guardians of the land.

CHARLES B. DREUX.

BY JAMES R. RANDALL.

Weep, Louisiana, weep thy gallant dead!
Weave the green laurel o'er the undaunted head!
Fling thy bright banner o'er the heart which bled
                    . Defending thee!

Weep—weep, Imperial City, deep and wild!
Weep for thy martyred and heroic child,
The young, the brave, the free, the undefiled—
                    Ah! weep for him! .

Lo! the wail surges from embattled bands,
By Yorktown's plains and Pensacola's sands,
Re-echoing to the golden sugar lands,
                    Adieu! Adieu!

The death of honor was the death he craved,
To die where weapons clashed and pennons waved,
To welcome freedom o'er the opening grave,

And live for aye.

His blood had too much lightning to be still;
His spirit was the torrent, not the rill;
The gods have loved him, and the Eternal Hill

Is his at last.

He died while yet his chainless eye could roll,
Flashing the conflagrations of his soul!
The rose and mirror of the bold Creole,

He sleepeth well!

Lament, lone mother, for his early fate,
But bear thy burden with a hope elate,
For thou hast shrined thy jewel in the stake,

A priceless boon!

And thou, sad wife, thy sacred tears belong
To the untarnished and immortal throng,
For he shall fire the poets breast and song,

In thrilling strains.

And the fair virgins of our sunny clime
Shall wed their music to the minstrel's rhyme,
Making his fame melodious for all time—

It cannot die.

BEAUREGARD.

BY MRS. C. A. WARFIELD, OF KY.

[Written after the Battle of Shiloh, when Beauregard became Commander-in-Chief.]

Our trust is now in thee,
 Beauregard!
In thy hand the God of Hosts
 Hath placed the sword;
And the glory of thy name
Has set the world aflame—
Hearts kindle at thy name,
 Beauregard!

The way that lies before
 Is cold and hard;
We are lead across the desert
 By the Lord!
But the cloud that shines by night
To guard our steps aright,
Is the pillar of thy might,
 Beauregard!

Thou hast watched the southern heavens
 Evening starred,
And chosen thence thine emblems,
 Beauregard;

And upon thy banner's fold,
Is that starry cross enrolled,
Which no northman shall behold
 Shamed or scarred.

By the blood that crieth loudly
 From the sward,
We have sworn to keep around it
 Watch and ward,
And the standard of thy hand
Yet shall shine above a land,
Like its leader, free and grand—
 Beauregard!

BEAUREGARD'S APPEAL.

Yea! since the need is bitter,
  Take down those sacred bells,
Whose music speaks of our hallowed joys,
  And passionate farewells!

But ere ye fall dismantled,
  Ring out, deep Bells! once more:
And pour on the waves of the passing wind
  The symphonies of yore.

Let the latest born be welcomed
  By pealings glad and long,
Let the latest dead in the churchyard bed
  Be laid with solemn song.

And the bells above them throbbing,
  Should sound in mournful tone,
As if in the grief for a human death,
  They prophesied their own.

Who says 'tis a desecration
  To strip the Temple Towers,
And invest the metal of peaceful notes
  With death-compelling powers?

A truce to cant and folly!
  With Faith itself at stake,

Shall we heed the cry of the shallow fool,
　Or pause for the bigot's sake?

Then, crush the struggling sorrow!
　Feed high your furnace fires,
That shall mould into deep-mouthed guns
　　　bronze,
　The bells from a hundred spires.

Methinks no common vengeance—
　No transient war eclipse—
Will follow the awful thunder burst
　From their "adamantine lips."

A cause like ours is holy,
　And useth holy things,
And over the storm of a righteous strife,
　May shine the Angel's wings.

Where'er our duty leads us,
　The Grace of God is there,
And the lurid shrine of War may hold
　The Eucharist of prayer.

SABBATH BELLS. *

Those Sabbath bells! Those Sabbath bells!
No more their soothing music tells
Of boyhood's dawn and manhood's prime,
Cheered by their morn and evening chime.

No more those notes shall float through air
To call us to the House of Prayer!
No more their silvery welcome greet
The Christian at the Mercy Seat!

A fiercer warning now they tell—
Let the oppressor hear it well!
Nor dare the stern, relentless might,
Upholding truth—defending right!

And still we hail the voice that swells
In thunder from those Sabbath bells,
Proclaiming, in defiant tone,
We own no Master, save the ONE!

Charleston Mercury.

* A number of Churches in the South gave their bells to the Confederate authorities to be cast into cannon.

MARCH ON! CAROLINIANS, MARCH ON!

Written on reading the notice of the death of Dr. E. S. Buist, one of
Carolina's noblest sons and most accomplished gentlemen.

BY MRS. FARLEY.

The chief is arming in his hall,
   The farmer by his hearth,
The mourner hears the thrilling call
   And rises from the earth.
The mother on her first-born son
   Looks with a boding eye,
They come not back though all be won,
   Whose young hearts leap so high.—*Hemans.*

March on, Carolinians! "our hearts leap so high,"
When the young and devoted martyr-like die;
Oh! we'll deem it joy to stand 'mid the showers
Of shot and of shell in a cause such as ours.
        March on! Carolinians, march on!

At his post in the conflict he fearlessly fell,
Let us snatch one moment to murmur—farewell!
He has gone, his career was brilliant as brief,
"So *to-day* for revenge, *to-morrow* for grief."
        March on! Carolinians, march on!

Too indignant our feelings, too solemn for tears,
In our hearts let them sleep for long-coming years.

The blood of our brother cries up from the ground,
In all Carolina no laggard is found.
         March on! Carolinians, march on!

The flag of his country to the breeze we will cast,
His dirge shall be heard in the war-trumpet's blast!
To arms! then, to arms! all ye sons of the South!
Speak, ye dauntless of soul, from the cannon's loud
    mouth.
         March on! Carolinians, march on!

So proudly their ships ride the waves of the sea,
Away! then, away! to the coast let us flee,
We burn! oh! we burn now to meet them in strife,
To hurl back their insults, and take "life for life."
         March on! Carolinians, march on!

Fear not to meet death, since it comes once to all,
In defence of our country 'tis glorious to fall;
Far better in death to lie down with the slain
Than to languish out life in disgrace and in pain.
         March on! Carolinians, march on!

LAURENSVILLE, *Nov.* 20, 1861.

CAROLINA.

BY MRS. ANNA PEYRE DENNIES.

INSCRIBED TO THE PEE DEE LEGION—GEN. W. W. HARLLEE.

———

"Breathes there a man with soul so dead,
Who never to himself has said,
This is my own—my native land?—*Scott.*

———

In the hour of thy glory,
     When thy name was far renowned,
When Sumter's glowing story
     Thy bright escutcheon crowned;
Oh, noble Carolina! how proud a claim was mine,
That through homage, and through duty, and bithright,
     I was thine.

Exulting as I heard thee,
     Of every lip the theme,
Prophetic visions stirred me
     In hope's illumined dream—
A dream of dauntless valor, of battles fought and won,
Where each field was but a triumph—a hero every son.

And now when clouds arise,
     And shadows round thee fall,
I lift to Heaven my eyes
     Those visions to recall;

For I cannot deem that darkness will rest upon thee
    long—
Oh, lordly Carolina! with thy heart so brave and
    strong.

      Thy serried ranks of pine,
        Thy live oaks spreading wide,
      Beneath the sunbeams shine
        In fadeless robes of pride ;
Thus marshaled on their native soil thy gallant sons
    stand forth,
As changeless as thy forest green, defiant of the North.

      The deeds of other days
        Enacted by their sires,
      Themes long of love and praise,
        Have wakened high desires
In every heart that beats within thy proud domain,
To cherish their remembrance, and live those scenes
    again.

      Each heart the home of daring,
        Each hand the foe of wrong,
      They'll meet with haughty bearing
        The war-ships thunder song ;
And though the base invader pollutes thy sacred shore,
They'll meet him as undaunted as their fathers did of
    yore.

      His feet may press thy soil,
        His numbers bear thee down,
  6

In his vandal raid for spoil
    His sordid soul to crown;
But his triumph will be fleeting, for the hour is drawing
    near
When the war-cry of thy cavaliers shall strike his
    startled ear.

A fearful time shall come
    .When thy gathering bands unite,
And the larum sounding drum
    Calls to struggle for the right;
"*Pro aris et pro focis,*" from rank to rank shall fly,
As they meet the dastard foeman to conquer or to die.

Oh! then a tale of glory
    Shall yet again be thine,
And the record of thy story
    The laurel shall entwine;
Oh, noble Carolina! oh, proud and lordly State!
Heroic deeds shall crown thee, and the Nations own
    thee great!

New Orleans, *December* 1, 1861.

THE TENNESSEE EXILE'S SONG.

I hear the rushing of her streams,
   The murmuring of her trees,
The exile's anguish swells my heart
   And melts with each soft breeze.
'Midst other scenes her corn-hills wave,
   Her mountains pierce the sky—
Where, where are they who swore to save—
   To conquer, or to die?

They come, from every blue hill-side,
   From every lovely dale,
The heart, the soul, the very pride
   Of mountain, hill, and vale;
They court, like Anak's stalwart sons,
   The rapture of the strife,
Drink in the earthquake of the guns,
   To them, the breath of life.

Spare not the invading mongrel hordes,
   But slay them as they stand!
Strike! Tennessee has living swords,
   The best in all the land!
Strew o'er her plains their hostile lines,
   Drench her fair fields with blood,
Fill their long ranks with bitter groans—
   Let blood flow like a flood!

Ay, sow the seeds of lasting hate
   At Johnson's, Hatton's graves,
And do their deeds and dare their fate,
   Or live the oppressors' slaves!
Bleed freely, as you bled of yore,
   In every well-fought field,
Press round the flag you always bore
   The foremost—as a shield.

.   ·   ·   ·   ·   ·   ·   ·   ·

I feel her pulse beat high and quick,
   Her sinews stretch for strife,
Full come her heart-throbs deep and thick,
   She kindles into life!
Though Donelson has told her tale,
   And Shiloh's page is bright,
There's yet a bloodier field to win,
   For Nashville and the right!

LINES ON THE DEATH OF COL. B. F. TERRY,

*The gallant commander of "The Texas Rangers," who fell at the
battle of Green River, in defense of the rights and liberties of
Kentucky, his native State, and of his adopted South.*

BY J. R. BARRICK.

There is a wail
As if the voice of sadness long and deep,
Had given its low tones to the Southern gale,
   Sweeping o'er vale and steep.
There is a voice
As if of mingled mourning in the land,
And nature, stricken, ceases to rejoice,
   As if at grief's command.

There is a grief
As if of hearts that were unused to mourn,
And sighs and sorrow fail to bring relief
   To those that thus bemoan.
There is a tear
As if of eyes that were unused to tears—
A link of friendship broken that was dear—
   A shadow on past years.

There is a pall
As if of darkness o'er our sun-land spread,
A weight of weariness, and grief on all—
   Who mourn the heroic dead.

The south winds moan,
The south winds murmur in a plaintive strain,
The south birds warble in a saddened tone,
And the land groans with pain.

The Lone Star shines
Less brilliant in her glow of Southern skies,
Since he, the idol of her cherished shrines,
In death's cold slumber lies.
Back to the State
That gave him birth, his spirit bade him come
To share the peril of her pending fate,
Far from his chosen home.

There, where his life
First coursed the channel of its future fame,
He fell, the foremost in the deadly strife,
With glory to his name.
Tho' dead to earth,
While man may boast that he is not a slave
Of tyranny, his valor and his worth
The tide of time will brave.

Dear unto those
To whom his voice in battle gave command,
Who, now, amid the terror of his foes,
Shall head that gallant band?
Dear to the State
Of his adoption, to the people dear
Whose cause he proudly strove. to illustrate,
Who now shall fill his sphere?

GLASGOW, KY., *Dec.* 18, 1861.

THE STRANGER'S DEATH.

No mother bends with tender care
  To kiss his burning brow,
No father kneels in earnest prayer
  Beside the sufferer now.

No sister's gentle voice is near,
  In accents mild and low,
To breathe into his languid ear
  The love that sisters know.

Far from his land and friends and home,
  Across the Mississippi's wave,
His restless spirit bade him roam
  To find a stranger's grave.

The dews of death are on his brow,
  He feels the tyrant's power,
But, hark! he speaks of kindred now,
  In this last trying hour:

" O, Texas! dearest, best beloved,
  Land of my father's home—
Though from thee I have vainly roved,
  For thee I've come—I've come.

" Land of the mountains, heath and stream
  O'er Mississippi's foam,
Thou lingerest in my dying dreams,
  My Texas, and my home !

" How gently could I sink to rest,
  If but my dying gaze
Could rest on those, the kindly-blest,
  The loved of other days !

" Ah ! ye are there, but this is death,
  Friends, I am with you still,
And must I yield this fleeting breath,
  In a last, and sad farewell ?

" I must—I must—then, fare ye well,
  Home, and loved kindred too,
Death soon will break this life's vain spell,
  Friends of my youth—adieu ! "

Beneath the prairie sod he sleeps,
  The wild flowers o'er him wave,
Few friends or kindred there to weep,
  His is a Stranger's Grave.

SONG OF THE TEXAS RANGERS.

INSCRIBED TO MRS. JOHN H. WHARTON.

———

AIR—Yellow Rose of Texas.

———

I.

The morning star is paling,
  The camp fires flicker low,
Our steeds are madly neighing
  For the bugle bids us go;
So put the foot in stirrup,
  And shake the bridle free,
For to-day the Texas Rangers
  Must cross the Tennessee!
    With Wharton for our leader,
      We'll chase the dastard foe,
    Till our horses bathe their fetlocks
      In the deep blue Ohio.

II.

Our men come from the prairies
  Rolling broad, and proud, and free,
From the high and craggy mountains,
  To the murmuring Mexic sea;
And their hearts are open as their plains,
  Their thoughts are proudly brave
6*

As the bold cliffs of the San Bernard,
  Or the Gulf's resistless wave.
    Then quick into the saddle,
      And shake the bridle free,
    To-day with gallant Wharton,
      We cross the Tennessee.

III.

'Tis joy to be a Ranger;
  To fight for dear Southland;
'Tis joy to follow Wharton,
  With his gallant, trusty band;
'Tis joy to see our Harrison
  Plunge, like a meteor bright,
Into the thickest of the fray,
  And strike with deadly might.
      Oh! who would not be a Ranger,
        And follow Wharton's cry,
      To battle for their country—
        And if it need be—die!

IV.

Up with the crimson battle-flag!
  Let the blue pennon fly!
Our steeds are stamping proudly,
  They hear the battle-cry.
The thundering bomb, the bugle's call,
  Proclaim the foe is near,
We strike for God and native land,
  And all we hold most dear.

Then spring into the saddle,
    And shake the bridle free—
For Wharton leads thro' fire and blood,
    For Home and Victory!

THE FLAG OF THE LONE STAR.

BY TENELLA.

Hurrah for the Lone Star!
    Up, up to the mast,
With the honored old bunting,
    And nail it there fast.
The ship is in danger,
    And Texans will fight,
'Neath the flag of the Lone Star,
    For God and their right.

Shall we who have conquered
    Our freedom so late,
Turn traitors, and yield
    Our rights as a State?
No! No! we will battle
    With head, heart and hand,
And the shades of our Fathers
    Around us shall stand.

The Alamo heroes
    Shall wake from their sleep,

Round the Lone Star of Texas
    A vigil to keep.
Oh let them not find us
    Unworthy to guard,
That freedom for which
    They struggled so hard.

The Star Spangled Banner
    Shall never more wave
O'er the heads of the Texans,
    Determined as brave.
At first, when beneath it
    Our rights were denied,
We reverently furled it
    And laid it aside.

But now, with a yell
    Of defiance and hate,
We'll tear down the flag
    We honored so late.
'Tis stamped by "The Beast"
    With indelible shame,
And the blood of a Texan
    Grows hot at its name.

Then up with the "Lone Star,"
    We'll stand with our Hood,
By Davis and Lee,
    As we often have stood.
The ship is in danger,
    And Texans will fight
'Neath the flag of the "Lone Star,"
    For God, and their right.

THERE'S LIFE IN THE OLD LAND YET.

BY JAMES R. RANDALL.

By blue Patapsco's billowy dash,
  The tyrant's war-shout comes,
Along with the cymbal's fitful clash,
  And the roll of his sullen drums.
We hear it! we heed it, with vengeful thrills,
  And we shall not forgive or forget—
There's faith in the streams, there's hope in the hills--
  "There's life in the Old Land yet!"

Minions! we sleep, but we are not dead;
  We are crushed, we are scourged we are scarred;
We crouch—'tis to welcome the triumph-tread
  Of the peerless Beauregard!
Then woe to your vile, polluting horde,
  When the Southern braves are met,
There's faith in the victor's stainless sword—
  "There's life in the Old Land yet!"

Bigots! ye quell not the valiant mind
  With the clank of an iron chain;
The Spirit of Freedom sings in the wind,
  O'er Merryman, Thomas, and Kane!
And we, though we smite not, are not thralls—
  We are piling a gory debt,

E'en down by McHenry's dungeon walls,
  "There's life in the Old Land yet!"

Our women have hung their harps away,
  And they scowl on your brutal bands,
While the nimble poignard dares the day
  In their dear, defiant hands;
They will strip their tresses to string our bows,
  Ere the Northern sun is set,
There's faith in their unavenged woes—
  "There's life in the Old Land yet!"

There's life, though it throbbeth in silent veins;
  'Tis vocal, without noise;
It gushed o'er Manassas' gory plains
  In the blood of the *Maryland boys!*
That blood shall cry aloud, and rise
  With an everlasting threat,
By the death of the brave!—by the God in the skies!—
  "There's life in the Old Land yet!"

ALL QUIET ALONG THE POTOMAC TO-NIGHT.

The authorship of this poem has been disputed with us, but we have every reason to believe that it was written by Lamar Fontaine, Second Virginia Cavalry

" All quiet along the Potomac to-night,"
    Except now and then a stray picket
Is shot, as he walks on his beat to and fro,
    By a rifleman hid in the thicket.
'Tis nothing—a private or two now and then,
    Will not count in the news of the battle;
Not an officer lost—only one of the men—
    Moaning out, all alone, the death rattle.

" All quiet along the Potomac to-night,"
    Where the soldiers lie peacefully dreaming,
Their tents in the rays of the clear autumn moon,
    Or the light of the watch-fires are gleaming.
A tremulous sigh, as the gentle night-wind
    Through the forest leaves slowly is creeping,
While the stars up above, with their glittering eyes,
    Keep guard—for the army is sleeping.

There is only the sound of the lone sentry's tread,
    As he tramps from the rock to the fountain,
And thinks of the two on the low trundle-bed,
    Far away in the cot on the mountain.

His musket falls slack—his face, dark and grim,
    Grows gentle with memories tender,
As he mutters a prayer for his children asleep—
    For their mother, may Heaven defend her!

The moon seems to shine as brightly as then,
    That night, when the love yet unspoken
Leaped up to his lips, and when low murmured vows,
    Were pledged to be ever unbroken.
Then drawing his sleeve roughly over his eyes,
    He dashes off tears that are welling,
And gathers his gun close up to its place,
    As if to keep down the heart-swelling.

He passes the fountain, the blasted pine-tree,
    The footstep is lagging and weary,
Yet onward he goes, through the broad belt of light,
    Towards the shades of the forest so dreary.
Hark! was it the night-wind that rustled the leaves?
    Was it moonlight so wondrously flashing?
It looked like a rifle—ha! Mary, good-bye!
    And the life-blood is ebbing and splashing!

"All quiet along the Potomac to-night,"
    No sound save the rush of the river;
While soft falls the dew on the face of the dead—
    The picket's off duty forever!
1861.

FAST-DAY, NOVEMBER, 1861.

BY MISS R. POWELL, OF VIRGINIA.

Hark! to the silvery chiming,
    That stirs the quiet air,
Calling with solemn summons
    A nation unto prayer.

And now from every dwelling
    Within our Southern land,
The people come, with humble hearts,
    Before their God to stand.

Virginia's sons and daughters
    Bow low before His shrine,
And Carolina's maidens
    Beseech His aid divine.

While on the Gulf's fair sunny shore,
    Where the sparkling waters play,
All with united voice implore
    God's benison to-day.

We plead for all that Thou hast made
    To human hearts most dear,
For home, for life, for liberty,
    Lord, our petitions hear!

Be Thou to us as Thou hast been—
    Our sword, our strength, our shield,

Grant us Thy counsel in the camp,
　　Thy presence in the field.

Hear us, O Lord, for those who go
　　Forth at their country's call,
To fight in our defense, perchance
　　In our defense to fall.

Strengthen each hand, and nerve each heart,
　　And for our Savior's sake,
Into Thy heaven of joy and peace,
　　Each parting spirit take.

What though our enemies declare
　　Their boasted power and sway,
We know the God who reigns on high
　　Is mightier far than they.

Stretch forth Thine hand to aid us, Lord,
　　Do Thou our prayers receive;
Hear Thou in heaven, Thy dwelling-place,
　　And when Thou hearest, forgive.

And when at last the strife is o'er,
　　When all our work is done,
And by Thy blessing on our arms,
　　The victory has been won,

Grant us with steadfast hearts to tread
　　The paths Thy saints have trod,
And be throughout all future time
　　A nation serving God.

THE WAR-CHRISTIAN'S THANKSGIVING.

RESPECTFULLY DEDICATED TO THE WAR-CLERGY OF THE UNITED STATES,
BISHOPS, PRIESTS, AND DEACONS.

BY S. T. WALLACE.

Cursed be he that doeth the work of the Lord negligently, and cursed be he
that keepeth back his sword from blood.—*Jeremiah* 48 : 10.

O God of battles! once again,
　With banner, trump, and drum,
And garments in Thy wine-press dyed,
　To give Thee thanks, we come!

No goats or bullocks, garlanded,
　Unto thine altars go—
With brothers' blood, by brothers shed,
　Our glad libations flow.

From pest-house and from dungeon foul
　Where, maimed and torn, they die;
From gory trench and charnel-house,
　Where, heap on heap, they lie;

In every groan that yields a soul,
　Each shriek a heart that rends—
With every breath of tainted air—
　Our homage, Lord, ascends.

We thank thee for the sabre's gash,
　The cannon's havoc wild,
We bless Thee for the widow's tears,
　The want that starves her child.

We give Thee praise, that Thou hast lit
　The torch and fanned the flame;
That lust and rapine hunt their prey,
　Kind Father! in Thy name;

That, for the songs of idle joy
　False angels sang of yore,
Thou sendest War on Earth, Ill Will
　To Men, forevermore.

We know that wisdom, truth, and right,
　To us and ours are given—
That Thou hast clothed us with Thy wrath,
　To do the work of Heaven.

We know that plains and cities waste
　Are pleasant in Thine eyes;
Thou lov'st a hearthstone desolate,
　Thou lov'st a mourner's cries.

Let not our weakness fall below
　The measure of Thy will,
And while the press hath wine to bleed,
　Oh! tread it with us still!

Teach us to hate—as Jesus taught
　Fond fools, of yore, to love—

Grant us Thy vengeance as our own,
  Thy Pity, hide above.

Teach us to turn, with reeking hands,
  The pages of Thy word,
And hail the blessed curses there,
  On them that sheathe the sword.

Where'er we tread, may deserts spring,
  Till none are left to slay;
And when the last red drop is shed,
  We'll kneel again—and pray!

FORT WARREN.

CHRISTMAS CAROL, FOR 1862.

From "Beechenbrook," a Poem of the War.

BY MRS. M. J. PRESTON, OF VIRGINIA.

'Tis Christmas, the season of mirth and of cheer,
The happiest holiday known to the year,
The one that we oftenest love to recall—
Most ancient, most sacred, and dearest of all!
Turn the records of memory over and see,
What days of your childhood were fullest of glee—
What scenes are remembered as brightest with joy,
For the old and the young—for the maiden and boy—
When home with its festive and innocent mirth,

Seemed the sweetest and sunniest spot upon earth,
And the chimes of your heart most responsively rung,
To the song that the angels at Bethlehem sung;
Be sure that these white-letter days will be drawn,—
Now is it not so?—from your Christmasses gone.

How saddening the change is! The season's the same,
And yet it is Christmas in nothing but name:
No merry expression we utter to-day—
How can we, with hearts that refuse to be gay?
We look back a twelvemonth on many a brow
That graced the home hearthstone—and where are
       they now!
We think of the darling ones clustering there,
But we see thro' our tears, an untenanted chair;
We wait for a footstep—we wait, but in vain—
It will never return from the battle again:
The dear face is hidden cold under the clay—
His Christmas is kept with the angels to-day!
Thank God! there is joy in the sorrow for all—
He fell—but it surely was blessed to fall;
For never shall murmur be heard from the mouth
Of mother or wife thro' our beautiful South,
Or sister or maiden yield grudging her part,
Tho' the price that she pays, must be coined from
       her heart!

We drop the close curtains—we stir up the fire,
And pile up the blazing hearth higher and. higher;
We wheel up our chair, and with friends and good
       cheer,

We try to shut from us all visions of fear.
But the spectre *will* come—thro' the warmth and the
    light,
The camp gleams before us, all shrouded in white;
We tread the soft carpet, and lo! there's the sound
Of the half-frozen sentinel pacing his round.
Come hither, my pretty musician,—we say,
Come chase us this gloomy oppression away,
Her hand o'er the instrument gently she flings,
And this is the song of the Snow that she sings:

I.

Halt! the march is over;
    Day is almost done;
Loose the cumbrous knapsack,
    Drop the heavy gun:
Chilled, and worn, and weary,
    Wander to and fro,
Seeking wood to kindle
    Fires amidst the snow.

II.

Round the camp-blaze gather,
    Heed not sleet nor cold;
Ye are Spartan soldiers,
    Strong, and brave, and bold.
Never Xerxian army
    Yet subdued a foe,
Who but asked a blanket
    On a bed of snow!

III.

Shivering midst the darkness,
  Christian men are found
There devoutly kneeling
  On the frozen ground ;
Pleading for their country
  In its hour of woe,
For its soldiers marching
  Shoeless through the snow !

IV.

Lost in heavy slumbers,
  Free from toil and strife,
Dreaming of their dear ones—
  Home, and child, and wife ;
Tentless they are lying,
  While the fires burn low—
Lying in their blankets,
  Midst December's snow !

A PICTURE.

We were sitting round the table
  Just a night or two ago,
In the little cozy parlor,
  With the lamp light burning low;
And the window blinds half opened,
  For the summer air to come,
And the painted curtain waving
  Like a busy pendulum.
O! the cushion on the sofa,
  And the pictures on the wall,
And the gathering of comforts
  In the old familiar hall;
And the wagging of the pointer,
  Lounging idly by the door,   ·
And the flitting of the shadow
  From the ceiling to the floor.
O! they wakened in my spirits,
  Like the beautiful in Art,
Such a busy, busy thinking,
  Such a dreaminess of heart,
That I sat amongst the shadows
  With my spirit all astray,
Thinking only—thinking only
  Of the soldiers far away!
And the tent beneath the moonlight,
  Of the stirring tattoo's sound,

7

And the soldier in his blanket—
  In his blanket on the ground.
Of the icy winter coming,
  Of the bleak, bleak winds that blow,
And the soldier in his blanket—
  In his blanket on the snow!
Then I linger in my dreaming,
  In my dreaming far away,
Till the spirit's picture-painting
  Seemed as vivid as the day;
And the moonlight faded softly
  From the window open wide,
And the ever faithful pointer
  Nestled closer at my side.
And I know, beneath the starlight,
  Tho' the chilly frosts may fall,
That the soldier will be dreaming,
  Dreaming often of us all.
So I give my spirit's painting
  Just the breathing of a sound,
For the dreaming, dreaming soldier
  In his slumber on the ground.

Savannah Morning News.

A SOUTHERN SCENE.—1862.

"Oh, mammy, have you heard the news?"
   Thus spake a Southern child,
As, in the nurse's aged face,
   She upward glanced and smiled.

"What news you mean, my little one?
   It must be mighty fine,
To make my darling's face so red,
   Her sunny blue eyes shine."

"Why, Abram Lincoln, don't you know?
   The Yankee President,
Whose ugly picture once we saw,
   When up to town we went,

"Why, he is going to free you all,
   And make you rich and grand,
And you'll be dressed in silk and gold,
   Like the proudest in the land.

"A gilded coach shall carry you
   Whene'er you wish to ride,
And, mammy, all your work shall be
   Forever laid aside."

The eager speaker paused for breath,
   And then the old nurse said,

While closer to her swarthy cheek
    She pressed the golden head:

"My little missus, stop an' res,
    You 's talking mighty fas,
Jes look up dere an' tell me what
    You see in yonder glass?

"You see ole mammy's wrinkled face,
    As black as any coal,
An' underneath her handkerchief
    Whole heaps of knotty wool.

"My darlin's face is red and white,
    Her skin is sof and fine,
And on her putty little head
    De yaller ringlets shine.

"My chile, who made dis difference
    'Twixt mammy and twixt you?
You reads it in de dear Lord's book,
    An' you kin tell me true.

"De dear Lord said, it must be so,
    An' honey, I, for one,
Wid tankful heart will always say,
    'His holy will be done.'

"I tanks Mass Linkum all de same,
    But when I wants for free,
I'll ask de Lord ob glory,
    Not poor buckra man, like he.

" And as for gilded carriages,
  Deys berry fine to see,
But massa's coach what carries him
  Is good enough for me.

" An' honey, when your mammy wants
  To change her homespun dress,
She'll pray, like dear old missus,
  To be clothed with righteousness.

" My work's been done dis many a day,
  An' now I takes my ease;
A waiten for de Master's call,
  Jes when de Master please.

" An' when at last de time done come,
  An' poor ole mammy dies,
Your own dear mother's sof white han'
  Shall close dese tired old eyes.

" De dear Lord Jesus soon will take
  Ole mammy home to Him,
An' he can wash my guilty soul
  From eb'ry stain of sin.

" An' at his feet I shall lie down,
  Who died and rose for me,
An' den, an' not till den, my chile,
  Your mammy shall be free.

"Come, little missus, say your prayers,
  Let ole Mass Linkum 'lone.
De debil knows who b'longs to him
  An' he'll take care ob his own."

SONG OF THE FREEDMAN.

[On Orleans street, near Adams, yesterday afternoon, there sat
upon the curbstone a gray-haired negro man; his face was
buried in his hands; tears crept through his toughened fingers,
and his groans melted the heart of the passers-by. When
questioned, he said he must die; that he had no home, that
he was sick; and no one cared for him now. Listen to his
story. It is in truthful verse by A. R. WATSON :]

A freedman sat on a pile of bricks,
  As the rain was pattering down,
His shoes were worn and his coat was torn,
  And his hat was without a crown.
He viewed the clouds and he viewed himself,
  And he shook the wet from his head,
A tear dimmed his eye as he saw go by
  A boy with a loaf of bread.
And he raised his voice in a dolorous tone,
  That sounded like a gong,
While the rain came down on his nappy crown,
  And sang to himself this song:

De wind blows cold, but I's done wid toil,
  And leff de cotton patch;
I guess ole massa tink he count
  De chickens 'fore dey hatch.
I totes no more de heaby load,
  Nor drives ole missus round,
I wonder who dey's gwine to get
  To work de patch ob ground?
Den fling away de rake and hoe,
  Dis am de jubilee,
De rain may come, de wind may blow,
  But bress de Lord I's free!

But I tink last night as I tried to sleep
  Upon de muddy ground,
While de rain was drippin' on my head
  And de wind was whizzin' round,
I'd like to hab my light'ood fire,
  And my cabin back again,
For de wedder's gettin' berry cold
  Out here in all dis rain;
But den I's done wid de rake and hoe,
  Dis am de jubilee,
De rain may come, de wind may blow,
  But bress de Lord I's free!

I's got all ragged 'bout de knees,
  My shoes is worn-out too,
My coat so ole dat from each sleeve
  De elbow's commin froo.
And dere's de children dat once played
  In shirt-tail bout de yard,

I cannot buy a shirt for dem,
  De time's so berry hard.
But fling away de rake and hoe,
  Dis am de jubilee,
De rain may come, de wind may blow,
  But bress de Lord I's free!

De udder day when Pinky 'died,
  I tink it berry good,
Dat de dear Lord should take her off
  Before dis cold wind blowed.
But den 'twas hard to see her die—
  I wish she'd not been born—
I's 'fraid she perished, for she asked
  About de rice and corn.
But den I's done wid de rake and hoe,
  Dis am de jubilee,
De rain may come, de wind may blow,
  But bress de Lord I's free!

And Dinah sits here on de ground
  And looks so thin and poor,
She cannot sing de song she sung
  About de cabin door.
Her poor old limbs are almost bare,
  Her cheek bone's comin froo;
I almost wish de Lord would come
  And take her up dere too.
But den she's done wid de rake and hoe,
  Dis am de jubilee,
De rain may come, de wind may blow,
  But bress de Lord she's free!

I dreamt las' night ole massa come
  And took us home wid he,
To de log cabin dat we lef
  When first dey set us free;
And dere I built de light'ood fire,
  And Dinah cook'd de yam,
Dey say dat dreams are sometimes true,
  I wonder if dis one am?
But den I's flung away de hoe,
  To hab a. jubilee,
De rain may come, de wind may blow,
  But bress de Lord I's free!

ATLANTA, GA.

THE UNRETURNING.

The swallow leaves the ancient eaves,
     As in the days agone;
The wheaten fields are all ablaze
And in and out the west wind plays,
     Amid the tasseled corn.

The sun's rays light as warm and bright
     On clover fields all red;
The wild bird wakes his simple song
As joyfully, the whole day long,
    As if *he* were not dead!

7*

The summer skies, with softest sighs,
          Their rain and sunshine send,
And, standing in the farmhouse door,
I see—dotting the landscape o'er—
          The flocks he used to tend.

The woodbine grows—the jasmine blows—
          Beside the window-sill;
Their soft sweet sigh is in the air,
For the dear hands that placed them there
          On the red field are still.

Around the wolds the summer folds
          Her wealth of golden light,
And, past the willows' silvery gleam,
I catch the glimmering of the stream
          And lilies, cool and white.

But oh! one shade has solemn made
          The sunshine and the bloom,
His voice, whose sweet and gentle words,
Were sweeter than the song of birds,
          Is silent in the tomb.

How can the day, so bright and gay,
          Glare round the farmhouse door?
When all the quiet ways he trod
By leafy wood, or blooming sod,
          Shall know him nevermore!

ZOLLICOFFER.

Killed Battle of Somerset, Ky., 19*th Jan'y*, 1862.

BY H. L. FLASH.

First in the fight, and first in the arms
  Of the white-winged angels of glory,
With the heart of the South at the feet of God,
  And his wounds to tell the story.

For the blood that flowed from his hero heart,
  On the spot where he nobly perished,
Was drunk by the earth as a sacrament
  In the holy cause he cherished!

In heaven a home with the brave and blessed,
  And for his soul's sustaining,
The atoning blood of his Savior, Christ,
  And nothing on earth remaining

But a handful of dust in the land of his choice—
  A name in song and story,
And fame to shout with immortal voice,
  " Dead on the field of glory !"

THE BURIAL OF CAPT. O. JENNINGS WISE.

Killed at Roanoke Island, February 8th, 1862.

BY ACCOMAC.

Mournfully the bells are tolling,
And the muffled drums are rolling
With a sad and dreamy echo,
Through Richmond's crowded streets;
And the dead-march slowly pealing,
On the solemn air now stealing,
Hushing every lightsome feeling,
Our saddened senses greet;
And a look of settled sorrow
Is on every face we meet.

To his last, long home they're bearing
One, whose many deeds of daring,
One, whose noble, high-toned spirit
Has endeared him to us all;
Now, his sleep shall know no waking,
Now, his rest shall have no breaking,
And no more, amid war's thunders,
Shall his soldiers hear his call.
He has laid aside his armor,
And his banner is his pall!

But his deeds will never slumber,
For we'll ever proudly number

Him among the brave who've perished
  Struggling for our liberty;
And Virginia, when she's weeping
O'er the sons that now are sleeping
On her bosom, shall forget not
  That he died to set her free;
And graven on her sacred tablets
  Shall his name forever be!

FORT DONELSON — THE SIEGE, FEB'Y, 1862.

BY MRS. C. A. WARFIELD, OF KY.

I cannot look on the sunshine
  That breaks thro' the clouds to-day,
I can only lie in the shadow,
  And close my eyes and pray;
Pray, with my pale lips moving,
  While my breath comes thick and short,
For that band of beleaguered heroes
  Shut up in that doomed Fort.

Constant and true, yet hopeless,
  Desperate and stern and brave,
With the black flag waving o'er them,
  Each stands by his yawning grave;
Their foes gather thick around them,
  In numbers as five to one,

And more follow fast in the distance,
　As motes in the noonday sun.

The strength of the strong man faileth,
　He panteth for needful rest,
He is changed as by years of anguish,
　By the fever in his breast.
Fierce and grim and grizzly,
　As wolves on the Lapland wold,
They gaze on their spent munition,
　And the fourth day nearly told.

Oh! God, from Thy throne in heaven,
　Put forth Thy saving hand,
Succor them, oh! my Father,
　Our death-devoted band.
It is not in human wisdom,
　It is not in mortal skill,
To stay the bolt of perdition—
　All resteth with Thy will.

The evening is closing around us—
　The evening cold and gray—
We hear the booming cannon
　In the city far away.
We know the Fort has fallen,
　We mourn our bitter loss,
Yet we glory in our heroes—
　Our martyrs of the cross.

THE BATTLE OF HAMPTON ROADS.

BY TENELLA.

Now, once again, let Southern hearts unite in thank-
    ful praise
To the mighty God of battles, mysterious in His ways;
For He hath rent the cloudy veil which late con-
    cealed His face,
And in the fiery pillar's light revealed His wondrous
    grace.
At noon, the hated Cumberland, the Congress by her
    side,
Our iron-clad Virginia most scornfully defied;
Ere night the waves were rolling o'er stem, and stern,
    and mast,
While from her burning consort a lurid glare was cast;
And silenced were the batteries that, from the neigh-
    b'ring shore,
Rained shot and shell upon her with hoarse and sullen
    roar.
The good ship Minnesota lies many a fathom deep,
And 'neath the silent waters three hundred foemen
    sleep,
For, ah! the sunken Merrimac, Antæus-like, arose,
And re-baptized " Virginia," deals death unto our foes.
They boasted that the serpent lay coiled around our
    hearts,

But from its iron cradle our infant navy starts,
And at one grasp has strangled the base, insidious foe,
Who, *with the white flag flying*, dared strike a coward's
    blow.
Oh, brethren ! can you wonder, while 'neath this brand
    he burns,
Upon your wives and children his dastard arms he
    turns ?
Nor scorns on flying women to pour his murd'rous fire,
And vent on wailing infants his baffled, savage ire !
But, Southerners, take courage ; sink not beneath the
    rod ;
Rise, buckle on your armor, and put your trust in
    God.
What though your homes be vacant, or worse, in
    ashes lie—
" Like the bird unto the mountain," your helpless
    women fly ?—
Though the changing tide of fortune may ebb as well
    as flow,
'Tis the hand that crowned with victory that deals
    the chastening· blow.
We are battling for our freedom, our sacred rights
    and laws,
And the God that gave these blessings himself be-
    friends our cause.
Yes, like a treach'rous serpent, our foe around us coils,
But, though he's hydra-headed, we are not in his toils ;
Like the scorpion, he shall perish by his own poisoned
    bite,
If undismayed we battle for God and for our right.

Then, maiden, arm your lover ; oh ! mother, gird
 your son ;
And, wife, cheer on your husband, till liberty is won.
Like the steed in strength rejoicing, the eagle free of
 wing,
O'er ocean, plain, and mountain, our banner outward
 fling !

THE TURTLE.

Cæsar, afloat with his fortunes !
 And all the world agog,
Straining its eyes
At a thing that lies
 In the water, like a log !
It's a weasel ! a whale !
I see it's tail ;
 It's a porpoise ! a pollywog !

Tarnation ! it's a turtle !
 And blast my bones and skin,
My hearties ! sink her,
Or else you'll think her
 A regular terror-pin !

The frigate poured a broadside !
 The bombs they whistled well,
But, hit old Nick
With a sugar stick !
 It didn't "phase" her shell !

Piff, from the creature's larboard—
  And dipping along the water,
A bullett hissed
From a wreath of mist
  Into a doodle's quarter!

Raff, from the creature's starboard—
  Rip, from his ugly snorter,
And the Congress, and
The Cumberland
  Sunk, and nothing—shorter.

Now here's to you, "Virginia,"
  And you are bound to win,
By your rate of bobbing round,
  And your way of pitchin in;
For you are a cross
Of the old sea-horse,
  And a regular terror-pin!

ALBERT SIDNEY JOHNSTON.

Killed Battle of Shiloh, April, 1862.

BY FLEMING JAMES.

'Mid dim and solemn forests, in the dawning chill
    and gray,
Over dank, unrustling leaves, or through the stiff
    and sodden clay,
With never a fife or bugle, or mutter of rumbling
    drum,
With shivering forms and solemn souls the Southern
    soldiers come;
Their long lines vanishing in mist as onward they
    are sweeping
With step as silent as the dawn's to where the foe
    is sleeping.
Hark! a challenge! "Halt!" Th' expected shot—
    and then a dozen more,
Like pebbles pattering down the steep the avalanche
    before;
And then a rush, and then a yell, and then a blind-
    ing glare,
And then a crash to lift the feet, resounding every-
    where!
Now vanish chill and solemn thoughts, now burns
    the frenzied blood!

The tottering tents toss to and fro upon the driving
    flood,
And the camp-fires flash and darken fast beneath the
    masses' tread—
Now smoke behind in scattered brands 'mid wounded
    men and dead.
And forward crowd the fugitives in panic-driven
    race;
In vain in bush, ravine and brake they hunt a hid-
    ing place;
For still that long line onward sweeps unbroken far
    and near
As War himself, with pinions bowed, were screaming
    in their rear!

But far beyond the panic's reach the foe is forming
    fast—
And in our path stands rank on rank of long bat-
    talion's massed.
Now, Southern soldiers, nerve your hearts and gather
    up your strength,
The time of trial waited for is come to you at
    length!
Remember how you left your homes—that cruel part-
    ing, men,
And all the weary months of toil and suffering since
    then!
Remember now, ye refugees, your olden homes that be
By Cumberland's green waters or the crystal Ten-
    nessee—
And your waiting wives and sisters, and your chil-
    dren at their play,

Or your homeless, helpless wanderers—how many!
    who can say?
Two chimneys tall and a crumbling wall are all the
    home I have,
And all I love are on the world or sheltered in the
    grave!
If ever you have thought to fight because our cause
    is just,
And in the god of battles, boys, have put the freeman's
    trust;
And if ever you have dreamed of home and prayed
    to set it free,
Oh! pray to-day, and fight to-day for Southern liberty;
For Southern rights and Southern homes, and South-
    ern liberty!

Now a hundred pieces open and their shrieking mis-
    siles pour,
And full ten thousand muskets flash and mingle in
    the roar,
Till the cannon's boom is swallowed in the din of
    musketry,
As the booming of the ocean when the thunders crash
    on high.
But momently our laboring lines are charging o'er the
    field,
And forcing back the stubborn ranks which only
    inches yield;
For at every fence they rally and oppose our surging
    flood,
Till their dead lie heaped before us wherever they have
    stood.

Here a Southern regiment is matched against a full
    brigade,
Not a hundred yards apart in open field arrayed—
And a brook half-way between them through a copse
    of willows glides,
There's not a rock, fence, log or . tree to shelter ours
    besides.
But stubbornly, undauntedly, with ne'er a cheer or
    shout—
With hands too busy for their lips they deal their
    vollies out !
Oh ! unavailing courage !   How the bullets beat you
    down !
I fear, ye gallant Southrons, ye can never hold your
    own !
But the Colonel passes down the lines, in clear and
    steady voice
He tells : " The order's come at last ; 'tis bayonets,
    my boys ! "
And their eyes exchange their lightnings and their
    hearts exchange a thrill—
Then the word—a clank of muskets—and they for-
    ward with a will.
Ah ! woe betide the enemy who tarries in their path,
Death bends him to his iron scythe to cut a bloody
    swath !

Again the battle gathers strength on yonder wooded
    hill,
Behind whose awful batteries fresh ranks are forming
    still ;

A reeking vail of undergrowth divides the hostile
    lines, ·

But lurid through its tangled web the vivid lightning
    shines !

And so appalling death appears behind that dreadful
    pall—

The stoutest spirit hesitates and flinches from his call.

Now who will pierce that curtain dire and meet the
    battle's brunt,

Before their armies gather there and burst upon our
    front ?

Again the stern portentous cry of bayonets is heard,

But not again the serried line springs forward at the
    word ;

Behind the trees as skirmishers the cowering soldiers
    hide,

And from afar the harmless trade of musket balls is
    plied.

In vain, in vain their leaders shout, they cannot make
    them stir,

But perish singly in the lead with scarce a follower !

But hark ! a sound of hoofs behind, a clang of sabres
    loud !

I see a squad of mighty men go by me like a cloud !

As the immortals rode to war when Hector fought for
    Troy,

These ride as if immortals too, inspired with awful
    joy.

Before them rides their leader with a form that fills
    the air,

So does his bearing fill their eyes as if a god were
 there !

Look how he rides to battle with a glory on his brow,

As if prophetic victory held her laurels o'er it now.

They are riding to the rescue; it is Johnston rides
 before !

God grant they be in time to turn the battle's tide
 once more.

I hear their shoutings in the din, I hear the cries to
 "form,"

I see a stiffening battle line take shape within the
 swarm;

And again the rank advances with an impetus of
 wrath,

Their chieftain's rage in every heart impels them on
 their path !

A thousand rifles level'd low, but every rifle dumb,

The beating of a thousand feet upon a monster drum,

A surging of the war-cloud as they disappear beneath,

A sickening of my spirit and a gasping of my breath;

Redoubled din—a lull—a cheer; I would the smoke
 would go !

Oh ! see our swooping battle-flags ! Oh ! see the fleeing foe !

Now glory to those gallant men ; and, Father, to thy
 hand,

To-morrow shall thy praises ring throughout our
 stricken land !

But where is he who rallied them ? I miss his charger
 there ;

I see him now midst yonder three whose saddles all
    are bare ;
And two men staggering with a load this side of
    them I see ;
Oh ! who is it they carry in their arms so tenderly ?
They lay him gently on the leaves. Ah ! well I
    know him now ;
I know that lordly figure and that grand imperial
    brow !
'Tis he, but, oh ! how prostrate that form which filled
    the air,
And his the pallid face ; but look, the glory still is
    there !

Oh ! ye daughters of Kentucky, ere your peans are
    begun,
Your lips shall falter when they tell how Shiloh's
    fight was won !
Oh ! ye " hunters of Kentucky," how your hunting
    grounds are poor,
For the noblest of the " hunters of Kentucky " hunts
    no more !
And oh ! country, whose reproaches made him weary
    of his life,
But never made him traitor in that hour with traitors
    rife,
Thou shalt lift thy voice repentant but in unavailing
    praise,
The stony ear shall never hear in his last resting
    place !

8

And thy daughters' hands shall weave the crown of
    laurels, but in vain,
His marble brows shall never feel, nor pulse beat quick
    again.
Oh! South, be sure a heart so pure had never loved
    so well
A country which had wronged him sore, he pardoned
    ere he fell!

LINES WRITTEN DURING THESE GLOOMY TIMES—TO HIM WHO DESPAIRS.

[Spoken at the Richmond "Varieties," by Mr. Ogden, Wednes-
day night, May 7th, 1862.]

BY PROF. J. H. HEWITT.

Tho' our roofs be on fire, tho' our rivers run blood,
Tho' their flag's on the hill, on the plain, on the
    flood,
Tho' their bayonets bristle and shouts rend the air,
Faint heart, do not utter the cry of despair!

The red morn looks down on the field of the slain,
The gaunt vulture soars over the desolate plain;
By the loved ones that mantled in glory lie there,
Arouse from thy stupor and never despair!

We have mountains that lift their grey peaks to the
    skies,
We have rifles whose crack to the war-yell replies,
We have sinewy arms, we have souls. that will dare,
While these are our safe-guards, why, doubters, de-
    spair ?

The great God is just and he blesses the right,
He makes the weak rise like a giant in might;
When he strikes for his home and the tender ones
    there,
There's hope in each blow—there is shame in despair !

Then, shoulder to shoulder, push on with a tread
That will shake the loose earth that is heaped o'er
    the dead ;
Bear the torch and the sword to the proud tyrant's
    lair,
Let the wild battle-shout drown the wail of despair !

Despair ? while the old man can flourish his staff ;
Despair ? while the boy at the invader can laugh ;
Despair ? while our daughters and wives kneel in
    prayer,
And our mothers cry out, Don't despair ! don't despair !

Go preach to the rock on the lone ocean shore,
And tell it to battle the billows no more ;
While there's life, there is hope ; for the death-blow
    prepare,
It is glorious to battle—'tis base to despair !

"AWAY WITH THE DASTARDS WHO WHINE OF DEFEAT."

BY PAUL H HAYNE, OF SOUTH CAROLINA.

Away with the dastards who whine of defeat,
  And hint that the day of destruction draws near,
Who counsel "submission," or whisper "retreat,"
  With the traitor's mistrust and the renegade's fear.

What! doff the strong armor, and yield us as slaves
  To lust and to robbery, banded with might,
While the standard that symbols our liberty waves,
  Still flaming and fair in the front of the fight?

By the souls of our fathers! I hold them accurst,
  The caitiffs who falter and flee from the strife,·
Who would slake at Dishonor's foul cess-pool the
      thirst
  Of a passion—the meanest and· basest—for life!

Go! crouch in the forest! Go! hide 'neath the rock!
  Slink, pallid and scared, into mountain and den;
We have maidens to fill your lost ranks in the field
  Of death and of conflict—most gallant of men!

The soul of the brave saint of Orleans is here,
  It thrills in the voices, it burns on the cheek

Of women who heed not the wail of despair,
   And scorn the false words which the craven would
      speak.

"Submission," ah! yes! we'll submit when the sod,
   Lies blackened and bare on the tombs of our race,
And "retreat" when the call of our merciful God,
   Shall bid us disband in His kingdom of grace!

CHARLESTON, *May* 10, 1862.

STEADY AND READY.

Steady, when fortune's dark shadows surround us,
   Calm, when the winds of adversity blow;
Brave, when the world's hollow voice would confound
      us,
   Strong, though its wild waves tumultuously flow;
Steady in tempest, in strife and commotion,
   Hope as our anchor to stem the rude sea,
Fierce though the billows, and wrathful the ocean,
   Steady and ready our maxim shall be.

Ready, when sinister foes would oppose us,
   Dauntless in conflict to do and to dare;
Ready to echo the voices which bless us
   When shielding our offspring from want and despair;
Ready—to calm the low wailing of sorrow,
   To battle with wrong till the enemy flee;

Hoping and trusting to win the bright morrow,
  Steady and ready our maxim shall be.

Steady—while dark streams around us are flowing,
  Steady—the rocks and the quicksands to shun;
Firmer in faith and full-heartedness growing,
  Till the conflict is over, the victory won.
Glimpses of sunshine steal o'er the dark river,
  Star-light and moon-light illumine the sea;
Hail to the symbol both now and forever,
  Steady and ready our maxim shall be.

PRAYER.

[These verses were written by a deaf and dumb girl of Savannah,
Ga., on the occasion of a fast-day.]

Before Thy throne, O God!
Upon this blood-wet sod,
  We bend the knee:
And to the darkened skies
We lift imploring eyes,
  We cry to Thee.

The clouds of gloom untold
Have deepened fold on fold,
  By Thy command;
And war's red banner waves,
Still o'er the bloody graves,
  That fill the land.

Our trampled harvest field,
No more its bounty yields—
  Of corn and wine;
Thy suffering children see,
They crave no friends but Thee,
  No help but Thine.

Behold how few we stand,
To guard our native land
  From shame and wrong;

How weak without Thine aid!
Yet by Thy hand arrayed,
　We shall be strong.

Hark! through the vernal air
The foemen's shout we hear—
　They come! they come!
From valley, hill, and coast
They throng, a countless host,
　Around our homes.

O God! save us from harm!
Stretch forth Thy mighty arm,
　Thy glittering spear!
We fight beneath Thy shield,
We cannot fear nor yield
　For Thou art near.

And Thou, O Christ, so fair,
Who did'st our sorrows bear,
　Prince of Peace!
Breathe out Thy love divine,
Through all this world of Thine,
　And war shall cease!

A SUNDAY REVERIE.

BY JAMES R. RANDALL.

Beyond my dingy window pane,
  This beaming Sunday morn,
I watch the red-breast on the vane,
  And the ravens robbing corn;
Hard by, the Alabama boils
  Its sallow flood along,
With drift-wood full and forest spoils—
  A melancholy throng!

The rich horizon melts away
  To an illumined arch,
With Summer glories all astray
  Upon the brows of March;
The birds, inebriate with glees,
  Seem happiest when they sing,
Filling the aromatic trees
  With melodies of Spring.

The pulse of nature throbs anew,
  Impassioned by the sun;
The violet, with eyes of blue,
  Is modest as a nun;
The roses reck not of the strife
  That crashes from the North—

8*

Alas! the mockery of life,
  When Death is striding forth.

An alien in this lovely land,
  I sound an alien strain,
Until my own fair State shall stand,
  Inviolate again.
The long-lost Pleiad of our sky
  Is glimmering still afar,
The nations yet shall see on high,
  That bright and blessed star.

The church bells toll their solemn chime,
  Above the minster eaves,
Knelling some old religious rhyme,
  Half-stifled by the leaves.
A thousand miles away, I hear,
  Those grand Cathedral notes,
Which made my youth a fairy sphere,
  With cymbal-clashing throats.

And oh, I feel as men must feel
  Who have not wept for years!
Upon my cheek behold the seal
  Of consecrated tears.
A mighty Sabbath calm is mine,
  That baffles human lore;
A resurrection of "Lang Syne"—
  A guiltless child once more!

And Mother's schoolboy, with his mimes,
  This beaming Sunday morn,

Forgets the grim, tumultuous times
  That hardened him in scorn ;
Forgets terrific ocean days
  Beyond the tropic gates,
Where the Magellan clouds gaze down
  On Patagonian straits.

He nothing heeds the long despair
  Within the savage swamp,
The jungle and the thicket, where
  The serpent tribes encamp :
He little heeds the sport of fame,
  Its treason or its trust ;
The hope of a sonorous name—
  A requiem from the dust.

But oh, he heeds elysian hours,
  That tell of Long Ago !
Those dreamy days in College towers,
  He nevermore shall know ;
The home he never more may see,
  A Paradise to him—
The books he read at Mother's knee,
  When her dear eyes grew dim.

O, Mother ! Mother ! years must fleet,
  Along the battle track,
Ere yet thy lonely heart can greet
  Its weary wanderer back ;
A deathless love these tears bespeak,
  For thy devotion shed,
With thy pure kisses on my cheek,
  Thy blessings on my head !

THE SOLDIER'S FAREWELL TO HIS WIFE.

BY WILLIAM K. CAMPBELL, OF GREENEVILLE, S. C.

Side by side, and hand in hand,
　Silently we sit;
For the parting hour is near,
　Swift the moments flit !
Scarce a word is uttered now
　But our eyelids fill;
And the children too, are sad,
　Their rosy lips are still.

Looks. and tears are all that speak,
　And the smothered sigh;
Hark—the rolling carriage wheels,
　And the coachman's cry !
Hurriedly " Good bye " is said,
　One fond pressure more—
Then the prayer " May God bless you !"
　And the parting 's o'er !

Oh, the pain that parting brings !
　Sorrow weighs the heart,
And the aching breast will heave,
　And the tears will start;
For the painful thought will rise
　That, when now we sever,

We perchance will meet again,
　Nevermore—oh, never !

Shall thy eyes, my dearest wife,
　Beam once again on me ?
Shall I kiss those loving lips
　Oft pressed so tenderly ?
Thy sweet smile and welcome home,
　Will kind Heaven restore ?
Shall I meet my little ones
　Happily, once more ?

Oh ! 'tis hard to part from home,
　Feeling, day by day,
That the loved ones left behind,
　Slowly pine away !
Thoughtless children may forget—
　Oh ! their happy lot !
But their mother's grief flows on,
　She forgetteth not !

JAMES' ISLAND, 1862.

THE SOLDIER'S GRAVE.

BY PEARL.

'Tis where no chisel's tracing tells,
  The humble sleeper's name,
No storied marble proudly swells,
  The measure of his fame.

Nor while the pensive moonbeams sleep,
  Upon the dim blue wave,
Do mourning kindred come to weep,
  Beside the *soldier's grave.*

But poised upon her gleaming wings,
  The beauteous summer bird,
In sweet and melting strains to sing
  His requiem is heard.

And oft as spring her garland weaves,
  There blooms her dewy rose,
And autumn strews her yellow leaves,
  Above his deep repose.

So true is Nature to his tomb,
  So true I almost crave,
While musing on the soldier's doom,
  To fill a soldier's grave.

Victoria Advocate.

THE SOLDIER'S LAST COMBAT.

BY MRS. ELIZA E. HARPER.

The soldier girded his armor on,
The fire of hope in his bright eyes shone,
He knew he must meet his foe ere long,
But his heart was beating high and strong.
Feeling naught of fear or dread,
As he heard the swift approaching tread—
Not with the sound of stirring drums,
Not as an earthly foeman comes,
Not with the din of the cannon's rattle,
Nor with the pomp and blaze of battle;
The severed cord and the broken bowl,
Marked the foe—a foe of old !
He must prepare to meet him *alone,*
Of all the thousands there, not one
Could go forth now, by his side to fight,
For his foe was hidden from mortal sight.
He looked on his brothers, the friends of his youth,
Who had gathered round his pain to soothe,
His thoughts went back, to the southern home,
To which he nevermore might come.
The view of the dear ones gathered there,
Spread o'er his soul, the gloom of despair,
He girded his armor closer on,
Shut out the sight of joys that are gone,

With a. prayer, and a blessing they could not hear,
He turned to the foeman drawing near.
He looked on his "*Captain*," whose tearful eyes,
Whose compressed lips, and smothered sighs,
And heart too full for words of cheer,
Told how he loved his brave soldier. ·
He smiled, as he bade his "*Captain*" "good-bye,"
He saw beside him, with faith's clear eye,
Jesus, the "*Captain of Israel's host,*
And all his pain in that vision, was lost.
Tired nature at length gave way,
And sleep, o'er the soldier, held her sway,
Till he woke again from visions bright,
Saw in his room a glorious light,
Knew from angels' wings it shone,
And girded his armor closer on.
Stronger his heart to meet the foe,
Whose coming now seemed but too slow,
Triumph in his dimmed eyes glistened,
His friends drew near, and eagerly listened
To the sound of his clear, though feeble voice,
"*I have fought a good fight, I have finished my course,*
I have kept the faith —"   *   *   *   *   *
*   *   *   *   *   and· all was past!
He had met his foe and conquered at last.

October, 1861.

HOME AGAIN!

Written in Prison.

BY JEFF. THOMPSON.

My dear wife awaits my coming,
  My children lisp my name,
And kind friends wait to welcome
  Me to my own home again.
My father's grave lies on the hill,
  My boys sleep in the vale,
I love each rock and murmuring rill,
  Each mountain, hill, and dale,
                    Home again!

I'll suffer hardships, toil and pain,
  For the good times that are to come,
I'll battle long that I may gain
  My freedom and my home.
I will return, though foes may stand,
  Disputing every rod;
My own dear home—my native land—
  I'll win you yet through God,
                    Home again!

MY FATHER.

[The following beautiful lines were written by Brigadier-General
HENRY R. JACKSON, of Georgia, who was re ently operating in
the Confederate Army, below Richmond :]

As die the embers on the hearth,
    And o'er the hearth the shadows fall,
And creeps the chirping cricket forth,
    And ticks the death-watch in the wall,
I see a form in yonder chair,
    That grows beneath the waning light,
There are the wan, sad features—there
    The pallid brow and locks of white.

My father! when they laid thee down,
    And heaped the clay upon thy breast,
And left thee sleeping all alone
    Upon thy narrow couch of rest,
I know not why, I could not weep—
    The soothing drops refused to roll,
And oh! that grief is wild and deep,
    Which settles tearless on the soul.

But when I saw thy vacant chair,
    Thine idle hat upon the wall,
The book—the penciled passage where
    Thy eye had rested last of all—

The tree beneath whose friendly shade,
　Thy trembling feet had wandered forth,
The very prints those feet had made,
　When last they feebly trod the earth;

And thought while countless ages fled,
　Thy vacant seat would vacant stand—
Unworn the hat—thy book unread—
　Effaced thy footsteps from the sand—
And widowed in this cheerless world,　.
　The heart that gave its love to thee—
Torn, like the vine whose tendrils curled
　More closely round the falling tree—

O, father! then for her and thee
　Gushed madly forth the scorching tears;
And oft and long, and bitterly
　Those tears have gushed in later years;
For as the world grows cold around,
　And things assume their real hue,
'Tis sad to find that love is found,
　Alone above the stars with you.

MY WIFE AND CHILD.

BY HENRY R. JACKSON.

The tattoo beats—the lights are gone,
  The camp around in slumber lies,
The night with solemn peace moves on,
  The shadows thicken o'er the skies;
But sleep my weary eyes hath flown,
  And sad, uneasy thoughts arise.

I think of thee, oh, dearest one,
  Whose love my early life hath blest;
Of thee and him—our baby son—
  Who slumbers on thy gentle breast.
God of the tender, frail and lone,
  Oh, guard the tender sleepers' rest!

And hover gently, hover near
  To her, whose watchful eye is wet—
To mother, wife—the doubly dear,
  In whose young heart have freshly met
Two streams of love so deep and clear,
  And cheer her drooping spirits yet.

Now, while she kneels before Thy throne,
  Oh, teach her, Ruler of the skies,
That, while by Thy behest alone,
  Earth's mightiest powers fall or rise,

No tear is wept to Thee unknown,
  No hair is lost, no sparrow dies !

That Thou can'st stay the ruthless hand
  Of dark disease, and sooth its pain,
That only by Thy high command
  The battle's lost, the soldier's slain—
That from the distant sea or land,
  Thou bring'st the wanderer home again.

And when upon her pillow lone
  Her tear-wet cheeks are sadly prest,
May happier visions beam upon
  The brightening current of her breast ;
No frowning look or angry tone,
  Disturb the Sabbath of her rest.

Whatever fate those forms may show,
  Loved with a passion almost wild—
By day—by night—in joy or woe—
  By fears oppressed, or hopes beguiled,
From every danger, every foe,
  Oh, God ! protect my wife and child !

A MOTHER'S PRAYER.

[We venture to say that there are few mothers whose hearts will
not swell respousively to the tender sentiment expressed in the
following lyric. Every stanza is brimful of unshed tears :]

Father ! in the battle fray,
Shelter his dear head, I pray !
Nerve his young arm with the might
Of Justice, Liberty and Right !
Where the red hail deadliest falls,
Where stern duty loudest calls,
Where the strife is fierce and wild,
Father ! guard, oh ! guard my child !

Where the foe rush swift and strong,
Madly striving for the wrong ;
Where the clashing arms men wield
Ring above the battle-field ;
Where the stifling air is hot
With bursting shell and whistling shot—
Father ! to my boy's brave breast
Let no bloody blade be pressed !

Father ! if my woman's heart—
Frail and weak in every part—
Wanders from the mercy-seat
After these dear roving feet,

Let thy tender, pitying grace
Every selfish thought erase ;
If this mother's love be wrong—
Pardon, bless and make me strong.

For, when silent shades of night,
Shut the bright world from my sight—
When around the cheerful fire—
Gather brothers, sisters, sire—
There I miss my bright boy's face
From his old familiar place,
And my sad heart wanders back
To tented field and bivouac.

Often in my troubled sleep—
Waking, wearily to weep—
Often dreaming *he* is near,
Claiming every anxious fear,
Often started by the flash
Of hostile swords that meet and clash,
Till the cannons' smoke and roar
Hide him from my eyes once more !

Thus I dream, and hope and pray
All the weary hours away ;
But I know *his* cause is just,
And I centre all my trust
In Thy promise : " As thy day
So shall thy strength be "—alway !
Yet I need Thy guidance still !
Father ! let me do Thy will !

If now sorrow should befall—
If my noble boy should fall—
If the bright head I have blessed,
On the cold earth find its rest;
Still, with all the mother heart
Torn, and quivering with the smart,
I yield him, 'neath Thy chast'ning rod,
To his country and his God.

THE MOTHER TO HER SON IN THE TRENCHES
AT PETERSBURG.

BY W. D. PORTER.

The winter night is dark and chill,
The winter rains the trenches fill—
Oh! art thou on the outposts still,
  My soldier boy?

Thy mother's heart is sick with fear,
The moaning winds sound sad and drear,
The foeman lurks in ambush near
  My soldier boy!

One treacherous shot may lay thee low;
My stricken heart, with such a blow,
Nor rest nor peace again would know,
  My soldier boy!

Thy tender years and soft brown eyes
Ill suited seem to such emprise,
But in thy soul the manhood lies,
  My soldier boy !

I think by day and dream by night,
I start at tidings of the fight,
And learn thee safe with such delight,
  My soldier boy !

Cheerful and bright, thou dost essay
To chase my every fear away,
And turn the darkness into day,
  My soldier boy !

In thee I gave what most I love.
For thy return, thou weary dove,
I lift my fervent prayer above,
  My soldier boy !

Temper the wind to my dear child,
O God ! and curb the winter wild,
And keep in Thy embraces mild
  My soldier boy !

9

THE LADIES OF RICHMOND.

A correspondent of the *Charleston Courier*, who writes with equal
grace and facility, in verse and prose, thus refers to the ladies
of Richmond, who, to do them justice, have fully come up to
the measure of his poetic praise in their ministrations to the
sick and wounded soldiers during the war.

Fold away all your bright-tinted dresses,
   Turn the key on your jewels to-day,
And the wealth of your tendril-like tresses
   Braid back, in a serious way :
No more delicate gloves—no more laces,
   No more trifling in boudoir or bower,
But come—with your souls in your faces—
   To meet the stern needs of the hour!

Look around! By the torch-light unsteady,
   The dead and the dying seem one,
What! paling and trembling already,
   Before your dear mission's begun?
These wounds are more precious than ghastly,
   Time presses her lips to each scar,
As she chaunts of a glory which vastly
   Transcends all the horrors of war.

Pause here by this bedside—how mellow
   The light showers down on that brow!

Such a brave, brawny visage! Poor fellow!
  Some homestead is missing him now:
Some wife shades her eyes in the clearing,
  Some mother sits moaning, distressed,
While the loved one lies faint, but unfearing,
  With the enemy's ball in his breast.

Here's another; a lad—a mere stripling—
  Picked up on the field, almost dead,
With the blood through his sunny hair rippling,
  From a horrible gash in the head.
They say he was first in the action,
  Gay-hearted, quick-handed, and witty;
He fought, till he fell with exhaustion,
  At the gates of our fair Southern city.

Fought and fell 'neath the guns of that city,
  With a spirit transcending his years.
Lift him up, in your large-hearted pity,
  And wet his pale lips with your tears.
Touch him gently—most sacred the duty
  Of dressing that poor shattered hand!
God spare him to rise in his beauty,
  And battle once more for his land!

Who groaned? What a passionate murmur—
  "In Thy mercy, O God! let me die!"
Ha! surgeon, your hand must be firmer,
  That grapeshot has shattered his thigh.
Fling the light on those poor furrowed features;
  Gray-haired and unknown, bless the brother!

O God! that one of Thy creatures
   Should e'er work such woe on another!

Wipe the sweat from his brow with your kerchief,
   Let the stained, tattered collar go wide,
See! he stretches out blindly to search if
   The surgeon still stands at his side.
"My son's over yonder! he's wounded—
   Oh! this ball that has broken my thigh!"
And again he burst out, all a-tremble,
   "In Thy mercy, O God! let me die!"

Pass on! It is useless to linger,
   While others are claiming your care,
There's need of your delicate finger,
   For your womanly sympathy, there.
There are sick ones, athirst for caressing—
   There are dying ones, raving of home—
There are wounds to be bound with a blessing—
   And shrouds to make ready for some.

They have gathered about you the harvest
   Of death, in its ghastliest view,
The nearest, as well as the farthest,
   Is here with the traitor and true!
And crowned with your beautiful patience,
   Made sunny, with love at the heart,
You must bind up the wounds of a nation,
   Nor falter, nor shrink from your part!

Up and down, through the wards, where the fever
   Stalks noisome, and gaunt, and impure,

II.

See ye the fires and flashings still leaping,
Hear ye the pelting and beating of storm,
See ye the banners of proud Alabama—
In front of her columns move steadily on?
Hear ye the music that gladdens each comrade—
As it floats through the air amid the torrent of sounds,
Hear ye! booming adown the red valley,
Carter unbuckles his swarthy old hounds.

III.

Twelfth Mississippi, I saw your brave columns
Rush through the channels of living and dead;
Twelfth Alabama, why weep your old war horse,
He died as he wished, in the gear at your head.
Seven Pines, ye will tell on the pages of glory,
How the blood of the South ebbed away 'neath the
    shade,
How the lads of Virginia fought in the red valley,
And fell in the columns of Rodes' Brigade.

IV.

Fathers and mothers, ye weep for your jewels,
Sisters, ye weep for your brothers in vain,
Maidens, ye weep for your sunny-eyed lovers,
Weep, for they never will come back again!
Weep ye, but know what a halo of glory,
Encircles each chamber of death newly made,
And know ye that victory, the shrine of the mighty,
Stands forth on the banners of Rodes' Brigade.

v.

Daughters of Southland, come bring ye bright flowers,
Weave ye a chaplet for the .brow of the brave,
Bring ye some emblem of freedom and victory,
Bring ye some emblem of death and the grave;
Bring ye some motto befitting a hero,
Bring ye exotics that never will fade,
Come to the deep crimsoned valley of Richmond,
And crown the young chieftain who led his Brigade.

LINES

On the death of Lieut. Henry Lewis, commanding Company B,
of the 47th Virginia Volunteers, who was killed in the battle
of Seven Pines, on the 31st of May, 1862; written by a lady
who knew his virtues and loved him well:

He lay among the dying, and the battle raged near by,
Upon the moist sod lying he was left to bleed and die,
Yet comrades came to seek him, and raised his droop-
    ing head—
"Go win our country's cause," he said, "and leave me
    with the dead."
Whole squadrons swept beside them, and the cannon
    thundered on,
His friends rushed with the tide of war, and he was
    left alone!

Oh! not alone! for one was there, the mighty "Prince
　　of Peace,"
Who whispered in his dying ear, and bade his sufferings
　　cease,
And to his weary, dying eyes a beauteous sight was
　　given—
The starry portals of the skies and peaceful fields of
　　Heaven.
He dreamed of waters pure and clear, the crystal
　　streams of life,
Untainted by the human tear or battle's bitter strife.
His thoughts were with the loved and lost, and radi-
　　ant forms were there,
While voices from the angel host came floating on the
　　air—
Lower and lower sunk his head, and fainter came his
　　breath,
The Christian lay among the dead, and slept the sleep
　　of death.
The battle ceased—the evening sun looked down upon
　　the field,
Where thousands died for freedom's cause, and dying,
　　scorned to yield.
While weeping comrades made his grave beneath the
　　bloody sod,
His soul was with the radiant hosts around the throne
　　of God!

" INFORMATION WANTED

"Of my son, —— ——. He was known to be engaged in
last ——'s fight, and cannot now be found. Was a private in
Company —, — Regiment, —— Volunteers. Any tidings of
him will be gratefully received by his anxious father at ——
House."

" Oh ! stranger, can you tell me where,
    Where is my boy—my brave bright boy !
He was the light of my failing eye,
    His gentle mother's life and joy.
All day I've walked the crowded street
    Piercing the groups with eager glance,
Vainly questioning all I meet—
    Searching the slow drawn ambulance.

" The sounding war-trump rung afar,
    We heard it by the South sea wave,
'Mid the orange groves of Florida,
    It summoned forth the true and brave.
I gave him the sword I used to wear,
    To wield again for his country's right ;
I gave him my blessing and heard him swear
    He would falter not in the coming fight.

" His mother's eyes were dimmed with tears,
    She pressed her first-born to her heart—
His dark-eyed sister scorning fears,
    With hidden woe, bade him depart.
        9*

But say—oh say—you've seen him well,
  Or how shall I meet Mary again—
How shall my palsied tongue e'er tell,
  Our noble boy's among the slain?"

"Alas! I saw the boy too well,
  Dead on the gory battle-field—
Saw where in thickest fight he fell,
  While through our ranks the cannon pealed;
I saw him mount the battery's· side,
  Over the mortars grim and dread—
Where Southrons like an ocean tide,
  Swept o'er the heaps of mangled dead.

"After the fight I found him there
  Under the murderous cannon's mouth—·
While many heads of raven hair,
  Near by, spoke of the sunny South.
Brave hearts! on gory beds they fell,
  With wounds that still their daring show,
How loved they were our tears· shall tell,
  How well they fought the foemen know."

"Oh! stranger, lead me where he lies,
  To kiss away the powder stain—
And let me close his glazing eyes,
  Ere mother sees his face again!
My boy! my boy! my brave, bright boy!.
  Could not the cruel death shot spare!
From thy loved home has fled the joy,
  And dark 'twill be without thee there."

I left him mourning 'o'er his dead,
　That saddened father, old and gray—
O'er that boy on his martial bed,
　Stricken alas! before his day.
Oh! Richmond, queen of the gory plain—
　List to thy Southern sisters' wail,
Think of the precious ones that stain,
　With their best blood, thy crimsoned vale!

THE DRUMMER BOY.

A drummer boy in the agony of death being asked where he
was from, replied that his mother had sent him from Mississippi
"to fight and defend her home," and that "he did not regret
it, and was ready to do it again." He wanted to see his
mother, and said, "My mother is a good woman, too; she
would treat a poor sick prisoner kindly, and if she were here
she would kiss me." "I will kiss you, my child," said a
lady, "for your mother," and she did so. The child was
already at the last gasp, and in a few moments he expired.

N. Y. Post.

BY JAMES R. BREWER.

All pallid upon his couch he lay,
　As death fast dimm'd his eye,
And his wandering thoughts were far away,
　For he knew that he must die.
His parching lips must thirst in vain,
　For his blood went with his breath,

And the racking pain that rent life's chain,
　Would leave him still in death;
And the tear that·nature bade him weep,
Should glaze his eye when cold in sleep.

And they asked the slowly dying child,
　Why one so young should roam?
And the ashen lips, replying, smiled,
　" To defend my Mother's home!"
" She kissed me with a tearful smile,
　And bade me be a man,
So I marched where Death its victims piled,
　And led the battle's van,
Till, where the streams of carnage flow,
I fell beneath a cruel blow.

" But though my body's racked with pain,
　I cherish no regret,
And I would again, through the leaden rain,
　Lead Freedom's legions yet;
And glory-crowned, ·in peace, draw near
　The scene of childish joy,
 And a mother's prayer and a mother's tear
　Should welcome back her boy—
But no, ah, no! I feel the smart,
The hand of death is on my heart!

" My God! Oh, would that she were here,
　To kiss me, ere I die — "
With a vacant stare of wild despair,
　He struggled back to die.
His strength was gone, his frame was weak,

And dull his gasping sigh,
For the hectic streak and the sunken cheek
  Proclaimed the destroyer nigh ;
Whilst a prayer escapes his lips of foam,
" Oh, God ! defend my Mother's home ! "

'Tis done—his gentle spirit's flown,
  With the youthful hero's breath,
And the Angel throng with his soul is gone,
  And he smiles alone in death.
While fellow Angels watch his grave,
  To her home he flits away, .
In her hours of sleep his vigils to keep
  And guard her through the day.
And now no longer doomed to roam,
He watches above his Mother's home.

ANNAPOLIS, *July* 23, 1862.

THE OLD BRIGADE.

VIRGINIA'S 1ST, 7TH, 11TH AND 17TH.

BY MAURICE D'BELL.

Behold yon throng of heroes!
  Their eyes are heavy and dim,
With weary watching—with weight of war,
  Worn every aching limb;
But, if ever a band of warriors won
A pæan for deeds of valor done,
They deserve indeed the glorious meed,
  And the proud triumphal hymn!

'Tis the Old Brigade of Longstreet,
  Virginia's loved Brigade,
The brave Brigade of Ewell,
  That glorious Hill has swayed;
That wherever the storm of battle burst,
In *place*, as in *name*, has been the "First,"
That has met the foe, and by bolt and blow,
  Their strong advance has stayed.

Ah yes, their ranks are meagre,
  And their lines are worn and thin,
For long they have dared the death-shots,
  Amidst the battle's din;

The first to check the invading host,
In the last dread strife, to bleed the most;
They have courted fate, for themselves and State
   The victor's crown to win.

With tearful joy Virginia,
   Her share of their proud praise claims,
For they came from the broad Potomac,
   And the beauteous banks of James;
With the men of the mountain, side by side,
To weave for their mother a chaplet of pride,
That her brows shall wear, whenever and where
   Are named heroic names.

On the fields that glow with their glory,
   The shrines of their martyrs we see,
Of Humphries, and Mitchell and Waller,
   Of Harrison, Carter and Lee.
And wherever their gallant ranks have stood,
From the foes' footsteps in the foes' best blood,
With bayonet sharp and furious fire,
   The have washed their loved soil free !

And hark ! as we gaze, the thunder
   Bursts on the startled air,
And the ominous order issues forth—
   " For the conflict now prepare !"
And eyes that *were* heavy and limbs that *are* scarred
When their banners are pointing battle-ward,
Beaming and bright—active and light,
   Boldly and bravely bear ! ·

And lo! on these flashing banners,
  What splendid deeds are told!
Bull Run, Manassas, Williamsburg,
  Their story now unfold,
While Frazier's Farm and Seven Pines,
Tell how o'er their steady lines,
Hissing and hot, the shell and shot,
  In mortal waves have rolled!

Then forward! veteran legion,
  With your free and fearless tread,
With your banners, blazoned with glory,
  To the battle-breezes spread!
We will help you on with such hearty cheers,
As you send up when the foe appears,
And your onward way they may not stay,
  Though they block it with their dead!

Oh! God preserve those heroes
  Of the sturdy heart and will!
The old brigade of Longstreet—
  The loved brigade of Hill;
Their praise shall live in every mouth—
In Virginia's heart and the heart of the South,
Though their banners are torn, and their frames are
      worn,
  There's a warm place for them still!

THE BURIAL OF LATANÉ.

In General Stuart's famous raid around the rear of McClellan's army, Capt. Latané was the only man killed. His brother, returning after the fight, carried the body to Dr. Brockenbrough's plantation near by, and left it with Mrs. Brockenbrough to be interred. Mrs. B. sent for a clergyman to perform the funeral rites, but he not being permitted to pass, she read the burial service herself, some ladies of the family, and a few faithful servants, forming a small, sad audience. This scene has been made the subject of a touching picture by Mr. Washington.

BY JNO. R. THOMPSON.

The combat raged not long, but ours the day;
　And, through the hosts that compassed us around,
Our little band rode proudly on its way,
　　Leaving one gallant comrade, glory-crowned,
　　　Unburied on the field he died to gain—
　　　Alone of all his men, amid the hostile slain.

One moment on the battle's edge he stood—
　Hope's halo, like a helmet, round his hair—
The next beheld him, dabbled in his blood,
　　Prostrate in death; and yet, in death how fair!
　　　Even thus he passed through the red-gates of
　　　　　strife,
　　　From earthly crowns and palms, to an immor-
　　　　　tal life.

A brother bore his body from the field,
   And gave it unto strangers' hands, that closed
The calm blue eyes, on earth forever sealed,
   And tenderly the slender limbs 'composed :
      Strangers, yet sisters, who, with Mary's love,
      Sat by the open tomb, and weeping, looked
        above.

A little child strewed roses on his bier—
   Pale roses, not more stainless than his soul,
Nor yet more fragrant than his life sincere,
   That blossomed with good actions—brief, but whole;
      The aged matron and the faithful slave
      Approached, with reverent feet, the hero's lowly
        grave.

No man of God might say the burial rite
   Above the " rebel "—thus declared the foe
That blanched before him in the deadly fight;
   But woman's voice, with accents soft and low,
      Trembling with pity—touched with pathos—
        read
      Over his hallowed dust the ritual for the dead.

" *'Tis sown in weakness, it is raised in power !* "
   Softly the promise floated on the air,
While the low breathings of the sunset hour,
   Came back responsive to the mourner's prayer.
      Gently they laid him underneath the sod,
      And left him with his fame, his country, and
        his God !

Let us not weep for him, whose deeds endure !
  So young, so brave, so beautiful ! He died
As he had wished to die ; the past is sure ;
  Whatever yet of sorrow may betide
      Those who still linger by the stormy shore,
      Change can not harm him now, nor fortune
        touch him more.

And when Virginia, leaning on her spear,
  Victrix et Vidua—the conflict done—
Shall raise her mailed hand to wipe the tear
  That starts as she recalls each martyred son,
      No prouder memory her breast shall sway
      Than thine, our early lost, lamented Latané !

THE BELEAGUERED CITY.

BY ROSA VERTNER JEFFREY.

There 's a beautiful city, far, far away,
  In the land of the myrtle and rose,
The fair land of my birth—which, I hear them say,
  Is beleaguered, by deadliest foes ;
And my spirit goes forth with those braves to stand,
  Who are striking for home and for hearth,
God of mercy ! defend that heroic band,
  In this beautiful land of my birth !

'Tis hard, when the pulse of a soldier doth thrill
  In the heart of a woman—for there
While burning in vain—it enkindles the will
  Of a soldier to suffer and dare.
When war-bugles sound where the brave win or fall,
  Then I burn with the feverish unrest
A ringdove might feel, at the falconer's call,
  Reared by chance in some proud falcon's nest!

As one in a light-house, who watches the deep
  Through a tempest, my sad spirit seems
A vigil of love o'er that fair land to keep,
  Where the red blood is flowing in streams.
Though mingled with tears, yet the sod where it flows
  Groweth greener—the butterflies' wings
Are brighter, and even the blush of the rose
  Deepens—down by those dark crimson springs.

Yet he in the light house is void of the power
  To fetter the storms as they rove,
No legions of watchers can stay that red shower,
  Polluting the land of my love.
But there is a light-house beyond the blue steeps,
  Where the star-lamps eternally burn,
And there dwells a watcher whose eye never sleeps,
  In the darkness to Him let us turn.

RICHMOND ON THE JAMES.

BY ANNIE MARIE WELBY.

A soldier boy from Bourbon, lay gasping on the field,
When the battle's shock was over and the foe was
    forced to yield;
He fell, a youthful hero, before the foemen's aims,
On a blood-red field near Richmond, near Richmond
    on the James.

But one still stood beside him, his comrade in the fray,
They had been friends together through boyhood's
    happy day,
And side by side had struggled, on fields of blood
    and flames,
To part that eve, near Richmond, near Richmond on
    the James.

He said, "I charge thee, comrade, the friend in days
    of yore,
To the far, far distant dear ones that I shall see no
    more,
Tho' scarce my lips can whisper their dear and well-
    known names,
To bear to them my blessing from Richmond on the
    James.

"Bear my good sword to my brother, and the badge
upon my breast,
To the young and gentle sister, that I used to love
the best;
One lock take from my forehead for the mother still
that dreams
Of her soldier boy near Richmond—near Richmond
on the James.

"Oh, I wish that mother's arms were folded round
me now,
That her gentle hand could linger one moment on my
brow;
But I know that she is praying where our blessed
hearth-light gleams,
For her soldier's safe return from Richmond on the
James.

"And on my heart, dear comrade, close lay those
nut-brown braids,
Of one that was the fairest of all our village maids;
We were to have been wedded, but death the bride-
groom claims,
And she is far, that loves me, from Richmond on the
James.

'Oh, does the pale face haunt her, dear friend, that
looks on thee?
Or is she laughing—singing, in careless, girlish glee?
It may be she is joyous,—she loves but joyous themes,
Nor dreams her love lies bleeding near Richmond on
the James.

" And though I know, dear comrade, thou'lt miss me
    for awhile,
When their faces—all that loved thee—again on thee
    shall smile,
Again thou'lt be the foremost in all their youthful
    games,
But I shall lie near Richmond—near Richmond on
    the James."

And far from all that loved him that youthful soldier
    sleeps,
Unknown among the thousands of those his country
    weeps ;
But no higher heart nor braver, than his, at sunset's
    beams,
Was laid that eve, near Richmond — near Richmond
    on the James.

The land is filled with mourning, from hall and cot
    left lone,
We miss the well known faces that used to meet our
    own,
And long, poor wives and mothers shall weep — and
    titled dames,
To hear the name of Richmond—of Richmond on the
    James.

LOUISVILLE, KY., *July*, 1862.

MISSING.

In the cool sweet hush of a wooded nook,
  Where the May buds sprinkle the green old sward,
And the winds, and the birds, and the limpid brook,
  Murmur their dreams with a drowsy sound;
Who lies so still in the plushy moss,
  With his pale cheek presséd on a breezy pillow,
Couched where the light and the shadows cross
  Thro' the flickering fringe of the willow,
      Who lies, alas!
So still, so chill, in the whispering grass?

A soldier clad in the zouave dress,
  A bright-haired man, with his lips apart,
One hand thrown up o'er his frank, dead face,
  And the other clutching his pulseless heart,
Lies here in the shadows, cool and dim,
  His musket swept by a trailing bough;
With a careless grace in his quiet limbs,
  And a wound on his manly brow;
      A wound, alas!
Whence the warm blood drips on the quiet grass.

The violets peer from their dusky beds,
  With a tearful dew in their great pure eyes,
The lilies quiver their shining heads,
  Their pale lips full of sad surprise;

And the lizard darts thro' the glistening fern—
  And the squirrel rustles the branches hoary;
Strange birds fly out with a cry, to bathe
    Their wings in the sunset glory,
        While the shadows pass
O'er the quiet face and the dewy grass.

God pity the bride who awaits at home
  With her lily cheeks, and her violet eyes,
Dreaming the sweet old dream of love,
  While her lover is walking in Paradise;
God strengthen her heart as the days go by,
  And the long, drear nights of her vigil follow,
Nor bird, nor moon, nor whispering wind
  May breathe the tale of the hollow;
        Alas! alas!
The secret is safe with the woodland grass.

THE DYING SOLDIER.

Lay him down gently where shadows lie still
And cool, by the side of the bright mountain rill,
Where spreads the soft grass its velvety sheen,
A welcoming couch for repose so serene;
Where opening flowers their aroma breathe
From clustering tendrils that lovingly wreathe,
And quivering leaves their murmurous song
In whispers are chanting the bright summer long—
There lay the young hero. See, from his side
Flows swiftly the current whose dark pulsing tide
Is bearing away the bright sands of life,
And closing forever this wild dream of strife.
Feebly uncloses the fast dimming eye,
Once bright as the jewels that light up the sky;
A moment he looks on the blue arched dome,
Then whispers in anguish, "Oh take—take me home!
But no! far away o'er mountain and fen
Lies the home that I never shall enter again;
Where loving ones wait to welcome in joy
Back to its sun-light their own soldier boy.
Father, when proudly you gave up your child,
And crushed back the tears while your lip sadly smiled,
How vague was the thought that we nevermore
Should meet till we stood on eternity's shore!
And, mother, again I feel thy hot tears
Rain on my cheek. Not the mildew of years,

Nor shadows of death can tarnish the bliss,
The blessing you gave in that last holy kiss.
Oh! darkly shall gather clouds o'er the hearth
That echoed once gaily with music and mirth.
Oh, God! may Thy spirit be there to sustain,
When record shall mingle my name with the slain.
And one, too, whose fair cheek whiter still grew
As I pressed on her lip my last sad adieu!
"Will she soon forget?" Then, raising his hand,
He lovingly gazed on the small golden band
That circled his finger—while over his face
The gray shadows of death seemed stealing apace.
"Dear comrades, farewell! my battles are o'er,
Together in conflict we'll rally no more;
'Tis bitter to die erè my country is free;
But painted in glory her future I see;
Farewell! life is o'er, earth fades from my sight,
Around me is closing death's long, dreamless night."
Then, softly as star-light melts into day,
On pinions of angels his soul passed away.
Those strong men are bowed—in anguish they weep
O'er the dead, still so fair in death's quiet sleep.
Then, parting the flowers, they laid him to rest,
And heaped the green sod o'er the young martyr's
      breast.
Weep, heart of the South—weep, maiden and sire,
Wreathe darkly with cypress love's bright mystic lyre,
Weep for the heroes, so brave and so true,
Who nobly have yielded their life-blood for you.

READING THE LIST.

" Is there any news of the war?" she said,
" Only a list of the wounded and dead,"
        Was the man's reply,
        Without lifting his eye
        To the face of the woman standing by.
" 'Tis the very thing I want," she said;
" Read me a list of the wounded and dead."

He read the list—'twas a sad array
Of the wounded and killed in the fatal fray;
In the very midst was a pause to tell
That his comrades asked, " Who is he, pray?"
" The only son of the Widow Gray,"
        Was the proud reply
        Of his Captain nigh.
What ails the woman standing near?
Her face has the ashen hue of fear!

" Well, well, read on; is he wounded? quick!
Oh, God! but my heart is sorrow sick!"
" Is he wounded?"   " No! he fell, they say,
Killed outright on that fatal day!"
But see, the woman has swooned away!

Sadly she opened her eyes to the light;
Slowly recalled the events of the fight;
Faintly she murmured, " Killed outright!

It has cost me the life of my only son,
But the battle is fought and the victory won;
The will of the Lord, let it be done!"

God pity the cheerless Widow Gray,
And send from the halls of Eternal Day
The light of His peace to illumine her way!

THE LONELY GRAVE.

BY MRS. C. A. BALL.

In a sheltered nook on Potomac's shore,
Where the earth is crimsoned with Southern-gore,
Sparkles and bubbles a little spring,
Which never ceases its lay to sing
  Over a lonely grave.
'Tis a spot that was made for peace and rest,
Where Nature in richest robes is dressed,
Where the birds confidingly build their nests,
  And the weeping willows wave.

Many a wounded Southern brave
Has dragged himself here his brow to lave,
And to drink of the waters clear and bright,
Which flashed and glanced in the moon's soft light,
  Unheeding his anguished moan.
And the carpet of green around it spread,

Has pillowed full many a weary head;
And many a soul from that grassy bed
    Has passed to the dark unknown.

Yet only one hillock, mossy and green,
By that joyous dancing spring is seen,
Where the sighing winds wake a mournful wail,
And the ringdove moans through the evening gale,
    And the firs their tall heads rear.
Of the countless hosts who in battle fell,
Or of those whose death-hour none can tell,
Whose souls passed out from this shaded dell,
    But *one* lies buried here.

And who was he? a brave young boy,
Of his Southern home the pride and joy;
The pet and darling of every heart,
That in his bright life had shared a part,
    But seventeen summers old.
Oh! what a terrible grief was theirs,
As back in their souls they crushed their fears,
And sent him forth with prayers and tears,
    From the parental fold.

Precious as was the boy to all,
They gave him up at his country's call.
Honor to him was dearer than life,
And he panted to enter the field of strife,
    And shine on the roll of fame.
With a crown of blessing on his head,
He on to the field of glory sped,

The blood of his pure young heart to shed,
And to win himself a name.

Bravely he bore him in the fray,
And wonder-struck were our boys in gray,
To see the youth with flashing eye,
Press on while shouting the battle-cry,
To the thickest of the fight.
His dauntless mien, his bearing bold,
His face of rare and beauteous mould,
His head with its clustering waves of gold,
Seemed filling the field with light.

O'er the scene of blood came a joyous cry,
The enemy falter—they fly, they fly!
And as the smoke of battle rose,
In circling wreaths above their foes,
They were seen from the field to run.
The gallant boy, his proud head raised,
While every feature with triumph blazed,
And now he cried, May our God be praised
For the victory we have won.

With kindling cheek and glistening eye,
Aye *this* he said, were a time to *die!*
The words from his lips had barely passed,
When a rushing sound came on the blast,
And the boy fell on the plain.
'Twas a bullet that whistling through the air,
With pitiless blow struck the temple fair,
Right in the waves of his golden hair—
He never rose again.

Rude men shed tears o'er that noble boy,
So suddenly called in his hour of joy,
When closed had seemed the murderous strife,
And saved through all that bright young life,
    To shine on glory's rolL
They bore him away to the shaded dell,
And laid him to rest 'in his narrow cell,
Where the mourning pines sighed out a knell
    For the departed soul.

It was meet, they thought, that one so fair
Should be laid in that spot of beauty rare,
Where the birds might warble o'er his grave,
And the foliage green above him wave,
    With the bright spring singing near.
And this is the way with all who fell,
Or of those whose death-hour none can tell,
Whose souls passed out from this shaded dell,
    But *one* lies buried here.

CHARLESTON, *June 7.*

THE JACKET OF GRAY—TO THOSE WHO WORE IT.

BY MRS. C. A. BALL.

Fold it up carefully, lay it aside,
Tenderly touch it, look on it with pride,
For dear must it be to our hearts evermore,
The jacket of gray our loved soldier boy wore.

Can we ever forget when he joined the brave band,
Who rose in defense of dear Southern land;
And in his bright youth hurried on to the fray,
How proudly he donn'd it, the jacket of gray!

His fond mother blessed him and looked up above,
Commending to Heaven the child of her love,
What anguish was hers, mortal tongue may not say,
When he passed from her sight in the jacket of gray.

But her country had called him, she would not repine,
Tho' costly the sacrifice placed on its shrine;
Her heart's dearest hopes on its altar she lay,
When she sent out her boy, in his jacket of gray!

Months passed, and War's thunders rolled over the land,
Unsheathed was the sword and lighted the brand;
We heard in the distance the noise of the fray,
And prayed for our boy, in the jacket of gray.

10*

Ah! vain all,—all vain were our prayers and our tears,
The glad shout of victory rang in our ears;
But our treasured one on the cold battle-field lay,
While the life blood oozed out on the jacket of gray.

Fold it up carefully, lay it aside,
Tenderly touch it, look on it with pride;
For dear must it be to our hearts evermore,
The jacket of gray our loved soldier boy wore.

His young comrades found him and tenderly bore
His cold lifeless form to his home by the shore;
Oh! dark were our hearts on that terrible day
When we saw our dead boy in the jacket of gray.

Ah! spotted, and tattered, and stained now with gore,
Was the garment which once he so gracefully wore;
We bitterly wept as we took it away,
And replaced with death's white robes the jacket of
    gray.

We laid him to rest in his cold narrow bed,
And graved on the marble we placed o'er his head,
As the proudest of tributes our sad hearts could pay,
"He never disgraced the dear jacket of gray."

Then fold it up carefully, lay it aside,
Tenderly touch it, look on it with pride;
For dear must it be to our hearts evermore,
The jacket of gray our loved soldier boy wore.

" YOU'LL TELL HER, WON'T YOU ? "

" Another soldier, shot through the lungs, clasped a locket to his
breast and moved his lips till I put down my ear and listened for
his last breath—' You'll tell her, won't you ?' Tell whom or
what, I could not ask; but that locket was the picture of one
who might be wife, sweetheart or sister."—*Army Letter*, 1862.

You'll tell her, won't you ?   Say to her I died
   As a brave soldier should—true to the last;
She'll bear it better, if a thought of pride
   Comes in to stay her, the first shock o'erpast !

You'll tell her, won't you ?   Show her how I lay
   Pressing the pictured lips I loved so well,
And how my last thoughts floated far away
   To home and her, with love I could not tell.

You'll tell her, won't you ? not how hard it was
   To give up life—life for her sake so dear,
Nay, nay, not so ! Say 'twas a noble cause,
   And I died for it without a tear.

You'll tell her, won't you ?   She'll be glad to know
   Her soldier stood undaunted, true as steel,
His heart with her, his bosom to the foe,
   When struck the blow no human power could heal.

You'll tell her, won't you? Say, too, we shall meet
  In God's hereafter, where our love shall grow
More holy for this parting, and more sweet,
  And cleansed from every stain it knew below.

SOMEBODY'S DARLING.

The following exquisite little poem was written by Miss Marie
Lacoste, of Savannah, Ga., and originally published, we
think, in the *Southern Churchman*. It will commend itself by
its touching pathos to all readers. The incident it commemorates
was, unfortunately, but too common in both armies.

Into a ward of the whitewashed walls
  Where the dead and the dying lay—
Wounded by bayonets, shells and balls—
  Somebody's darling was borne one day.
Somebody's darling! so young and so brave,
  Wearing still on his pale sweet face—
Soon to be hid by the dust of the grave—
  The lingering light of his boyhood's grace.

Matted and damp are the curls of gold,
  Kissing the snow of that fair young brow,
Pale are the lips of delicate mould—
  Somebody's darling is dying now.
Back from the beautiful, blue-veined face
  Brush every wandering, silken thread,

Cross his hands as a sign of grace—
  Somebody's darling is still and dead !

Kiss him once for *somebody's* sake ;
  Murmur a prayer, soft and low,
One bright curl from the cluster take—
  They were somebody's pride you know.
Somebody's hand hath rested there ;
  Was it a mother's soft and white ?
And have the lips of a sister fair
  Been baptized in those waves of light ?

God knows best. He was somebody's love ;
  Somebody's heart enshrined him there ;
Somebody wafted his name above,
  Night and morn on the wings of prayer.
Somebody wept when he marched away,
  Looking so handsome, brave and grand ;
Somebody's kiss on his forehead lay,
  Somebody clung to his parting hand—

Somebody's watching and waiting for him,
  Yearning to hold him again to her heart :
There he lies—with the blue eyes dim,
  And smiling, child-like lips apart.
Tenderly bury the fair young dead,
  Pausing to drop on his grave a tear,
Carve on the wooden slab at his head,
  " *Somebody's darling lies buried here !* '

THE REAR-GUARD OF THE ARMY.

BY IRIS.

The hills were touched with sunset tints, the sky
    was painted bright,
When the rear-guard of our army came marching into
    sight.
All the Army of Potomac had passed us by but these,
The faint sound of their drum beat was dying on the
    breeze.
How Manassas was deserted, not a Southron left, not
    one !
Save the still forms in silent graves, whose marchings
    then were done ;
The pine huts with their roofing green are empty,
    quiet, sad,
They that all winter echoed with voices gay and
    glad.
Manassas ! proud Manassas ! and near by her battle
    plain !
Shall she ne'er hear the Southern shout of victory
    again ?
Shall the foe triumphant tread the soil where patriot's
    blood was shed,
Where many a noble hero sleeps, where Bee and
    Bartow bled ?
We fain would see the rear-guard, but our tears were
    flowing still ;

But hush they give the word to "Halt"—they pause
    upon the hill,
They wave the flag above them, but its folds *will* droop
    to earth,
They shout, but, ah ! it is no shout of victory or mirth.
Once more, along our vales and hills the words of Dixie
    ring,
But, alas ! full mournfully it grates upon both ear and
    mind,
For the Southern army *all* have gone, and we are
    left behind !
Left to the foeman's mercy, left to their cruel hate,
Left helpless babes and women to such a dreary fate !
Cease your triumphal music, play a dirge for those
    you leave,
For those who in this parting hour have naught to
    do but grieve ;
And breathe a dirge in plaintive tone for fair Vir-
    ginia's land,
That soon will feel a tyrant-rule with bold and heavy
    hand.
Keep back your stirring anthem till you have passed
    us by,
We have no cheer or smile to give, only a tear and
    sigh.
Altho' we had forgotten, we send our prayers with
    you—
Alas for woman ! this is all now left for her to do.

CHARLESTOWN, VA.

HEART VICTORIES.

BY A SOLDIER'S WIFE.

There's not a stately hall,
  There's not a cottage fair,
That proudly stands on Southern soil,
  Or softly ,nestles there,
But in its peaceful walls
  With wealth or comfort blessed,
A stormy battle fierce hath raged
  In gentle woman's breast.

There Love, the true, the brave,
  The beautiful, the strong,
Wrestles with Duty, gaunt and stern,
  Wrestles and struggles long.
He falls—no more again
  His giant foe to meet,
Bleeding at every opening vein,
  Love falls at Duty's feet.

O! Daughter of the South!
  No victor's crown be thine,
Not thine, upon the tented field
  In martial pomp to shine;
But with unfaltering trust
  'In Him who rules on high,

To deck thy loved ones for the fray,
  And send them forth to die.

With wildly throbbing heart—
  With faint and trembling breath,
The maiden speeds her lover on .,
  To victory or death;
Forth from caressing arms,
  The mother sends her son,
And bids him nobly battle on,
  Till the last field is won.

While she, the tried, the true,
  The loving wife of years,
Chokes down the rising agony,
  Drives back the starting tears;
"I yield thee up," she cries,
  In the country's cause to fight,
Strike for our own, our children's home,
  And God defend the right."

O, Daughter of the South!
  When our fair land is free,
When peace her lovely mantle throws
  Softly o'er land and sea,
History shall tell how thou
  Hast nobly borne thy part,
And won the proudest triumph yet—
  The victory of the heart.

ADDRESS TO THE EXCHANGED PRISONERS.

On the 31st of July, 1862, all the prisoners of war in Fort Warren (about 250 soldiers of the Confederate army) embarked for
Fortress Monroe, to be exchanged.   They left in Fort Warren
14 gentlemen who were imprisoned under the designation of
"political prisoners."   These were all Marylanders by birth,
all but one (Mr. Winder) were residents in that State when
arrested.   On their behalf the following lines were addressed
to their departing friends.

BY S. T. WALLIS.

The anchors are weighed, and the gates of your prison
    Fall wide, as your ship gives her prow to the foam,
And a few hurried hours, shall return you exulting,
    Where the flag you have fought for floats over your
        home.

God send that not long shall its folds be uplifted
    O'er fields dark and sad with the trail of the fight;
God give it the triumph He always hath given,
    Or sooner or later to valor and right!

But if peace may not yet wreathe your homes with
      her olive,
    And new victims are still round the altar to bleed,

God shield you amid the red bolts of the battle,
  God give stout hearts for high thought and brave
    deed!

No need we should bid you go strike for your freedom,
  You have stricken like men for its blessings before,
And your homes and your loved ones, your wrongs and
    your manhood,
  Will nerve you to fight the good fight o'er and o'er.

But will you not think, as you wave your glad banners,
  How the flag of old Maryland trodden in shame,
Lies sullied and torn in the dust of her highways?
  And will ye not strike a fresh blow in her name?

Her mothers have sent their first born to be with you,
  Wherever with blood there are fields to be won,
Her daughters have wept for you, clad you, and nursed
    you,
  Their hopes and their vows, and their smiles are your
    own.

Let her cause be your cause, and whenever the war-cry
  Bids you rush to the field, oh! remember her too!
And when freedom and peace shall be blended in glory
  Oh! count it your shame, if she be not with you!

And if in the hour when pride, honor, and duty,
  Shall stir every throb in the hearts of brave men,
The wrongs of the helpless can quicken such pulses,
  Let the captives at Warren give flame to them then.

FIAT JUSTITIA.

DEDICATED TO THE MARYLAND PRISONERS AT FORT WARREN.

BY A LADY OF BALTIMORE.

There is no day however darkly clouded,
  But hath a brighter sun,
There is no truth however falsely shrouded,
  But hath its martyrs won.
No grief that bringeth not some consolation,
  When the first pang is past,
No loss without its hidden compensation,
  To heal or soothe at last.
So in this hour, when even justice slumbers,
  Our courage shall not fail;
Might is not right, and strength lies not in numbers,
  Nor will the strong prevail.
The few, alas, must suffer for the many,
  Oh brave and chosen few!
The loss of freedom always sad to any,
  Is still more sad for you,
Whose native State is held in base subjection,
  A camp for armed men,
Whose native city waits in proud dejection
  Her liberty again!
Be yours the place of honor, yours the crowning,
  Yours is the leader's right,

Who, where those wave-washed dungeon walls are
    frowning,
  Have fought the noblest fight.
There, with the shield the Constitution granted,
  WALLIS defends our cause;
And good " King GEORGE," the fearless and undaunted,
  Resists a tyrant's laws.
There SCOTT has shown us how with faith unswerving
  E'en bondage may be borne,
How Roman firmness, patient in deserving,
  Can never be uptorn!
There, round the temples of another HOWARD,
  The " Old Line " laurels bloom,
There, BROWN, beneath whose rule all treason cowered,
  Receives a traitor's doom.
There, THOMAS, JORDAN, and a host of heroes,
  Do honor to their name,
While perjured *Seward*, last and worst of Nero's,
  Sets all the world aflame!
Dear Maryland! thy children will not shame thee,
  Nor aid thy feet to fall,
Let those who choose to question, dare to blame thee,
  Fort Warren answers all!

1862.

LINES WRITTEN IN FORT WARREN.

BY G. W. B.

Wild flowers gathered from the hills,
　Sunlit clouds on evening sky,
Shadows dancing o'er the rills,
　Brief as these our pleasures die.

Dews that fall from pitying skies,
　Sparkle in the morning ray,
Tears that dim the watcher's eye
　Change to smiles with dawning day.

Good and evil mingle so
　In the chequered web of life,
Whether best we do not know,
　Joy or sorrow, peace or strife.

Even may these prison walls,
　Preach a lesson large and free,
Vainly taught in stoic halls,
　Better sung by poesy.

Calmly moves the steadfast soul,
　On its Heaven appointed way,
Brave and strong in self-control,
　Rivet fetters as you may.

Doing battle, like a knight
  'Gainst a host in stricken field,
Trebly armed by sense of right,
  Christ's red cross upon his shield.

Bright flowers on the ramparts bloom,
  By the cannon frowning there,
Breathing all around perfume,
  While war's drum-beat rends the air.

Lives of captives have shed fragrance
  Sweet as breath of summer flowers,
And their deeds a holy radiance,
  Such as gild these evening hours.

FORT WARREN, *Sept.* 3, 1862.

THE CAPTAIN'S STORY.

We rested on the battle-field,
  The busy day was o'er,
Hushed was the angry clash of arms,
  The cannon's frightful roar ;
And twilight settled on the scene
  Of carnage and of strife,
Ah ! it was sad to gaze upon
  The fearful loss of life.

Beneath a tent of cedar boughs,
  By soft night breezes fann'd,
One of our braves lay dying now,
  A youth from Maryland.
Ah ! well we loved the fearless boy !
  When dangers round him pressed,
Through many an awful conflict
  He nobly stood the test.

Now, one by one his comrades all
  Had gathered round his bed,
And when each one had press'd his hand.
  He smiled, and then he said :
" Ah ! boys you'll take a message
  When I shall be no more,
To friends in dear old Maryland,
  On fair Patuxent's shore."

"Tell my father that I fell
  When victory was won,
But tell him not too hastily
  The tidings of his son.
And comrades, you will say to him
  I drew no coward's breath,
My last cry on the battle-field,
  Was LIBERTY or DEATH.

"Oh! to my mother gently tell
  The news—when I am dead,
And place her letters on my breast,
  Her Bible at my head.
Now boys, won't some of you repeat
  The prayer she sent to me—
When I was but a little boy,
  I learned it at her knee."

The tears coursed down our bronzed cheeks,
  We knelt at his request,
And when we rose to gaze on him
  The spirit was at rest.
We placed the letters on his breast,
  The Bible at his head,
And we wrapped him in our banner—
  'Twas the "Red, the White, the Red."

THE DEBT.

Remember men of Maryland,
  You have a debt to pay,
A debt which years of patience
  Will never wear away;
Which must be paid at last, although
  Our dearest blood it cost,
A debt which *shall* be paid unto
  The very. uttermost.

We owe for confidence betrayed
  By those we trusted best,
The sword we gave them to defend,
  They turned against our breast ;
For spies that noted down our words,
  The while they shared our bread,
For hounds that even dared disturb
  The quiet of the dead.

We owe for all the love they hid,
  The wolfish hate they showed,
For all those glittering bayonets
  That meet us on the road.
For black suspicion, deadlier far
  Than flash of Northern swords,
For treason threatened at our hearths,
  And poison at our boards.

For many a deed of darkness done
  Beneath the "stripes and stars,"
For women outraged in their homes,
  And fired on in the cars.
For those black tiers of cannon, trained
  To bear on Baltimore ;
We owe for friends in prison képt,
  And Davis* in his gore.

Wrongs such as these, aye more than these,
  Make up our fearful debt,
And many a gallant heart has sworn
  It shall be settled yet.
Each moment near and nearer brings,
  That solemn reckoning day,
And when it comes—and when it comes,
  Remember—and repay !

---

* Murdered in the streets of Baltimore, April, 1861, by Massachusetts soldiers.

BUTLER'S PROCLAMATION.

"It is ordered that hereafter when any female shall, by word, gesture, or movement, insult or show contempt for any officer or soldier of the United States, *she shall be regarded and held liable to be treated as a woman of the town, plying her vocation.*"

Butler's Order at New Orleans.

———

BY PAUL H. HAYNE, OF SOUTH CAROLINA.

———

Aye! drop the treacherous mask! throw by
  The cloak which veiled thine instincts fell,
Stand forth thou base incarnate lie,
  Stamped with the signet brand of hell.
At last we view thee as thou art—
A trickster with a demon's heart.

Off with disguise! no quarter now
  To rebel honor! thou would'st strike
Hot blushes up the anguished brow,
  And murder fame and strength alike.
Beware! ten millions hearts aflame
Will burn with hate thou canst not tame.

know thee now! we know thy race!
Thy dreadful purpose stands revealed
Naked before the nation's face!
Comrades! let mercy's fount be sealed,
While the black banner courts the wind,
And cursed be he who lags behind!

O! soldiers, husbands, brothers, sires!
Think that each stalwart blow ye give
Shall quench the rage of lustful fires,
And bid your glorious women live
Pure from a wrong whose tainted breath,   .
Were fouler than the foulest death.

O! soldiers, lovers, Christians, men!
Think that each breeze that floats and dies
O'er the red field, from mount or glen,
Is burdened with a maiden's sighs;
And each false soul that turns to flee,
Consigns his love to infamy!

No pity! let your thirsty brands,
Drink their warm fill at caitiff veins,
Dip deep in blood your wrathful hands,
Nor pause to wipe those crimson stains.
Slay! slay! with ruthless sword and will,
The God of vengeance bids you "kill!"

Yes ! but there's one who shall not die
  In battle harness ! one for whom
Lurks in the darkness silently
  Another and a sterner doom !
A warrior's end should crown the brave,
For *him*, strong cord and felon grave !

As loathsome charnel vapors melt,
  Swept by the rushing winds to nought,
So may this fiend of lust and guilt
  Die like a nightmare's hideous thought.
Nought left to mark the monster's name,
Save—immortality of shame !

THE GUERRILLAS.

BY S. T. WALLIS.

Awake and to horse! my brothers,
   For the dawn is glimmering gray,
And hark! in the crackling brushwood
   There are feet that tread this way!

"Who cometh?" "A friend!" "What tidings?"
   "O God! I sicken to tell;
For the earth seems earth no longer,
   And its sights are sights of hell!

"There's rapine, and fire, and slaughter,
   From the mountain down to the shore;
There's blood on the trampled harvest,
   And blood on the homestead floor!

"From the far-off conquered cities.
   Comes the voice of a stifled wail,
And the shrieks and moans of the houseless,
   Ring out like a dirge on the gale!

"I've seen from the smoking village,
   Our mothers and daughters fly!
I've seen where the little children
   Sank down in the furrows to die!

"On the banks of the battle-stained river
   I stood, as the moonlight shone;
And it glared on the face of my brother,
   As the sad wave swept him on !

"Where my home was glad are ashes,
   And horror and shame had been there;
For I found on the fallen lintel,
   This tress of my wife's torn hair !

"They are turning the slave upon us,
   And with more than the fiend's worst art,
Have uncovered the fires of the savage,
   That slept in his untaught heart !

"The ties to our hearths that bound him,
   They have rent with curses away,
And maddened him with their madness,
   To be almost as brutal as they.

"With halter, and torch, and Bible,
   And hymns, to the sound of the drum,
They preach the gospel of murder,
   And pray for lust's kingdom to come !

"To saddle ! to saddle ! my brothers !
   Look up to the rising sun,
And ask of the God who shines there,
   Whether deeds like these shall be done.

"Wherever the vandal cometh,
  Press home to his heart with your steel,
And where'er at his bosom ye can not,
  Like the serpent, go strike at his heel.

"Through thicket and wood go hunt him,
  Creep up to his camp-fire side!
And let ten of his corpses blacken
  Where one of our brothers hath died!

"In his fainting, foot-sore marches,
  In his flight from the stricken fray,
In the snare of the lonely ambush,
  The debts that we owe him, pay!

"In God's hand alone is judgment,
  But He strikes with hands of men,
And His blight would wither our manhood,
  If we smote not the smiter again.

"By the graves where our fathers slumber,
  By the shrines where our mothers prayed,
By our homes, and hopes, and freedom,
  Let every man swear on his blade—

"That he will not sheath nor stay it,
  Till from point to heft it glow,
With the flush of Almighty vengeance,
  In the blood of the felon foe!"

11*

They swore ; and the answering sunlight,
　Leapt red from their lifted swords,
And the hate in their hearts made echo
　To the wrath in their burning words !

There's weeping in all New England,
　And by Schuylkill's banks a knell,
And the widows there, and the orphans,
　How the oath was kept can tell.

FORT WARREN.

AT FORT PILLOW,

BY JAMES R. RANDALL.

You shudder as you think upon
　The carnage of the grim report—
The desolation when we won
　The inner trenches of the Fort.

But there are deeds you may not know,
　That scourge the pulses into strife,
Dark memories of deathless woe,
　Pointing the bayonet and knife.

The house is ashes where I dwelt,
　Beyond the mighty inland sea,
The tomb-stones shattered where I knelt
　By that old church in Pointe Coupee.

The Yankee fiends that came with fire,
   Camped on the consecrated sod,
And trampled in the dust and mire,
   The holy eucharist of God!

The spot where darling mother sleeps,
   Beneath the glimpse of yon sad moon,
Is crushed with splintered marble heaps,
   To stall the horse of some dragoon!

God! when I ponder that black day,
   It drives my frantic spirit mad,
I marched—with Longstreet—far away,
   But since have seen the ruin sad.

The tears are hot upon my face,
   When thinking what black fate befell
The only sister of our race—
   A thing too horrible to tell.

They say, that ere her senses fled,
   She, rescue of her brothers cried,
Then feebly bowed her stricken head,
   Too pure to live thus—so she died.

Two of those brothers heard no plea,
   With their proud hearts forever still—
John shrouded by the Tennessee,
   And Arthur there at Malvern Hill.

But I have heard it everywhere
  Vibrating like a passing knell,
'Tis universal as the air,
  And solemn as a funeral bell.

By scorched lagoon or murky swamp
  My wrath has known nor rest nor check,
I've slain the picket by his camp,
  And killed the pilot on the deck.

With deadly rifle, sharpened brand,
  A week ago upon my steed,
With Forrest and his warrior band,
  I made the hell-hounds writhe and bleed.

You should have seen our leader go
  Upon the battle's burning marge,
Swooping like falcon on the foe,
  Heading the gray line's iron charge!

The Southern yell rang loud and high
  The moment that we thundered in,
Smiting the demons hip and thigh,
  Cleaving them unto the chin.

My right arm bared for fiercer play,
  The left one held the rein in slack,
In all the fury of the fray
  I sought the white man, *not the black*.

Throbbing along the frenzied vein
  My blood seemed kindled into song,
The death-dirge of the sacred slain,
  The slogan of immortal wrong.

It glared athwart the dripping glaives,
  It blazed in each avenging eye—
The thought of desecrated graves,
  And some lone sister's desperate cry.

WILMINGTON, *April 25th.*

BOMBARDMENT OF VICKSBURG.

DEDICATED TO MAJOR-GENERAL EARL VAN DORN.

For sixty days, and longer,
  A storm of shell and shot
Rained round as in a flaming shower,
  But still we faltered not!
"If the noble city perish,"
  Our grand young leader said,
"Let the only walls the foe shall scale,
  Be ramparts of the dead!"

For sixty days, and longer,
  The eye of heaven waxed dim,
And e'en throughout God's holy morn,
  O'er Christian's prayer and hymn,

Arose a hissing tumult,
　　As if the fiends of air,
Strove to engulf the voice of faith,
　　In the shrieks of their despair.

There·was wailing in the houses,
　　There was trembling on the marts,
While the tempest raged and thundered,
　　'Mid the silent thrill of hearts;
But the Lord, our shield, was with us,
　　And ere a month had sped,
Our very women walked the streets
　　With scarce one throb of dread.

And the little children gambolled—
　　Their pure, bright faces raised,
Just for a wondering moment ·
　　As the huge bombs whirled and blazed;
Then turned with silvery laughter,
　　To the sports which children love,
Thrice mailed in this instinctive thought,
　　That the good God watched above.

Yet the hailing bolts fell faster,
　　From scores of flame-clad ships,
And above us, denser, darker,
　　Grew the conflict's wild eclipse—
Till a solid cloud closed o'er us,
　　Like a type of gloom and ire,
Whence shot a thousand·quivering tongues
　　Of forked and vengeful fire.

But the unseen hand of angels,
  These death-shafts warned aside,
And the dove of Heavenly mercy
  Ruled o'er the battle tide;
In the houses ceased the wailing,
  And through the war-scarred marts,
The people strode with a step of hope,
  To the music in their hearts.

COLUMBIA, S. C., *Aug.* 6, 1862.

GONE TO THE BATTLE-FIELD.

The reaper has left the field,
  The mower has left the plain,
And the reaper's hook and the mower's scythe,
  Are changed to the sword again;
For the voice of a hundred years ago,
When Freedom struck her mightiest blow,
  Thrills every heart and brain!

The wayside mill is still,
  And the wheel drips all alone,
For the miller's brother, and son, and sire,
  And the miller's self are gone;
And their wives and daughters tarrying still,
With smiles and tears about the mill,
  Wave, wave their heroes on!

The grain is full and ripe,
  And the harvest moon is nigh,
But the farmer's son is among the slain,
  And the father heard the cry;
And his ancient eyes flashed fires of old,
His hoary head rose strong and bold,
  As wild he hurried by!

The corn is yet afield,
  But many a stalk is red;
Yet not with the autumn tassel stained,
  But with blood of heroes shed.
And their blood cries out from heaps of slain,
Oh! brothers, leave the sheaves of grain—
  And haste to avenge your dead!

By every quiet farm,
  Whence father and son had gone,
The fairest daughters of the land,
  Brave hearted, cheered us on;
With the tender smiles that shelter tears,
And words to thrill a soldier's ears,
  When bloody fields are won!

Scarcely the form of man
  Was seen on the long highway,
But patriots aged, with withered hands
  Stretched feebly up to pray;
And children, whose voices haunt us still,
Gathered on every knoll and hill,
  Cheering us on our way!

Yonder with feeble limbs,
　A matron with silver hair,
Knelt trembling down on the soldier's path,
　And breathed to Heaven a prayer;
With quivering lips, with streaming eyes,
"Oh! God, preserve these gallant boys,
　In battle be Thou there!"

Oh, soldiers! such as these,
　Like household memories come,
For a thousand prayers ascend to-day
　From those we left at home;
For the red, red field to-night may be
Our couch, our grave—while victory
　Shall shout above our tomb!

In battle's bloody hour,
　These pictures shall arise
Of mothers, sisters, wives and homes,
　And sad and streaming eyes,
And every arm shall stronger be,
For home, for God, for liberty,
　And strike while Mercy dies.

THE VIRGINIANS OF THE VALLEY.

SIC JURAT.

Ticknor of Georgia, the true poet, has thus eloquently eulogized
in the lines below, the noble qualities of the sons of Virginia:

The knightliest of the knightly race,
  Who, since the days of old,
Have kept the lamps of chivalry
  Alight in hearts of gold—
The kindliest of the kindly band
  Who rarely hated ease,
Yet rode with Smith around the land
  And Raleigh round the seas!

Who climbed the blue Virginia hills,
  Amid embattled foes,
And planted there, in valleys fair,
  The lily and the rose;
Whose fragrance lives in many lands,
  Whose beauty stars the earth,
And lights the hearths of many homes,
  With loveliness and worth!

We thought they slept! these sons who kept
  The names of noble sires,
And slumbered, while the darkness crept
  Around their vigil fires!

But still the Golden Horse-shoe knights,
  Their Old Dominion keep,
Whose foes have found enchanted ground,
  But not a knight asleep !

THE VALLEY OF THE SHENANDOAH.

BY A SOLDIER OF THE ARMY OF NORTHERN VIRGINIA.

The peace of the valley is fled,
  The calm of its once happy bowers
Is disturbed by the rude soldier's tread,
  While the blood of its braves dyes the flowers.
These hearts that beat once but to love,
  Now broken, forsaken, and dead,
No time can their sorrows remove,
  The peace of the Valley is fled !

The vine round the cottage door clings,
  Its tendrils neglected and torn,
By the door may the widow long wait
  For a form that shall never return.
He lies far away 'mid the slain,
  His broken shield pillows his head,
And the loved ones await him in vain—
  The soldier of freedom is dead !

THE REAPER

The apples are ripe in the orchard,
  The work of the reaper's begun,
And the golden woodlands redden
  In the rays of the dying sun.

At the cottage door, the grandsire
  Sits pale in his easy chair,
While the gentle wind at twilight
  Sports with his silvery hair.

A maiden is kneeling beside him,
  Her fair young head is prest,
In the first wild passion of sorrow,
  Against his aged breast!

And far from over the distance
  The faltering echoes come,
Of the thrilling blast of trumpet,
  And the roll of the rattling drum.

And the grandsire speaks in a whisper—
  "The end no man can see,
But we gave him to his country,
  And we give our prayers to Thee."

The lark sings in the meadows,
  The jessamine scents the room,
And in the apple orchard
  The sweet pink blossoms bloom.

But the grandsire's chair is empty,
  The cottage is dark and still,
There's a nameless grave on the battle-field,
  And a new one under the hill.

And a pallid; tearless woman,
  By the cold hearth sits alone,
And the old clock in the corner
  Ticks on with a steady drone.

*   *   *   *   *   *

The clock stands mute in the corner,
  The meadows sleep in the sun ;
The maiden's borne from the cottage,
  For the task of the reaper's done.

Fort Taylord, N. C.

DIRGE FOR ASHBY.

Heard ye that thrilling word—
  Accent of dread!
Fall like a thunderbolt,
  Bowing each head?
Over the battle dun—
Over each booming gun—
    Ashby, our bravest one!
    Ashby is dead!

Saw ye the veterans—
  Hearts that had known
Never a quail of fear,
  Never a groan—
Sob 'mid the fight they win,
Tears their stern eyes within?
    Ashby, our paladin!
    Ashby is dead!

Dash, dash the tear away!
  Crush down the pain!
Dulce et decus be
  Fittest refrain.
Why should the dreary pall
Round him be flung at all?
Did not our hero fall,
    Gallantly slain?

Catch the last words of cheer
  Dropped from his tongue!
Over the volley's din
  Let them be rung!
"Follow me! Follow me!"
Soldier! oh! could there be
Pæan, or dirge for thee
      Loftier sung?

Bold as the Lion's Heart—
  Dauntless and brave,
Knightly as knightliest
  Bayard could crave;
Sweet—with all Sidney's grace—
Tender as Hampden's face—
Who, who shall fill the space,
      Void by his grave?

'T is not one broken heart,
  Wild with dismay—
Crazed in her agony—
  Weeps o'er his clay!
Ah! from a thousand eyes
·Flow the pure tears that rise—
Widowed VIRGINIA lies
     Stricken to-day!

Yet charge as gallantly,
  Ye whom he led!
Jackson the victor, still
  Stands at your head!

Heroes! be battle done,
Bravelier every one,
Nerved by the thought alone—
 Ashby is dead!

ASHBY.

BY JNO. R. THOMPSON.

To the brave all homage render!
 Weep, ye skies of June!
With a radiance pure and tender,
 Shine, oh, saddened moon!
"*Dead upon the field of glory!*"—
Hero fit for song and story—
 Lies our bold dragoon!

Well they learned, whose hands have slain him,
 Braver, knightlier foe
Never fought 'gainst Moor or Paynim—
 Rode at Templestowe:
With a mien how high and joyous,
'Gainst the hordes that would destroy us
 Went he forth, we know.

Never more, alas! shall sabre
 Gleam around his crest—
Fought his fight, fulfilled his labor,
 Stilled his manly breast—

All unheard sweet nature's cadence,
Trump of fame and voice of maidens,
  Now he takes his rest.

Earth, that all too soon hast bound him,
  Gently wrap his clay !
Linger lovingly around him,
  Light of dying day !
Softly fall, ye summer showers—
Birds and bees among the flowers,
  Make the gloom seem gay !

Then throughout the coming ages,
  When his sword is rust,
And his deeds in classic pages—
  Mindful of her trust,
Shall VIRGINIA, bending lowly,
Still a ceaseless vigil holy
  Keep above his dust !

12

GEN. JOHN B. FLOYD.

BY EULALIE

The noble hero calmly sleeps,
　Unheeding all life's surging woes,
An angel-guard its vigil keeps
　About his couch of deep repose.

How still that brain once full of thought!
　How calm that pulse, which wildly beat!
Grim death the mighty change hath wrought,
　And now he lies in rest most sweet.

Hush'd to his ear the siren's song,
　Hush'd is the clarion trump of fame;
No more applauds the list'ning throng,
　His bold tones thrill them not again!

Virginia mourns her gallant son,
　Whose voice of wisdom charm'd her heart;
How many a noble conquest won,
　When he from virtue would not part!

And on the battle's gory field,
　When foes assail'd our Southern land,
His dauntless spirit would not yield,
　But boldly met th' invading band.

What anxious cares his soul harass'd,
  What sleepless nights his pillow found,
But now those bitter pangs are passed—
  He heeds no more the bugle's sound!

He sleeps in Jesus, blissful sleep!
  His cares forgotten, sorrows o'er,
With lov'd ones, where no eye doth weep,
  He treads in peace th' Eternal shore.

That eagle eye now sweeps through space,
  And reads the open book of love.
That voice shall to the Lamb give praise,
  While endless cycles onward move!

WOODLAWN, VA., *April*, 1866.

VIRGINIA'S DEAD.

Proud mother of a race that reared
　The brave and good of ours,
Lo ! on thy bleeding bosom lie,
　Thy pale and perished flowers.
Where'er upon her own bright soil
　Hosts meet their blood to shed,
Where brightest gleams the victor's sword,
　There lie Virginia's dead.

And where upon the crimsoned field
　The cannon loudest roars,
And hero blood for liberty
　A streaming torrent pours,
Where fiercest glows the battle's rage,
　And Southern banners spread,
Where minions crouch and vassals kneel,
　There lie Virginia's dead.

Where bright Potomac's classic wave
　Flows softly to the sea,
And Shenandoah's valley smiles
　In her captivity ;
Where sullen Mississippi rolls,
　By foaming torrents fed,
And Tennessee's smooth ripple breaks,
　There sleep Virginia's dead.

And where mid dreary mountain heights,
  The frost-king sternly sate,
As Garnett cheered his followers on,
  And nobly met his fate;
Where Johnson, Lee and Beauregard,
  Their gallant armies led,
Thro' winter snows and tropic suns,
  There sleep Virginia's dead.

And where through Georgia's flowery meads,
  The proud Savannah flows,
And soft o'er Carolina's brow
  Atlantic's pure breeze blows;
Where Florida's sweet tropic flowers,
  Their dewy fragrance shed,
And night-winds sigh through orange groves,
  There sleep Virginia's dead!

Where sad Louisiana's eye,
  Looks darkly on her chains,
And proud New Orleans' noble street,
  The despot's heel profanes;
Where virtue shrinks in dread dismay,
  And beauty bows her head,
Where courage spurns the oppressors' yoke,
  There lie Virginia's dead!

'Neath Alabama's sunny skies,
  On Texas' burning shore,
Where blooming prairies brightly sweep
  Missouri's bosom o'er—

Where. bold Kentucky's lion heart,
   Leaps to her Morgan's tread,
And tyrants quail at freedom's cry,
   There sleep Virginia's dead.

And where the ocean's trackless waves
   O'er pallid corpses sweep,
As 'mid the cannon's thunder peal,
   "Deep calleth unto deep,"
Wherever Honor's sword is drawn,
   And Justice rears her head,
Where heroes fall and martyrs bleed,
   There rest Virginia's dead.

MY ORDER.

BY GORDON M'CABE.

Said to have been found in the pocket of a wounded soldier, in hospital.

This flower has set me a-dreaming
   Of the future for you and for me,
All radiant with golden sunlight,
   And as bright as the future must be,

When youth guides the pencil, and Fancy
   Holds his colors of crimson and gold,
When Heaven's own blue is above us,
   And it seems we shall never grow old.

Sweetly stern the voice that awakes me!
   Virginia is calling her sons,
I can hear the tramp of her legions,
   And her hill-sides are bristling with guns.

I look at my garb as her soldier,
   That is rusty and faded by rain,
And know 'tis no time to be dreaming,
   When her foemen are pressing amain.

I will do as did my brave namesake,
  Whose sad story our old ballads sing,
When his ladye-love gave him a flower,
  Ere he rode to strike for his king.

He placed it beneath his silk-doublet,
  With a tender and reverent care,
'Tis " My *Order*," he said, " that forever
  I will strive to be worthy to wear."

Charging home with fiery Rupert,
  In the van of old England's best blood,
The gallant went down upon Naseby,
  Where the stout-hearted pikemen had stood.

A cut 'cross the beautiful forehead,
  The dark love-locks all dripping with gore,
And his lips closely prest to a flower
  That was hid in the scarf that he wore.

So this flower you gave me, dear lady,
  I will place 'neath my jacket of gray,
As *my* " order " for which to strike boldly,
  Charging home, as he did, in the fray.

And if Fate should decree that my life,
  Like his to the cause should be given,
I will pray that my soul may be wafted
  On this flower's sweet perfume to Heaven.

RICHMOND, VA.

THE SOUTHERN CROSS.

Fling wide each fold, brave flag, unrolled
  In all thy breadth and length!
Float out unfurled, and show the world
  A new-born nation's strength.
Thou dost not wave all bright and brave
  In holiday attire;
'Mid cannon chimes a thousand times
  Baptized in blood and fire.

No silken toy to flaunt in joy
  Where careless shouts are heard;
Where thou art borne all scathed and torn,
  A nation's heart is stirred.
Where half-clad groups of toil-worn troops
  Are marching to the wars,
What grateful tears and heart-felt cheers
  Salute thy cross of stars!

Thou ne'er hast seen the pomp and sheen,
  The pageant of a court;
Or masquerade of war's parade,
  Where fields are fought in sport:
But thou knowest well the battle yell
  From which thy foemen reel,
When down the steeps resistless leaps
  A sea of Southern steel.

12*

Thou know'st the storm of balls that swarm
 In dense and hurtling flight,
When thy cross'd bars a blaze of stars
 Plunge headlong through the fight;
Where thou'rt unfurled are thickest hurled
 The thunderbolts of war,
And thou art met with loudest threat
 Of cannon from afar.

For thee is told the merchant's gold—
 The planter's harvests fall,
Thine is the gain of hand and brain,
 And the heart's wealth of all:
For thee each heart has borne to part
 With what it holds most dear,
Through all the land no woman's hand,
 Has stayed one volunteer.

Though from thy birth outlawed on earth,
 By older nations spurned,
Their full-grown fame may dread the name
 Thy infancy has earned.
For thou dost flood the land with blood
 And sweep the seas with fire,
And all the earth applauds the worth
 Of deeds thou dost inspire!

Thy stainless field shall empire wield
 Supreme from sea to sea,
And proudly shine the honored sign
 Of peoples yet to be.

When thou shalt grace the hard won place
  The nations grudge thee now,
No land shall· show to friend or foe
  A · nobler flag than thou !

HYMN TO THE NATIONAL FLAG.

BY MRS. M. J. PRESTON.

Float aloft, thou stainless banner,
  Azure cross and field of light,
Be thy brilliant stars the symbol
  Of the pure and true and right;
Shelter Freedom's holy cause,
Liberty and sacred laws,
Guard the youngest of the Nations—
  Keep her virgin honor bright.

From Virginia's storied border,
  Down to Tampa's furthest shore,
From the blue Atlantic's dashings
  To the Rio Grande's roar,
Over many a crimson plain,
Where our martyred one's lie slain,
Fling abroad thy blessed shelter,
  Stream and mount and valley o'er.

In thy cross of Heavenly azure,
  Has our faith its emblem high,   .
In thy field of white, the hallowed
  Truth, for which we'll dare and die.
In thy red, the patriot blood
Ah! the consecrated flood!
Lift thyself! resistless banner!
  Ever fill our Southern sky!

Flash with living lightning motion
  In the sight of all the brave,
Tell the price at which we purchased
  Room and right for thee to wave
Freely in our God's free air,.
Pure and proud and stainless fair—
Banner of the youngest nation,
  Banner we would die to save!

Strike thou for us—King of Armies!
  Grant us room in thy broad world,
Loosen all the despot's fetters,
  Back be all his legions hurled!
Give us peace and liberty!
Let the land we love be free!
Then oh! bright and stainless banner
  Never shall thy folds be furled!

THE COUNTERSIGN.

Alas! the weary hours pass slow,
  The night is very dark and still,
And in the marshes far below
  I hear the bearded whip-poor-will.
I scarce can see a yard ahead,
  My ears are strained to catch each sound,
I hear the leaves about me shed,
  And the springs bubbling through the ground.

Along the beaten path I pace,
  Where white rags mark my sentry's track,
In formless shrubs I seem to trace
  The foeman's form with bending back.
I think I see him crouching low,
  I stop and list—I stop and peer—
Until the neighboring hillocks grow
  To groups of soldiers far and near.

With ready piece I wait and watch,
  Until mine eyes familiar grown,
Detect each harmless earthen notch,
  And turn guerillas into stone.
And then amid the lonely gloom,
  Beneath the weird old tulip trees,
My silent marches I resume,
  And think on other times than these.

Sweet visions through the silent night,
  The deep bay-windows fringed with vine,
The room within, in softened light
  The tender, pure white hand in mine;
The timid pressure, and the pause
  That oftentimes o'ercame our speech—
That time when by mysterious laws,
  We each felt all in all to each.

So rose the dream—so pass'd the night—
  When distant in the darksome glen,
Approaching up the sombre height,
  I heard the measured march of men;
Till over stubble, over sward,
  And fields where lay the golden sheaf,
I saw the lantern of the guard
  Advancing with the night relief.

" Halt! who goes there?" my challenge cry,
  It rings along the watchful line;
" Relief!" I hear a voice reply,
  "Advance, and give the countersign!"
With bayonet at the charge I wait,
  The corporal gives the mystic spell,
With arms at port I charge my mate,
  And onward pass, and all is well.

But in the tent that night awake,
  I think if in the fray I fall,
Can I the mystic answer make
  Whene'er the angelic sentries call?

And pray that Heaven may so ordain,
  That when I near the camp divine,
Whether in travail or in pain,
  I too may have the countersign.

OUR "COTTAGE BY THE SEA."

LINES .WRITTEN IN FORT LAFAYETTE BY A PRISONER.

I dreamed that I dwelt in marble halls,
  And 'tis not so, you see;
For cold and gray are the granite walls
  Of " our cottage by the sea."

No balmy gentle zephyrs here,
  But " shrill winds whistle free,"
No " lowing kine " nor flowers are here,
  In " our cottage by the sea."

But we've bunches of grape, oh! heavier far,
  Than ever you did see;
And cannisters, too, we have, my dear,
  But they are not filled with tea.

Such beautiful shells, as we have here,
  Tho' not washed up by the sea,
And marine curiosities one may speer,
  In " our cottage by the sea."

The wild goose on its Southern flight,
  In lengthening lines we see,
And we hear the houk* in the morning light,
  In " our cottage by the sea."

We can only dream of marble halls,
  And beauties of the sea,
Disturbed the while by the sentry's calls,
  In " our cottage by the sea."

Alas ! alas ! for the " pleasures of hope,"
  They're our only pleasure, you see ;
And all we can do is sit and mope
  In " our cottage by the sea."

---

* Houk—cry of the wild goose.

THE QUAKER GIRL'S FAREWELL TO HER SOUTHERN LOVER.

BY MRS. ELIZA E. HARPER.

George, we must part—and part for aye,
    And thee must now forget
All our past love, for we must live,
    As tho' we ne'er had met.

I cannot leave my father, George,
    He has but me to love;
Our paths through life lie wide apart,
    Perhaps they'll meet above.

Life's path would brighter seem to me,
    If *thou* wert by my side—
But they'd not welcome thee at home,
    If *I* went as thy bride.

So we our plighted troth must break,
    Thy friends and mine are foes,
'Tis not that I do love *thee* less,
    But blood between us flows.

Thy country needs thy heart and hand,
    Yet let *me* keep thy ring,
And wear it for the memory
    That round my heart will cling.

And thou wilt wear the one I gave,
   But heed my parting word:
* *Not on thy trigger-finger, George,*
   Nor hand that grasps the sword!

And sometimes in thy Southern home,
   Which once I thought to share,
Think of the far-off *"Quaker girl,"*
   And breathe for her a prayer.

But now farewell, this is no time
   The heart's fond words to say,
We cannot wed—we must not love—
   But I will for thee pray.

MINDEN. LA., *Oct.* 186'.

---

* This little poem is founded on a true incident. My young cousin George ———— was being educated by a clergyman in Pennsylvania and boarded with a Quaker family, one of whom was a beautiful young girl sweet sixteen. Of course he " fell in love," and when he left to join the Southern army rings were exchanged, the " Quaker girl " saying " thee must not wear it on thy trigger-finger, George."

A CONFEDERATE OFFICER TO HIS LADYE LOVE.

Maj. McKnight, ("Asa Hartz") A. A. Q., Gen. Loring's staff, while a prisoner of war at Johnston's Island wrote the following:

My love reposes on a rosewood frame—
        A bunk have I;
A couch of feathery down fills up the same—
        Mine's straw, but dry;
She sinks to sleep at night with scarce a sigh—
With waking eyes I watch the hours creep by.

My love her daily dinner takes in state—
        And so do I(?);
The richest viands flank her silver plate—
        Coarse grub have I;
Pure wines she sips at ease, her thirst to slake—
I pump my drink from Erie's limpid lake!

My love has all the world at will to roam—
        Three acres I;
She goes abroad or quiet sits at home—
        So cannot I;
Bright angels watch around her couch at night—
A Yank, with loaded gun keeps me in sight.

A thousand weary miles do stretch between
        My love and I ;
To her, this wintry night, cold, calm, serene,
        I waft a sigh ;
And hope, with all my earnestness of soul,
To-morrow's mail may bring me my parole !

There's hope ahead ! We'll one day meet again,
        My love and I ;
We'll wipe away all tears of sorrow then,
        Her lovelit eye,
Will all my many troubles then beguile,
And keep this wayward reb. from Johnston's Isle.

THE HOMESPUN DRESS.

Air—Bonnie Blue Flag.

Oh! yes, I am a Southern girl,
    And glory in the name,
And boast it with far greater pride
    Than glittering wealth or fame.
We envy not the Northern girl
    Her robes of beauty rare,
Though diamonds grace her snowy neck,
    And pearls bedeck her hair.
            Hurrah! Hurrah!
            For the sunny South so dear,
            Three cheers for the homespun dress
            The Southern ladies wear!

The homespun dress is plain, I know,
    My hat's palmetto, too;
But then it shows what Southern girls
    For Southern rights will do.
We send the bravest of our land
    To battle with the foe,
And we will lend a helping hand—
    We love the South, you know.
            Hurrah! Hurrah!
            For the sunny South so dear,
            Three cheers for the homespun dress
            The Southern ladies wear!

Now Northern goods are out of date;
　　And since old Abe's blockade,
We Southern girls can be content
　　With goods that's Southern made.
We send our sweethearts to the war;
　　But, dear girls, never mind—
Your soldier-love will ne'er forget
　　The girl he left behind.
　　　　　Hurrah! Hurrah!
　　　　　For the sunny South so dear,
　　　　　Three cheers for the homespun dress
　　　　　The Southern ladies wear!

The soldier is the lad for me—
　　A brave heart I adore;
And when the sunny South is free,
　　And when fighting is no more,
I'll choose me then a lover brave
　　From out that gallant band.
The soldier-lad I love the best
　　Shall have my heart and hand.
　　　　　Hurrah! Hurrah!
　　　　. For the sunny South so dear,
　　　　　Three cheers for the homespun dress
　　　　　The Southern ladies wear!

The Southern land's a glorious land,
　　And has a glorious cause;
Then cheer, three cheers for Southern rights,
　　And for the Southern boys!

We scorn to wear a bit of silk,
  A bit of Northern lace,
But make our homespun dresses up,
  And wear them with a grace.
      . Hurrah ! Hurrah !
      For the sunny South so dear,
      Three cheers for the homespun dress
      The Southern ladies wear !

And now, young man, a word to you :
  If you would win the fair,
Go to the field where honor calls,
  And win your lady there.
Remember that our brightest smiles
  Are for the true and brave,
And that our tears are all for those
  Who fill a soldier's grave.
      Hurrah ! Hurrah !
      For the sunny South so dear,
      Three cheers for the homespun dress
      The Southern ladies wear !

CANNON SONG.

Aha! a song for the trumpet's tongue!
  For the bugle to sing before us,
When our gleaming guns, like clarions,
  Shall thunder in battle chorus!
Where the rifles ring, where the bullets sing,
  Where the black bombs whistle o'er us,
With rolling wheel and rattling peal
  They'll thunder in battle chorus!
    With the cannon's flash, and the cannon's crash,
      With the cannon's roar and rattle,
     Let Freedom's sons, with their shouting guns,
      Go down to their country's battle!

Their brassy throats shall learn the notes
  That make old tyrants quiver,
Till the war is done, or each TYRRELL gun,
  Grows cold with our hearts forever!
Where the laurel waves o'er our brothers' graves,
  Who have gone to their rest before us,
Here's a requiem shall sound for them
  And thunder in battle chorus!
    With the cannon's flash, and the cannon's crash,
      With the cannon's roar and rattle,
     Let Freedom's sons, with their shouting guns,
      Go down to their country's battle!

By the light that lies in our Southern skies,
  By the spirits that watch above us;
By the gentle hands in our summer lands,
  And the gentle hearts that love us!
Our fathers' faith let us keep till death,
  Their fame in its cloudless splendor—
As men who stand for their mother land,
  And die—but never surrender!
      With the cannon's flash, and the cannon's crash,
        With the cannon's roar and rattle,
      Let Freedom's sons, with their thundering guns,
        Go down to their country's battle!

ON A RAID.

BY IKEY INGLE.

We must lively move to night my men, brisk march-
    ing 's to be done!
For a stout blow must be struck, and true, by the
    morrow's rising sun,
A blow for Virginia's hearthstones, round which her
    daughters sit,
And weary and sad and famished toil, to fill the
    soldier's kit.
A blow for our fallen comrades, for liberty and life,
I will lead and who'd be near me must be foremost
    in the strife;

13

For 'twill be no oft tried combat with the rifle's range
    between,
But breast to breast and blow for blow with the sabre
    swift and keen.
Then on, my lads, no songs to night! e'en your spurs
    too noisy clank,
For a silent night must be our guide to the invader's
    trailing flank.

.   .   .   .

And the *lael Sothoron** kept his word, for his bugles
    rang from far,
And his gallant troop swept down in charge, with a
    shout and a wild huzza.
Like the storm down the Alpine gorge with its blast-
    ing lightning breath,
Leaving weird waste behind it, and flooding the tide
    of death.
At its head with flashing falchion, rode a *Cavalier* to
    life,
A man of mirth to his merry men, but a direful foe
    in strife ;
For the stroke of his trusty sabre fell, with the force
    of the vernal flood,
Like the swoop of the mountain eagle down, when the
    young ones cry for food.
And his deep blue eye flashed gorgeously, and a joy
    in his visage shone,

---

* No stranger could look upon the frank florid face of Stuart, meet the
glance of his honest sparkling blue eye, or the warm cordial grasp of his
hand without feeling a positive conviction of the Scottish origin of this
boon cavalier.

Like the gleam on the face of the dying saint when
    his crown is almost won.
His joy that a frame inured to toil, and a dauntless
    soul were lent,
In the cause of Right and Liberty to spend and to
    be spent.
'Tis an envied pride the mariner feels—his ship on
    the raging sea—
When at Nature's threat in the tempest's tread, e'en
    atheists bend the knee—
To feel that *his* skill and compass true can mock at
    old ocean's sport,
An hundred hearts from affliction save, and his bark
    bring safe to port;
'Tis exulting joy the orator feels as he bends o'er the
    enraptured throng,
By the impetuous tide of his eloquence, to his purpose
    borne along;
But give me the sense that thrills each vein, and wraps
    each nerve with fire,
As the patriot faces his country's foe, in his fierce yet
    holy ire;
As he measures each thrust of his trusty sword by the
    depth of his country's wrong,
Yields drop by drop a patriot's blood his country's foes
    among;
Reclaims with each blow of his lusty arm, the foot-
    steps his childhood trod,
And offers his life for liberty and the altars of his
    God.

RICHMOND, VA., 1862.

COMING AT LAST.

BY GEORGE H. MILES.

Up on the hill there,
  Who are they, pray,
Three dusty troopers
  Spurring this way?
And that squadron behind them?
  Stand not aghast—
Why, these are the rebels, sir,
  Coming at last!

Coming so carelessly,
  Sauntering on,
Into the midst of us,
  Into our town;
Thrice thirty miles to-day
  These men have passed,
Stuart at the head of them
  Coming at last!

Oh, sir! no gold lace
  Burns in the sun,
But each blooded war-horse
  And rider seem one.
These men could ride at need,
  Outride the blast—
O yes, sir, the rebels
  Are coming at last!

Circling Mac's army,
  Three days at work!
Under that smile of theirs
  Famine may lurk.
Out with the best you have,
  Fill the bowl fast,
For Jeff's ragged rebels
  Are coming at last!

FREDERICK Co., MD.

BEYOND THE POTOMAC.

BY PAUL H. HAYNE, OF SOUTH CAROLINA.

They slept on the field which their valor had won!
But arose with the first early blush of the sun,
For they knew that a great deed remained to be
      done,
      When they passed o'er the River:

They rose with the sun, and caught life from his
      light—
Those giants of courage, those Anaks in fight—
And they laughed out aloud in the joy of their
      might,
      Marching swift for the River.

On! on! like the rushing of storms thro' the
      hills—
On! on! with a tramp that is firm as their wills—
And the one heart of thousands grows buoyant, and
      thrills,
        At the thought of the River!

Oh! the sheen of their swords! the fierce gleam
      of their eyes!
It seemed as on earth a new sunlight would rise,
And king-like, flash up to the sun in the skies,
        O'er the path to the River.

But, their banners shot-scarred, and all darkened
      with gore,
On morning's fresh breeze streaming bravely before,
Like wings of Death's angels swept fast to the shore,
        The green shore of the River.

As they march, from the hill-side, the hamlet, the
      stream,
Gaunt throngs whom the Foeman had manacled, teem
Like men just aroused from some terrible dream,
        To pass o'er the River.

They behold the broad Banners, blood-darkened, yet
      fair,
And a moment dissolves the last spell of despair,
While a peal as of victory swells on the air,
        Rolling out to the River.

And that cry, with a thousand strange echoings spread,
Till the ashes of heroes seemed stirred in their bed,
And the deep voice of passion surged up from the dead,
    Aye! press on to the River!

On! on! like the rushing of storms through the hills,
On! on! with a tramp that is firm as their wills,
And the one heart of thousands grows buoyant; and
    thrills,
    As they pause by the River.

Then the wan face of Maryland, haggard and worn,
At that sight lost the touch of its aspect forlorn,
And she turned on the Foeman full statured in scorn,
    Pointing stern to the River.

And Potomac flowed calmly, scarce heaving her breast,
With her low lying billows all bright in the West,
For the hand of the Lord lulled the waters to rest
    Of the fair rolling River.

Passed! passed! the glad thousands march safe thro'
    the tide.
(Hark, Despot! and hear the deep knell of your pride,
Ringing weird-like and wild, pealing up from the side
    Of the calm flowing River!)

'Neath a blow swift and mighty the Tyrant shall fall,
Vain! vain! to his God swells a desolate call,
For his grave has been hollowed, and woven his pall,
    Since they passed o'er the River!

THE SOUTHERN OATH.

BY ROSA VERTNER JEFFREY.

By the cross upon our banner,
    Glory of our Southern sky,
We have sworn—a band of brothers, .
    Free to live or free to die,—
We have sworn as freemen never
    Swear, who live to break their vow,
North-men, by the rights denied us,
    Ye shall *never* rule us now.

By our dear ones lost in battle,
    Best and bravest of our land,
Fighting with your Northern hirelings
    Face to face and hand to hand,
By a sacrifice so priceless,
    By the spirits of the slain,
Swear we now, our Southern heroes
    Shall not thus have died in vain.

Wide and deep the breach between us,
    Rent by hatred's poisoned darts!
And ye cannot now cement it,
    With the blood from Southern hearts!
Streams of gore that gulf shall widen,
    Running deep and strong and red,
Severing us from you *forever*,
    While there is a drop to shed.

Think ye, we'll brook the insults
　Of your fierce and ruffian chief,
Heaped upon our dark-eyed daughters
　Stricken down and pale with grief?
Think ye, while astounded nations
　Curse such malice, *we* will bear
Foulest wrongs, with God to call on,
　Arms to do, and hearts to dare?

When we prayed in peace to leave you,
　Answering came a battle cry!
Then we swore that oath which freemen
　Never swear who fear to die;
North-men, come, and ye shall find us
　Heart to heart, and hand to hand,
Calling to the God of battles,
　"Freedom and our native land."

July 22, 1862.

13*

THE BRAVE AT HOME.

The maid who binds her warrior's sash,
  And smiling, all her pain dissembles,
The while beneath the drooping lash
  One starry tear-trop hangs and trembles,
Though Heaven alone records the tear,
  And fame shall never know her story,
Her heart has shed a drop as dear,
  As ever dewed the field of glory!

The wife who girds her husband's sword,
  'Mid little ones who weep and wonder,
And bravely speaks the cheering word,
  What tho' her heart be rent asunder—
Doomed nightly in her dreams to hear
  The bolts of war around him rattle,
Has shed as sacred blood as e'er
  Was poured upon the plain of battle!

The mother who conceals her grief,
  While to her breast her son she presses,
Then breathes a few brave words, and brief,
  Kissing the patriot brow she blesses,
With no one but her secret God
  To know the pain that weighs upon her,
Sheds holy blood as e'er the sod
  Received on Freedom's field of honor!

LITTLE FOOTSTEPS.

BY MARY J. UPSHUR, NORFOLK, VA.

I sit in the summer moonlight,
　And watch the fleckèd floor,
Where the sheen and the shimmering aspen trees
　Make shadows across the door.

And I list and list for a footstep
　That I have heard long ago,
Tripping the summer pavement,
　Treading the winter's snow.

Light little feet where are you?
　Never ye'll come again,
Making my heart's unfoldings
　Like flowers to the summer rain.

O little child in Heaven!
　Say, do the fairy feet
Lave in the seas of jasper?
　Traverse the golden street?

Wave your bright angel pinions,
　Fan the celestial air,
But oh! for the little footsteps
　If ever I get there!

Oh, little child in Heaven,
　If thou should'st be sent to greet
The home-bound, let me but listen
　To the sound of the little feet!

———

"MINDING THE GAP."

BY MOLLIE E. MOORE.

There is a radiant beauty on the hills,
　The year before us walks with added bloom,
But ah! 'tis but the hectic flush that lights
　The pale consumptive to an early tomb;
　　The dying glory that plays around the day
　　When that which made it bright hath fled away!

A mistiness broods in the air—the swell
　Of east winds slowly weaving autumn's pall,
With dirge-like sadness wanders up the dell;
　And red leaves from the maple branches fall
　　With scarce a sound! 'Tis strange, mysterious rest,
　　Hath nature bound the Lotus to her breast?

But hark! a long and mellow cadence wakes
　The echoes from their rocks! how clear and high
Among the rounded hills its gladness breaks,
　And floats like incense toward the vaulted sky!

It is the harvest anthem! a triumph tone,
　It rises like these swelling notes of old,
That welcomed Ceres to her golden throne,
　　When through the crowded streets the chariots rolled.
　　　It is the laborer's chorus, for the reign
　　　Of plenty hath begun—the golden grain!

How cheeks are flushed with triumph, as the fields
　Bow to our feet with riches! How the eyes
Grow full with gladness as they yield
　　Their ready treasures. How hearts arise
　　　To join with gladness in the mellow chime,
　　　"The harvest time—the glorious harvest time!"

It is the harvest, and the gathered corn
　Is piled in yellow heaps about the field,
And homely wagons from the break of morn
　　Until the sun glows like a crimson shield
　　　In the far West, go staggering homeward bound,
　　　And with the dry husks strew the trampled ground.

It is the harvest, and an hour ago
　I sat with half-closed eyes beside the "spring,"
And listened idly to its dreamy flow,
　　And heard afar the gay and ceaseless ring
　　　Of song and labor from the harvesters—
　　　Heard faint and careless as a sleeper hears.

My little brother came with bounding step,
　And bent him low beside the shaded stream,
And from the fountains drank with eager lip—
　　While I, half-rousing from my dream,
　　　Asked where he'd spent this still September day,
　　　"Chasing the wrens, or on the hills at play?"

Backward he tossed his golden head, and threw
  A glance disdainful on my idle hands,
And with a proud light in his eye of blue
  Answered, as deep his bare feet in the sands
    He thrust, and waved his baby hand in scorn—
    "Ah, no! down at the cornfield since the morn
        I've been
      Minding the gap!"

"Minding the gap!" My former dream was gone,
  Another in its place! I saw a scene
As fair as e'er an autumn sun shone on—
  Down by a meadow, large, and smooth, and green,
    Two little barefoot boys, sturdy and strong,
    And fair, here in the sun, the whole day long,
      Lay on the curling grass,
        Minding the gap!*

Minding the gap! and the years swept by
  Like moments, I beheld those boys again—
And patriot hearts within their breasts beat high,
  And on their breasts was set the seal of men,
    And guns were on their shoulders, and they trod
    Back and forth, with measured step, upon the sod
      Near where our army slept,
        Minding the gap!

---

* Our town readers will have to be told that at harvest time in the rural districts, a length or two of the fence is let down to allow the wagons to pass to and fro. To keep cattle out, the children are set "Minding the Gap." This has given our sweet young poetess a text for one of her finest gems.—EDITOR HOUSTON TELEGRAPH.

Minding the gap !   My brothers, while you guard
  The open places where a foe might creep—
A mortal foe—O ! mind those other gaps—
  The open places of the heart—my brothers,
      Watch over them !

The open places of the heart—the gaps
  Made by the ruthless hand of Doubt and Care—
Could we but keep, like holy sentinels,
  Innocence and Faith forever guarding there—
    Ah ! how much of woe and shame would flee,
    Affrighted back from their blest purity !

No gloom or sadness from the outer world,
  With feet unholy then would wander in,
To grasp the golden treasures of the soul,
  And bear them forth to sorrow and to sin !
    The heart's proud fields! its harvest full and fair,
    Innocence and Love could we but keep them there,
      Minding the gaps !

WHY THE ROBIN'S BREAST WAS RED.

The following exquisite little gem, originally appearing in the *Pacificator*, a Catholic journal, is from the pen of James R. Randall, Esq. :

The Saviour, bowed beneath his cross,
　　Clomb up the dreary hill,
And from the agonizing wreath
　　Ran many a crimson rill;
The cruel Roman thrust him on
　　With unrelenting hand—
'Till,' staggering slowly 'mid the crowd,
　　He fell upon the sand.

A little bird that warbled near,
　　That memorable day,
Flitted around and strove to wrench
　　One single thorn away;
The cruel spike impaled his breast,
　　And thus 'tis sweetly said,
The Robin has his silver vest
　　Incarnadined with red.

Ah, Jesu! Jesu! Son of man!
　　My dolor and my sighs
Reveal the lesson taught by this
　　Winged Ishmael of the skies.

I, in the palace of delight,
  Or cavern of despair,
Have plucked no thorns from thy dear brow,
  But planted thousands there!

LINES ON THE DEATH OF ANNIE CARTER LEE,

Daughter of General Robert E. Lee, C. S. A., who died at Jones'
Springs, Warren county, N. C., October 20th 1862.

BY TENELLA.

" Earth to earth, and dust to dust,
Saviour in thy word we trust.
Sow we now our precious grain,
Thou shalt raise it up again.
Plant we the terrestrial root
Which shall bear celestial fruit;
Lay a bud within a tomb,
That a flower in Heaven may bloom.
Severed are no tender ties
Though in Death's embrace she lies,
For the lengthened chain of love
Stretches to her home above.
Mother, in thy bitter grief,
Let this thought bring sweet relief,

Mother of an angel now—
God Himself hath crowned thy brow
With the thorns the Savior wore,
Blessed art thou evermore,
Unto him thou dost resign
A portion of the life was thine.

"Earth to earth, and dust to dust,"
Sore the trial—sweet the trust,
Father—thou who seest Death
Reaping grain at every breath,
As the sickle sharp he wields
O'er our bloody battle-fields,
Murmur not that now he weaves
This sweet flower in his sheaves;
Taken in her early prime,
Gathered in the summer time;
Autumn's blast she shall not know,
Never shrink from winter's snow.
Sharp the pang which thou must feel,
Sharper than the foeman's steel,
For thy fairest flower is hid
Underneath the coffin's lid.
O'er her grave thou dropst no tear,
Warrior stern must thou appear,
Crushing back the tide of grief
Which in vain demands relief.
Louder still thy country cries,
At thy feet it bleeding lies,
And before the patriot now,
Husband, Father, both must bow.

But unnumbered are thy friends,
And from many a home ascends
Earnest, heartfelt prayers for thee,
" As thy days thy strength may be."

————————

AT THE LAST.

The stream is calmest when it nears the tide,
And flowers the sweetest at the eventide,
And birds most musical at close of day,
And saints divinest when they pass away.

Morning is lovely, but a holier charm
Lies folded close in evening's robes of balm;
And weary man must ever love her best,
For Morning calls to toil, but Night to rest.

She comes from Heaven, and on her wings doth bear
A holy fragrance, like the breath of prayer;
Footsteps of angels follow in her trace,
To shut the weary eye of Day in peace.

All things are hushed before her as she throws
O'er earth and sky her mantle of repose;
There is a calm, a beauty and a power,
That Morning knows not, in the Evening hour.

"Until the Evening" we must weep and toil,
Plough life's stern-furrow, dig the weedy soil,
Tread with sad feet our rough and thorny way,
And bear the heat and burden of the Day.

Oh! when our sun is setting, may we glide,
Like Summer Evening, down the golden tide;
And leave behind us, as we pass away,
Sweet, starry twilight round our sleeping clay.

THE LONG AGO.

This poem is from the pen of Philo Henderson, who was born
near Charlotte, Mecklenburg county, North Carolina, and who
died in early manhood, leaving a large number of unpublished
poems of rare value behind him.

Oh! a wonderful stream is the river of Time,
    As it runs through the realm of tears,
With a faultless rhythm and a musical rhyme,
And a broader sweep and a surge sublime,
    And blends with the ocean of years!

How·the winters are drifting like flakes of snow,
    And the summers like buds between,
And the ears in the sheaf—so they come and they go,
On the river's breast, with its ebb and flow,
    As it glides in the shadow and sheen!

There's a magical Isle in the river of Time,
  Where the softest of airs are playing;
There's a cloudless sky and a tropical clime,
And a song as sweet as a vesper chime,
  And the Junes with the roses are staying.

And the name of this Isle is Long Ago,
  And we bury our treasures there;
There are brows of beauty, and bosoms of snow,
There are heaps of dust—but we loved them so!
  There are trinkets and tresses of hair.

There are fragments of song that nobody sings,
  And a part of an infant's prayer;
There's a lute unswept, and a harp without strings,
There are broken vows and pieces of rings,
  And the garments she used to wear.

There are hands that are waved when the fairy shore
  By the mirage is lifted in air;
And we sometimes hear through the turbulent roar,
Sweet voices heard in the days gone before,
  When the wind down the river is fair.

Oh! remembered for aye be that blessed Isle,
  All the day of life till night;
When the evening comes with its beautiful smile,
And our eyes are closing to slumber awhile,
  May that 'greenwood of soul be in sight.'

CHRISTMAS—1863.

BY HENRY TIMROD.

How grace this hallowed day?
Shall happy bells from yonder ancient spire
Send their glad greetings to each Christmas fire,
　　Round which the children play?

　　Alas! for many a moon
That tongueless *tower hath cleaved the Sabbath air,
Mute as an obelisk of ice, a glare
　　Beneath an Arctic moon.

Shame to the foes that drown
Our psalms of worship with their impious drum!
The sweetest chimes in all the land lie dumb
　　In some far rustic town.

There let us think they keep
Of the dead yules, which here beside the sea
They've ushered in with old world English glee,
　　Some echoes in their sleep.

How shall we grace the day?
With feast and song and dance and antique sports,
And shouts of happy children in the courts,
　　And tales of ghost and fay?

* St. Michael's, the oldest Church in the Southern States. The chime of
bells was imported before the Revolution.

Is there indeed a door
Where the old pastimes, with their cheerful noise
And all the merry round of Christmas joys,
 Could enter as of yore?

Would not some pallid face
Look in upon the banquet, calling up
Dread shapes of battle in the wassail cup,
 And trouble all the place?

How could we bear the mirth,
While some loved reveller of a year ago
Keeps his mute Christmas now, beneath the snow
 In cold Virginian earth?

How shall we grace the day?
Ah! let the thought that on this holy morn
The Prince of Peace, the Prince of Peace was born,
 Employ us while we pray.

Pray for the peace, which long
Hath left this tortured land, and haply now
Holds its white court on some far mountain's brow,
 There hardly safe from wrong.

Let every sacred fane
Call its sad votaries to the shrine of God,
And with the cloister and the tented sod
 Join in the solemn strain!

With pomp of Roman form,
With the grave ritual brought from England shore,
And with the simple faith which asks no more
 Than that the heart be warm.

He, who till time shall cease,
Shall watch that earth where once not all in vain
He died to give us peace, will not disdain
  A prayer, whose theme is peace.

Perhaps, ere yet the Spring
Hath died into the Summer—over all
The land, the peace of His vast love shall fall .
  Like some protecting wing.

Oh! ponder what it means!
Oh! turn the rapturous thought in every way,
Oh! give the vision and the fancy play,   .
  And shape the coming scenes.

Peace in the quiet dells,
Made rankly fertile by the blood of men,
Peace in the wood and in the lonely glen,
  Peace in the peopled vale;

Peace in the crowded town,
Peace in the thousand fields of waving grain,
Peace in the highway and the flowery lane,
  Peace on the wind swept down;

Peace on the farthest seas,
Peace in our sheltered bays and ample streams,
Peace whereso'er our starry garland gleams,
  And peace in every breeze.

Peace on the whirring marts,
Peace where the scholar thinks, the hunter roams,
Peace! God of peace! peace, peace in all our homes,
  And peace in all our hearts!

CHARLESTON.

BY HENRY TIMROD.

Calm as that second summer which precedes
  The first fall of the snow,
In the broad sunlight of heroic deeds,
  The city bides the foe.

As yet behind their ramparts stern and proud,
  Her bolted thunders sleep—
Dark Sumter, like a battlemented cloud,
  Looms o'er the solemn deep.

No Calpe' frowns from lofty cliff or scar,
  . To guard the holy strand,
But Moultrie holds in leash her dogs of war, ˙
  Above the level sand.

And down the dunes a thousand guns lie couched
  Unseen, beside the flood—
Like tigers in some orient jungle crouched,
  That wait and watch for blood.

Meanwhile thro' streets still echoing with trade,
  Walk grave and thoughtful men,
Whose hands may one day wield the patriot's blade
  As lightly as the pen.

14

And maidens, whose bright glances would grow dim
  At sight of bleeding wound,
Seem each one to have caught the strength of him
  Whose sword she proudly bound.

Thus girt without and garrisoned at home,
  Day patient following day,
Old Charleston looks from roof and spire and dome,
  Across the tranquil bay.

Ships through a hundred foes, from Saxon lands
  And spicy Indian ports,
Bring Saxon steel and iron to her hands,
  And summer to her courts.

But still along yon dim Atlantic line,
  The only hostile smoke,
Creeps like a harmless mist above the brine,
  From some frail floating oak.

Shall the spring dawn, and she, still clad in smiles,
  And with an unscathed brow,
Rest on the strong arms of her palm-crowned isles,
  As fair and free as now?

We know not: in the temple of the Fates
  God has inscribed His doom;
And all untroubled in her faith, she waits
  Her triumph—or her tomb.

January, 1863.

BY THE CAMP FIRE.

BY VIOLA.

The snow has fallen thick and soft,
  The cold wind mourns in murmurs harsh;
We've marched all day as only those
  Who follow Stonewall Jackson march.

I bore it all with patient strength,
  And cheered my men with spirits light—
Bear with me, if within my heart
  I feel a little sad to-night.

I'm thinking of my distant home,
  That Eden spot of earth to me,
And something comes across my eyes,
  I do not care my men should see.

I shut them tight, while o'er my mind,
  As in the old magician's glass,
My life, with all its varied scenes,
  In changing shadows seems to pass.

I see myself a happy child,
  With spirit high, untouched by pain,
I sing and shout in frolic glee,
  A merry hearted boy again.

The boy has changed into the man—
   A glowing beam from Heaven above
Illumes my life, and o'er it sheds
   The golden light of youth's first love.

A fairy vision fills the glass,
   And holds my sense in rapt delight,
I see her in her loveliness,
   As on our happy bridal night.

From out her snowy, mist-like veil,
   Her soft eyes shine with starry ray,
While pearls and orange blossoms gleam
   On neck and brow more pure than they.

We kneel before the altar now,
   I hold her little trembling hand,
And vow a faith for life and death,
   And seal it with a golden band.

Oh! days of love and happiness—
   Oh! life of pure unearthly bliss—
How dark your purple memory makes
   The horrors of a night like this!

I want you, darling—Oh! I faint
   And shrink before my bitter cup,
Come, cheer me with your happier thought—
   Come, bear my drooping spirit up!

She comes, she takes me to her heart,
   And in low accents soft and mild,
She lulls my wearied frame to rest,
   And soothes me like a little child.

She points my soul to thoughts sublime,
  And fills it with the noblest aim;
She kneels and prays to God for me,
  Then leaves me to myself again.

Not fainting now, but nerved with strength
  To bear what sufferings God may send—
To shape my life in noble acts,
  'Til He shall please that life to end.

The trumpet sounds! To arms, my men!
  Our haughty foes in triumph come,
We'll meet them with a welcome stern,
  Our battle cry, "the loved at home!"

JOHN PELHAM.

BY JAMES R. RANDALL.

Just as the Spring came laughing through the strife,
  With all its gorgeous cheer,
In the bright April of historic life
  Fell the great cannonier.

The sudden lulling of a hero's breath,
  His bleeding country weeps—
Hushed in the alabaster arms of Death,
  Our young Marcellus sleeps.

Nobler and grander than the Child of Rome,
  Curbing his chariot steeds,
The knightly scion of a Southern home,
  Dazzled the land with deeds.

Gentlest and bravest in the battle brunt,
  The champion of the Truth,
He bore his banner to the very front
  Of our immortal youth.

A clang of sabres 'mid Virginian snow,
  The fiery rush of shells—
And there's a wail of immemorial woe
  In Alabama dells.

The pennon drops that led the sacred band
   Along the crimson field;
The meteor blade sinks from the nerveless hand,
   Over the spotless shield.

We gazed and gazed upon that beauteous face,
   While round the lips and eyes,
Couched in the marble slumber, flashed the grace
   Of a divine surprise.

O, Mother of a blessed soul on high!
   Thy tears may soon be shed—
Think of thy boy with princes of the sky,
   Among the Southern dead.

How must he smile on this dull world beneath,
   Fevered with swift renown—
He—with the martyr's amaranthine wreath,
   Twining the victor's crown!

KELLEY'S FORD, *March* 17, 1863.

We pledge thee, chief!
　In the name of our nation,
　Her wide devastation,
　Her sore desolation,
Her grandeur and grief!
　Where'er thou warrest
　When our need is the sorest,
　Or in Fortress or forest,
Bidest thy time;
　Thou—Heaven elected,
　Thou—Angel-protected,
　Thou—Brother selected,
What e'er thy fate be,
Our trust is in thee,
And our faith is sublime.
　With swords raised on high,
　With hearts nerved to die,
Or to grasp victory,
　Hand to hand—knee to knee,
　With a wild three times three,
We pledge thee, LEE!

CHARADE.

The following Charade is given, not so much for its poetical beauty,
as for the name which it suggests:

My FIRST is seen, on a field of green,
And a lucky elf is he,
The joy and sport of all the court,
Though a SQUIRE of low degree.
He has no gold, (though I am told
He strips the richest bare,)
But four gray suits and a pair of boots,
Whilst kings his playmates are.
He's rarely LOW, he'd have you know,
E'en when he maketh GAME,
He wields the power of Court and BOWER!
Oh, guess that GALLANT's name.
The tenderest tie that you or I
May ever hope to own,
A precious trust of dust to dust,
Is by my SECOND shown.
My whole shall cause the world to pause,
And gaze with wondering eyes—
A living NAME, a deathless FAME,
A soldier, brave and wise.

STONEWALL JACKSON'S WAY.

We reproduce a lyric which was extremely popular in many parts
of the South. The unknown author draws a picture which ad-
dresses itself at once to the eye, and through the eye to the heart.
This poem deserves to be preserved among the literary relics of
the times. Every Southerner and Northerner of taste will read it
with interest :

Come, stack arms, men, pile on the rails, ·
  Stir up the camp fires bright,
No matter if the canteen fails,
  We'll make a roaring night!
Here Shenandoah brawls along,
  There lofty Blue Ridge echoes strong,
To swell the brigade's rousing song
  Of "Stonewall Jackson's Way."

We see him now—the old slouched hat
  Cocked o'er his eye askew;
The shrewd dry smile—the speech so pat—
  So calm, so blunt, so true.
The "Blue Light Elder" knows them well,
Says he, "That's Banks—he's fond of shell,
Lord save his soul! we'll give him"—well,
  That's Stonewall Jackson's Way.

Silence! ground arms! kneel all! caps off!
  Old Blue Light's going to pray,
Strangle the fool who dares to scoff!
  Attention! its his way :

Appealing from his native sod,
In *forma pauperis*, to God—
"Lay bare thine arm, stretch forth thy rod
  Amen!" that's Stonewall Jackson's way!

He's in the saddle now! fall in!
  Steady! the whole brigade!
Hill's at the ford, cut off! We'll win
  His way out ball and blade.
What matter if our shoes are worn?
What matter if our feet are torn?
Quick step! we're with him e'er the morn!"
  That's Stonewall Jackson's Way!

The sun's bright glances rout the mists
  Of morning—and by George!
There's Longstreet struggling in the lists,
  Hemmed in an ugly gorge.
Pope and his columns whipped before,
"Bay'nets and grape!" hear Stonewall roar;
"Charge, Stewart!—pay off Ashby's score!"
Is "Stonewall Jackson's Way!"

Ah! maiden, wait and watch and yearn
  For news of Stonewall's band,
Ah! widow read with eyes that burn,
  That ring upon thy hand!
Ah! wife, sew on, pray on, hope on,
Thy life shall not be all forlorn,
The foe had better ne'er been born
  Than get in "Stonewall's Way."

STONEWALL'S SABLE SEERS.*

BY MRS. C. A. WARFIELD, BEECHMORE, OLDHAM C UNTY, KY.

"I'll tell you wat, ole Cato,"
    Quoth Cuff by the bright camp fire,
"We's gwine to hab a battle;
    Nebber min' dis mud an' mire,
Nebber min' dis rain wat is fallin'
    Enuff to melt de stones,
We's gwine to hab a battle
    I feels it in my bones.

"You passes fur a prophit!
    I'se heerd dat all my life;
An' you gibs me de name ob 'Foolish'
    Before my berry wife.
But fur all dat—I tells you—
    (Does you hear me, Cato Jones?)
We's gwine to hab a battle,
    I feels it in my bones!"

Then up arose old Cato,
    That swart, yet reverend sage,
With hair as white as lamb's wool,
    And the stiffened limbs of age

* From a well authenticated anecdote

Yet stately in his presence,
　　And stalwart in his frame,
A man in his Maker's image,
　　And worthy his Roman name.

He grasps his thorn-stick tightly,
　　As he stood above the fire,
With a face in which derision,
　　Was blended well with ire;
Then gazing down on Cuffy
　　With an eye intense with scorn,
He spoke these words of wisdom—
　　"*You* feels it. *try a horn !*"

"Does you tink de great Commander,
　　Means such as you to know,
What orders he gibs *his* captins
　　In de night time, Cuffy Crow?
You hears de masta prayin',
　　You listens wen he groans,
And dats de way dis battle
　　Am stirrin' in your bones.

"I seed your bead eyes twinklin',
　　About de crack ob day—
When de masta stopped his groanin',
　　And 'pose his mind to pray.
But I tought you knewed your manners,
　　Too well to see or hear,
De soldier in de presence
　　Ob his hebbenly brigadier!

"He prayed like dat old King David
　　Wat loved de Lord so well;
He called on de God ob battles
　　To cus dem houns ob hell.
I felt my har uprisin'
　　Like Job's, upon my head,
When he 'voked de precious sperits,
　　Ob de ole Virginny dead.

" No organ in white folks' churches
　　Ebber pealed so grand a sound,
As the masta's voice discoursin'
　　'Bout habbin' Satan bound.
He prayed like dat holy Samuel,
　　Wat broke de pride ob Saul—
Den I knewed de white trash Linkum,
　　Boun' to hab anoder fall!

" Dis day dese words am proven,
　　We goes to meet de foe,
It takes no nigga prophit,
　　To guess dat—Cuffy Crow.
For whenever de masta's wakeful,
　　And whenever he prays and groans,
Why dem dat lies by his camp fire
　　Feel battle in dere bones!"†

† One of Stonewall Jackson's serving-men made these very observations.

RIDING A RAID.

Air—Bonny Dundee.

'Tis old Stonewall the Rebel that leans on his sword,
And while we are mounting prays low to the Lord;
Now each cavalier who loves honor and right,
Let him follow the feather of Stuart to-night.
  Come, tighten your girths and slacken your rein,
  Come, buckle your blanket and holster again,
   Try the click of your trigger and balance your blade,
   For he must ride sure who goes riding a raid.

Now gallop, now gallop, to swim or to ford!
Old Stonewall still watching, prays low to the Lord.
Good-bye, dear old Rebel, the river's not wide,
And Maryland's lights in the window's do shine.
  Come, tighten your girths and slacken your rein,
  Come, buckle your blanket and holster again,
   Try the click of your trigger and balance your blade,
   For he must ride sure who goes riding a raid.

Then gallop, then gallop by ravine and rocks,
Who would bar up the way takes his toll in hard knocks,
For with these points of steel up the lines of old Penn,
We have made some fine strokes and will make 'em again.
  Come, tighten your girths and slacken your rein,
  Come, buckle your blanket and holster again,
   Try the click of your trigger and balance your blade,
   For he must ride sure who goes riding a raid.

THE LONE SENTRY.

The Rev. Dr. Moore, of Richmond, in a sermon in memory of the much loved and lamented Stonewall Jackson, narrates the following incident:

"Previous to the first battle of Manassas, when the troops under Stonewall Jackson had made a forced march, on halting at night they fell on the ground exhausted and faint. The hour arrived for setting the watch for the night. The officer of the day went to the General's tent, and said:

"' General, the men are all wearied, and there is not one but is asleep. Shall I wake them?'

"' No,'' said the noble Jackson, 'let them sleep, and I will watch the camp to-night.'

"And all night long he rode round that lonely camp, the one lone sentinel for that brave, but weary and silent body of Virginia heroes. And when glorious morning broke, the soldiers awoke fresh and ready for action, all unconscious of the noble vigils kept over their slumbers."

BY JAMES R. RANDALL.

'Twas as the dying of the day,
   The darkness grew so still,
The drowsy pipe of evening birds
   Was hushed upon the hill.
Athwart the shadows of the vale
   Slumbered the men of might,
And one lone sentry paced his rounds
   To watch the camp that night.

A grave and solemn man was he,
 With deep and sombre brow ;
The dreamful eyes seemed hoarding up,
 Some unaccomplished vow. '
The wistful glance peered o'er the plain,
 Beneath the starry light,
And, with the murmured name of God,
 He watched the camp that night.

The future opened unto him,
 Its grand and awful scroll—
Manassas and the valley march
 Came heaving o'er his soul ;
Richmond and Sharpsburg thundered by,
 With that tremendous fight
That gave him to the angel host,
 Who watched the camp that night.

We mourn for him, who died for us,
 With one resistless moan,
While up the Valley of the Lord
 He marches to the Throne !
He kept the faith of men and saints
 Sublime, and pure, and bright ;
He sleeps—and all is well with him
 Who watched the camp that night.

Brothers ! the midnight of the cause
 Is shrouded in our fate—
The demon Goths pollute our halls
 With fire, and lust, and hate !

Be strong—be valiant—be assured—
　Strike home for Heaven and Right!
The soul of Jackson stalks abroad,
　And guards the camp to-night!

ON THE DEATH OF LIEUT.-GEN. JACKSON.

A DIRGE.

BY MRS. C. A. WARFIELD, OF KY.

Go to thy rest, great chieftain,
　In the zenith of thy fame,
With the proud heart stilled and frozen,
　No foeman e'er could tame;
With the eye that met the battle,
　As the eagle's meets the sun,
Rayless beneath its marble lid,
　Repose, thou mighty one!

Yet ill our cause could spare thee,
　And 'neath the blow of fate,
That struck its staunchest pillar
　From 'neath our dome of State.
Of thee as of the Douglas,
　We say with Scotland's king,
"There is not one to take *his* place
　In all the knightly ring!"

Thou wert the noblest Captain
Of all that martial host,
That front the haughty Northman
And put to shame his boast;
Thou wert the strongest bulwark
To stay the tide of fight,
The name thy soldiers gave thee
Bore witness of thy might.

That name was worth a legion
In charge or battle call,
'Twas joy to see the cravens fly
At the shouting of "Stonewall!"
'Twas pride to mark thy phalanx,
Sweep onward like a blast,
That clears the leaves of autumn
From the forest, fierce and fast.

'Twas glory—'twas derision
To mark the bloody rout,
When, as signal for the panic,
The Southern yell rang out;
And thou, oh mighty leader,
Breasting the battle's van,
Dids't seem amid its sullen roar,
More demi-god than man.

Go, warrior, it is over,
No more shall bugle note
Arouse thee, stern and prayerful,
Nor banner o'er thee float;

A PLEDGE TO LEE.

WRITTEN FOR A KENTUCKY COMPANY, BY MRS. C. A. WARFIELD,

OF KY.

We pledge thee, LEE!
  In water or wine,
  In blood or in brine,
  What matter the sign?
Whether brilliantly glowing,
Or darkly o'erflowing,
  So the cup is divine
That we fill to thee!
  Vanquished—victorious,
  Gloomy or glorious,
Fainting and bleeding,
Advancing, receding,
Lingering or leading,
Captive or free;
  With swords raised on high,
  With hearts nerved to die,
Or to grasp victory;
Hand to hand—knee to knee,
With a wild three times three
We pledge thee, LEE!

Nor sound of shell and cannon,
  Make music in thy ear,
In the sultry tide of battle—
  Thou liest on thy bier!

We may not weep above thee,
  This is no time for tears,
Thou would'st not brook their shedding,
  Oh, saint among thy peers!
Could'st thou look from yonder Heaven,
  Above us smiling spread,
Thou would'st not have us pause for grief,
  On the blood-stained path we tread.

Not while our homes in ashes
  Lie smouldering on the sod,
Not while our houseless women
  Send up wild wails to God.
Not while the mad fanatic
  Strews ruin in his track,
Dare any Southron give the rein
  To feeling—and look back!

No, still the cry is *onward*,
  This is no time for tears,
No, still the word is *vengeance*,
  Leave *ruth* for coming years.
We will snatch thy glorious banner
  From thy dead and stiffening hand,
(The one thy foeman spared the grave)
  And bear it through the land.

And all who mark it streaming—
  Oh ! soldier of the cross !
Shall gird them with a fresh resolve
  Of loyalty for loss.
Whilst thou, enrolled a martyr,
  Thy sacred mission shown,
Shalt lay the record of our wrongs
  Before the *eternal Throne !*

LINES ON THE DEATH OF STONEWALL JACKSON.

  The city stirs this morn ;
From careless or from eager lips there fleets
A rumor onward through the busy streets,
  Of one to burial borne—
  A man of heroic mould,
And yet the starred flag in the dun closed air,
Floats at its highest from the shut house of prayer,
  No passing bell is tolled,
And men move on as on yesterday, nor deem
Their words, my burning tears, have but one bitter
        theme.

  For he is gone !
Gone in the bright meridian of his fame !
Gone with his words of power, his soul of flame !
  And I live on,

Groaning that I should live,
That all the worthless thousands round me, those
Who were, but dared not prove themselves his foes,
   Death's malice should reprieve;
And he, the victor-chief, even on the day
Which he made glorious, yields, subdued to its dark
     sway.

Oh can it be, that name
Which brought such cheer to the desponding heart,
Forcing the woe-closed lips in smiles apart,
   Whose lightest whisper came
   Like thoughts of Heaven's suspended wrath,
Swift, unexpected, to the despot Three
Quailing by the Potomac; can it be,
   That on the crowded path,
Whereon he now is borne, that name is known,·
A synonym of woe to those he loved alone?

Still hostile watch-fires glow
Upon his native soil, still the artillery's roar,
Is nightly heard on Rappahannock's shore;
   And the ungenerous foe
   Still doth our captive cities sway:
But oh, no more, no more, shall he arise
Before the morning star is in the skies,
   And ere the night of day
Bring down to naught the invader's lying boast,
Offering himself and his, one fiery holocaust!

Forgive, forgive, oh, Lord!
If to the living ingrate as unjust,
There lurks in my sad speech that weak distrust
   By him I mourn, abhorred:

Not such, not such the wail
That rises from his own loved land to-day.
He was their pride, their hope,—*Thou*, Lord, their
       stay :
  Nor wilt Thou fail
To raise for them, even in this hour of blight,
A warrior like to him, as strong, as sure to smite !

  We bless Thee, Lord, for him
Who, in a day of cold and sordid vice,
Held out against the world this proud device—
  "*Fidelity supreme.*"
  Even in this mammon hold,
Men, honoring him, proclaim, with loftier crest,
Faith, *Loyalty*, despite the cynic's jest
  Things real are as gold,
And feel the age which their lost aims defile,
Brightening in his pure fame, become less base, less
      vile !

  Take him, Virginia, to thy soil,
Now more than ever sacred ; guard his dust,
Ye generations, as a sacred trust,
  Till hushed in earth's turmoil,
  The loved, the venerated ;
Let him repose where by Shenandoah's flood,
A red *Asperges* of young Southern blood
  His grave has consecrated !
Where sleep they well 'neath many a grassy heap,
Who shared on earth his deeds, his grand compan-
      ionship.

The weak heart throbs
To think how great we would have made him ; now
A dirge, this little rood of glebe, the flow
  Of woman's tears, and strong men's sobs,
  Are all that we can give.
Vain murmurer! End thy plaints! When of all
          these
Who mourn his fate, the merest memories
  Have ceased for aye to live,
It shall be told, while earth is man's abode,
How the great soul which to all coming time
Made Stonewall Jackson's name a sound sublime,
  Went on it's way to God!

PHILADELPHIA, *May*, 1863.

THE FUNERAL DIRGE OF STONEWALL
JACKSON.

BY ROSA VERTNER JEFFREY.

Muffled drum and solemn bugle,
    Sound a dirge as on ye move,
Never soldiers mourned a chieftain,
    Worthier of their trnst and love.
As ye look your last upon him,
    Swear to fight as he has fought,
Swear to follow up the victory,
    By *his* life so *dearly* bought.

15

'Twas no North-man's hand that slew him,
　　No such honor shall they claim,
Those who would have *died* to save him,
　　Smote their leader as he came
Conquering towards them, in the darkness—
　　They mistook him for that foe
He bade them strike—alas ! *too* watchful,
　　All their anguish *none* can know.

Bravest chieftain !—good as· valiant,
　　Who, his sword—like Aaron's rod
Held as powerless—unless guided
　　By the strength and power of God.
Eve of battle never found *him*,
　　Making vain and idle boasts,
But, in humblest mood beseeching,
　　Victory, from the " Lord of Hosts."

As the mighty shade of Theseus,
　　Led the Athenian armies forth,
Southrons,—when ye go to battle
　　With the fierce hordes of the North,
Let the spirit of your hero,
　　Stand where erst he stood in life,
Cheering you to win or *perish*,
　　In the thickest of the strife.

Southern ranks will never falter,
　　Southern hearts will never faint,
Guided, guarded, by the spirit,
　　Of a hero and a *saint* /

Stand ye firm—the name deserving
    By your mighty Stonewall won,
Let his fame, on morn of battle,
    Be your valor's *rising sun !*

Kneel,—as erst ye saw him kneeling—
    Southern soldiers,—learn to *pray*,
Jackson prayed,—if ye would ·conquer
    Lo an angel points the way.
On ! where his bright form is leading,
    There behold your banner wave,
Soldiers, follow on—to Freedom,
    Or a Freeman's honored grave.

May 20, 1863.

STONEWALL JACKSON.

BY H. L. FLASH.

Not midst the lightning of the stormy fight,
  Nor in the rush upon the vandal foe,
Did kingly Death, with his resistless might
  Lay the great leader low.

His warrior soul its earthly shackles broke
  In the full sunshine of a peaceful town,
When all the storm was hushed, the trusty oak
  That propped our cause, went down.

Though his alone the blood that flecks the ground,
  Recalling all his grand heroic deeds,
Freedom herself is writhing with the wound,
  And all the country bleeds.

He entered not the nation's promised land,
  At the red belching of the cannon's mouth,
But broke the house of bondage with his hand—
  The Moses of the South.

O gracious God! not gainless in the loss,
  A glorious sunbeam gilds the sternest frown,
And while his country staggers 'neath the cross,
  He rises with the crown!

May 10, 1863.

STONEWALL.

"Let my men have the name—
It belongs more to them than to me."

Weep for the mighty dead,
  The nation's joy and pride,
Send forth the mournful tidings
  On hill and mountain side;
Virginia, shroud thy banners,·
  Thou had'st no nobler son,
Weep, fettered Maryland, for he
  Thy freedom would have won.

Weep for the hero chieftain,
  He met your greatest need,
Each Southern home is darkened,
  Each Southern heart must bleed;
A thousand would have fallen
  To win him from the grave,
What were a thousand lives to his—
  The pure, the good, the brave!

Weep for the good man fallen,
  Ye mothers and ye wives,
Teach your children how his virtues
  May brighten their young lives—
And to his pure example
  Each mother point her son
To the dead—he shall live on
  As liveth Washington.

Weep for the great and gifted,
　We all have cause for tears,
For him in whom shone brightly　·
　Each virtue that .endears;
And nightly in our prayer
　For those who rule our land,
At his dear name we falter,
　Then pray for Stonewall's band.

When the trumpet calls to battle
　They'll miss the olden spell
That ever led to victory
　O'er mountain, brake and dell;
They'll miss his voice in battle,
　And in the hour of prayer,
By council and by camp-fire,
　They'll miss him everywhere.

Oh! wreathe your brightest laurel
　With cypress that shall wave
Above the spot ye hallow
　As Stonewall Jackson's grave;
There, with reverence and with love,
　Years hence shall pilgrims stand,
Sweet memories to garner
　Of Stonewall and his band.

STONEWALL JACKSON'S GRAVE.

BY MRS. M. J. PRESTON, OF LEXINGTON, VA.

A simple, sodded mound of earth,
   With not a line above it—
With only daily votive flowers
   To prove that any love it;
The token flag that, silently,
   Each breeze's visit numbers,
Alone keeps martial ward above
   The hero's dreamless slumbers.

No name? no record? Ask the world—
   The world has heard his story—
If all its annals can unfold
   A prouder tale of glory?
If ever merely human life
   Hath taught diviner moral—
If ever round a worthier brow
   Was twined a purer laurel?

Humanity's responsive heart
   Concedes his wondrous powers,
And pulses with a tenderness
   Almost akin to ours;
Nay, not to ours—for us he poured
   His life—a rich oblation,
And on adoring souls we bear
   His blood of consecration.

A twelvemonth only since his sword
 Went flashing through the battle—
A twelvemonth only since his ear
 Heard war's last deadly rattle;
And yet have countless pilgrim feet
 The pilgrim's guerdon paid him,
And weeping women come to see
 The place where they have laid him.

Contending armies* bring, in turn,
 Their meed of praise or honor,
And Pallas here has paused to bind
 The cypress wreath upon her.
It seems a holy sepulchre
 Whose sanctities can waken
Alike the love of friend or foe—
 The Christian or the Pagan!

They come to own his high emprise
 Who fled in frantic masses
Before the glittering bayonet
 That triumphed at Manassas;
He witnessed Kernstown's fearful odds,
 As on their ranks he thundered,
Defiant as the storied Greek
 Amid his brave three hundred.

---

* In the month of June, 1864, this singular spectacle was presented at Lexington, of two hostile armies in turn reverently visiting the grave of Stonewall Jackson.

They will recall the tiger spring,
  The wise retreat—the rally—
The tireless march—the fierce pursuit
  Through many a mountain valley.
Cross Keys unlocks new paths to fame,
  And Port Republic's story
Wrests from his ever vanquished foes
  Strange tributes to his glory!

Cold Harbor rises to their view,
  The Cedar gloom is o'er them,
And Antietam's rough-wooded heights
  Stretch mockingly before them.
The lurid flames of Fredericksburg
  Right grimly they remember,
That lit the frozen night's retreat
  That wintry, wild December.

The largesse of this praise is flung,
  With bounty rare and regal,
Is it because the vulture fears
  No longer the dead eagle?
Nay, rather far accept it thus:
  An homage true and tender,
As soldier unto soldier's worth—
  As brave to brave will render!

But who shall weigh the wordless grief
  That leaves in tears its traces,
As round their leader crowd again
  Those bronzed and veteran faces?

15*

The "old brigade" he loved so well—
  The mountain men who bound him
With bays of their own winning, ere
  A tardier fame had crowned him.

The legions who had seen his glance
  Across the carnage flashing,
And thrilled to catch his ringing "charge"
  Above the volley crashing;
Who oft had watched the lifted hand
  The inward trust betraying,
And felt their courage grow sublime
  While they beheld him praying.

Cool knights, and true as ever drew
  Their swords with knightly Roland,
Or died at Sobieski's side
  For love of martyred Poland;
Or knelt with Cromwell's "Ironsides,"
  Or sung with brave Gustavus,
Or on the field of Austerlitz
  Breathed out their dying "aves."

Rare fame! rare name! if chanted praise,
  With all the world to listen,
If pride that swells a nation's soul—
  If foeman's tears that glisten—
If pilgrim's shining love—if grief
  Which nought can soothe or sever,
If these can consecrate, this spot
  Is sacred ground forever.

"OVER THE RIVER."

Dr. Hunter Maguire thus concludes his account of the last moments of Stonewall Jackson : "Then his manner changed, and he murmured, 'Let us cross over the river, and rest under the trees.' "

———

BY J. DAFFORE.

———

"Over the river—over the river—
    There where the soft lying shadows invite,"
And fanned by the South wind the forest leaves
      quiver,
    And fire-flies dance through the sweet summer night.

"Soldiers and comrades, we'll cross that broad river,
    Far from the tumults of trumpet and drum,
And the cannon's deep boom, and the fierce squadron's
      shiver,
As they reel in their saddles—then come, brothers,
    come.

"Over the river—over the river—
    Come ere the sun goeth down in the West,
Angel forms beckon us, sent to deliver
    The weary from labor, to offer him rest."

Over the river—a fathomless river,
　In the land where no shadow is needed or seen,
Where the leaves of the forest trees wither—no, never,
　And the fruits are all golden, the pastures all green.

From the couch where the warrior lay stricken and
　　　dying,
　He saw in a vision the country so fair—
All its streams and its valleys, its mountains outlying,
　And the city whose gates are of pearls rich and rare.

Over the river—the dark flowing river,
　Death bore the hero and victor and saint,
Great in earth's conflict, greater than ever
　When they had left him bleeding and faint.

Waiting to cross it, all radiant with glory,
　Strong in the faith which is born of pure life,
Bequeathing a name to the record of story,
　That tells of bold deeds in the patriot's strife.

"LET US CROSS OVER THE RIVER AND REST UNDER THE SHADE OF THE TREES."

Last words of Stonewall Jackson.

BY JAMES.

" Over the river," a voice meekly said,
Whose clarion tones had thousands obeyed,
As in ranks upon ranks they grandly rushed on,
To battle for liberty, country, and home !

" Over the river," immortality's plains,
In verdure eternal where peace ever reigns,
Rejoice with their beauty his vision of faith,
As his spirit approaches the river of death !

" Over the river, 'neath the shade of the trees,"
Advancing to meet him bright angels he sees,
They beckon him over to rest in the shade,
And dwell in the mansions the Saviour hath made.

" Over the river, 'neath the shade of the trees,"
Whose fruit of twelve manners his taste shall e'er
       please ;
Beneath whose soft foliage his spirit may rest,
" Over the river," in the home of the blest.

"Over the river, 'neath the shade of the trees,"
Freed from earth's sorrows he'll rest at his ease;
Life's conflict is over, its battle is won,
And his brow will be wreathed with the victor's
        bright crown.

"Over the river," now a Heavenly guest!
"'Neath the shade of the trees," forever at rest!
In that glorious land, enraptured he'll sing,
The praises of Him who of Kings is the King!

THE "STONEWALL" CEMETERY.

Lines written by Mrs. M. B. Clark, of North Carolina, ("Tenella")
in behalf of the "Stonewall" Cemetery, Winchester, Va.

The storm of war which swept our country wide,
Like snow-flakes, scattered graves on every side,
Here, heaped in drifts, on battle fields they lie,
There, dropped like leaves where soldiers chanced
        to die.
Back to their homes our State has brought,
Some honored sons who for her freedom fought,
And where their feet in youth and manhood strayed,
Beneath their native sod her children laid,
That kindred hands with loving care may keep
The graves in which her cherished soldiers sleep.

Thus to her heart in close embrace she drew
Her GORDON, PENDER, BRANCH and PETTIGREW.
But ah! there's many a one as leal and brave,
Who slumbers in a soldier's unmarked grave,
Buried just where he fell, by friend or foe,
Without one sign by which his State may know,
Now that the fearful conflict's wholly done,
What grave enfolds the ashes of her son.
Right nobly did she do her part to fill,
Those unmarked graves which dot each vale and hill,
Where bravely fought—and oh! how bravely died,
Virginia's boast and Carolina's pride!
The grand, gigantic "Stonewall" of our cause,
Whose name we breathe, and then in reverence
      pause.
And shall they lie uncared for where they fell,
Without one mark the soldier's grave to tell?
Were they not *Jackson's boys?* and does not he
Stand in our hearts beside immortal Lee?
Ah! for his sake, Virginia's daughters ask
Each sister State to aid them in their task,
And ere their graves like snowflakes melt away,
The bones of JACKSON'S boys together lay,
That they in death may sleep beneath that name,
Which shed upon their lives, its rays of fame!

A VOICE FROM THE SOUTH.

INSCRIBED TO QUEEN VICTORIA, BY ROSA VERTNER JEFFREY.

From our ancient moss-veiled forests,
    Jasmine bowers, savannahs green,
From the South a voice comes pleading,
    Pleading to thee, gracious Queen.
From our broad palmetto thickets,
    From each deep and fragrant vale,
Groves of orange and magnolia,
    Now breathes forth a plaintive wail.
From the graves of many heroes,
    While their life-blood soaks the sod,
From the hearts that mourn them, turning
    In their wretchedness to God.
From our fair homes desolated
    By a selfish tyrant's greed,
From the noble bosoms bleeding,
    And from those that still must bleed,
Plaintive comes a sad voice pleading
    Wafted to thee o'er the sea,
From a proud, brave, tortured people,
    Struggling fiercely to be free.
Struggling not for gain or conquest,
    But to *strike* the foes who spoil
Roof-trees, fire-sides, homes and altars,
    And to drive them from our soil.

Thus it is we stand exalted
  High before the world to-day,
Thus that twenty million North-men
  We have proudly held at bay!
Like the great Goliath boasting
  Of their wondrous power and might,
Went these North-men forth exultant,
  And defiant to the fight.
Thus we met them, few to many,
  Strong beneath the Almighty's wing,
As that youth who slew Goliath,
  With a pebble from a sling!
Years of bitter strife have left us
  Full of strength and prowess still,
Wearing freedom's mail, whose breast-plate
  Is a freeman's iron will.
And our prayer is not for treasure,
  Not for aid by sea or land,
But to stand among the nations,
  Where we have won a *right* to stand.
By the crown whose gems have gathered
  Brightness since they graced thy brow,
By that royal heart, so tender, .
  Hear us, sovereign lady, now.
When the British Lion shall greet us,
  All the world will find a voice,
To hail us, then, a nation, making
  Death or liberty her choice!

Jan., 1863.

THE AUTUMN RAIN.

BY SUSAN ARCHER TALLEY, (MRS. VON WEISS.)

Softly, mournfully, slowly,
   Droppeth the rain from the eaves,
It falls on the head of the drooping flowers,
   In the hearts of the withered leaves.

Sadly, mournfully, slowly,
   Over the darkening hills,
The funeral clouds are gathering low,
   As the rain from the sky distils.

My tears could fall as sadly
   For pleasant days that are past,
And dark as the clouds on the lovely hills,
   Are the shadows around me cast.

But holier far in its sadness,
   Is the desolate autumn time,
Than the light that parcheth the fainting flowers
   In the fullness of summer's prime.

Holier, gentler, and purer,
   Are thoughts that hallow the heart,
Which hath seen the buds of its hope decay,
   And the light of its joy depart.

For they were the April flowers,
    And these are the golden sheaves—
The sad, sweet thoughts on 'the hearts that fall,
    As droppeth the rain from the eaves.

RICHMOND, VA.,

NIL DESPERANDUM—TO THE SOUTHERN SOLDIER.

BY IKEY INGLE.

Wheel in the rut? then shoulder to the wheel;
Make muscle and sinew nerve force feel;
In the Slough of Despond sinks the nation's weal?
Let purpose speak in connon's peal!
             Learn to will and to do!

The ship's yet steady, the tempest sweeps past,
No leak's discovered, unsprung's the mast,
Let new spars be fitted, the seamen stand fast,
Beware but of breakers, she'll weather the blast,
             Her helmsman is true.

Bare the brawny arm, the anvil full swing!
Hands to the bellows, fresh fuel bring;
Iter, Iterumque, make the anvil sing,
Not cotton, not gold, but labor is king.
             Unite will and might!

Hand to the plough! Let us never look back!
Hold the reins steady, make the thong smack;
Strike deep the furrow, and hold fast to the track,
Sow the seed! The harvest! oh, let it not lack
     Fruit for posterity.

Remember the past, and rival its fame,
Barter not birthright for sorrow and shame!
Bequeath what was willed thee, thine honor, thy
  name,
To the true, death or victory are but the same
     Keys to eternity.

RICHMOND, VA., *Jan.* 18, 1864.

DESPONDENCY.

BY TENELLA.

The waters in life's goblet sink,
Which late were foaming to its brink
  With happiness aglow;
From every bubble flashing bright,
The sparkling opalescent light,
  That only it can show.

Now cold and dark the sluggish creep,
Not bounding on with vigorous leap
  O'er cares which clog the way,

From every struggle gaining strength,
Until the rocks o'erleaped at length,
 In limpid pools they lay.

But sinking, sinking, every hour,
'Neath care and sorrow's carping power,
 They daily run to waste.
No bubbles now upon them rise,
They glisten not with rainbow dyes,
 And bitter is their taste.

So bitter that the unwelcome draught
My thirsty spirit will not quaff,
 And scarcely is restrained
From dashing from my fevered lip
The stagnant lees I yet must sip
 Before the goblet's drained.

But in its waters dark I see
Reflected faces turned to me,
 And when of them I think,
I crush despondent thoughts like these,
Resolving to its bitter lees
 Life's goblet I will drink.

Nor has its beauty wholly fled,
Submissively I bow my head—
 And murmuring thoughts restrain,
For while each well beloved face,
In life's dark waters I can trace,
 They do not flow in vain.

LILIES OF THE VALLEY.

INSCRIBED TO THE FRIEND WHO SENT THEM. — BY ROSA VERTNER
JEFFREY.

Lady,—the fairy blossoms you have culled for me to-
    day,
Modest, dainty, vestal lilies, clustering on the path of
    May,
A deep and tender meaning, to my haunted heart may
    bring,
With their faint, delicious breathings from the bosom
    of the spring.

They mind me of a home beloved, *my home* in by-
    gone years,
Then beautiful beyond compare,—now dark with blood
    and tears !
They mind me that a storm of strife has strown my
    native shore,
With wrecks of hope and happiness,—lost, lost, for-
    evermore.

Lady, they prate of battles, they tell thee of the war,
And thou dost read of, nay lament, its horrors from
    afar,
But oh ! thy heart would grieve like mine, did that
    red deluge flow,
Dividing thee from cherished scenes, and friends of
    long ago.

I have wept above your lilies, for they lure my heart
        away,
Mid memories of the light and love of many a bygone
        May,
'Neath warm, bright skies, when joy was throned on
        every beaming brow,
The sun shines on!—mocking our gloom of desolation
        now.

Woe to the then thrice blessed,—who now must suffer
        and endure,
Woe to the countless bleeding hearts no earthly hope
        can cure,
Woe to that cry of carnage—making all the airs of
        spring
Like the voice of grief in Ramah—with lamentations
        ring.

Fled is the guardian spirit of a land once blest and
        good,
His white plume soiled with battle smoke, his banner
        steeped in blood,
And lo! one universal prayer from North and South
        should pour:
"Oh! Father send the angel *Peace*, to dwell with us
        once more."

ROCHESTER, *May*, 1864.

THE BOY PICKET; OR CHARLEY'S GUARD.

BY A LADY OF KENTUCKY.

Wearily my footsteps their measured cadence keep,
While my tired comrades are wrapped in slumber
 deep,
Cheerily on pinion whose range no limits bind,
My truant soul is speeding, floating on the wind,
Nor cold nor hunger heeding, floating on the wind.

Winter's gems are gleaming on crested glade and hill,
As my spirit wanders back and forth at will,
Onward to the cottage, nestling 'mid the trees,
Homeward to the dear ones there, floating on the
 breeze—
Sweetest words of joy to hear floating on the breeze.

Starry eyes bend o'er me in calm and holy love,
The sleepy earth beneath me, silence and God above;
A tender spell enfolds me, a soft breath stirs my hair,
It is my mother's blessing floating on the air—
Her weary boy caressing, floating on the air.

Hark! the note of warning, the low and muffled hum,
Ere another dawning the battle's crash shall come,
Ere another sunset, ten thousand heart throes warm,
The battle-fiend shall gather, floating on the storm—
Shall seek Thy presence, Father, floating on the storm.

Oh, Thou Guide of Israel! my country cries to Thee,
Lead her, Lord! to glory—to truth—to liberty,
Repel the invading spoiler, nor let her banner quail
Until the shout of victory is floating on the gale—
Till Liberty's hosanna is floating on the gale.

Father! hear and pardon Thine erring child to-night,
Clothe my soul in valor, and gird my limbs with might,
Bless, oh bless my mother, my friends beloved and
     dear ;
Father! listen to the cry, floating to Thine ear—
Father! take me if I die, take me to Thy care!

"TRUE TO THE LAST."

We give the following pathetic verses to our readers, premising
that they were written upon an incident, which occurred in the
last battle of one of the author's friends. Having a foreboding of
his fate, he penciled. on the plating of his scabbard, the name of
his lady love, and the words, "In the face of death, my thoughts
are thine." A faithful comrade removed from his body, and bore
to the weeping maiden, this sad token of his constancy. Col. W.
Stewart Hawkins, of Tennessee, is one of the most chivalrous and
accomplished gentlemen of the South, and, though a foeman, has
won the esteem of his opponents, on the field, and his captors,
while in prison, by his noble and manly spirit, his gallant and
generous bearing. He is very youthful, and, with the enthusiasm
of his years, seems to unite in himself the literary tastes of Sidney,
the valor of Bayard, and the endurance of Roderick.
New York Knickerbocker.

BY COL. W S. HAWKINS.

The bugles blow the battle-call,
   And through the camp each stalwart band,
To-day, its serried columns forms,
   To fight for God and native land!
Brave men are marching by my side,
   Our banners floating glad and free,
But yet, amid this brilliant scene,
   I give my thoughts to thee.
16

The horsemen dashing to and fro,
  The drums with wild and thunderous roll,
The sights and sounds—all things that tend
  To kindle valor in the soul;
These are all here, but in the maze
  Of squadrons, moved with furious glee,
Still true to every vow we made,
  I give my thoughts to thee.

The deep booms smite the troubled air,
  Each throb proclaims the foeman near,
And faintly echoed from the front,
  I hear my gallant comrades cheer—
Wild joy of heroes, marching on,
  Through blood, their glorious land to free!
I give to freedom, here, my life,
  But all my thoughts to thee.

And yet, beloved, I must not think
  What undreamed bliss may soon be mine:
It would unman me in the work
  Of guarding well our country's shrine.
Here, on this sword, I write my troth,
  These words shall yet thy solace be,
They'll tell how, in this last fierce hour,
  I gave my thoughts to thee.

Along the east, the holy morn
  Renews life's many cares and joys:
This hour, I hope, some wish for me,
  Thy pure and tender prayer employs..
Another beauteous dawn of light
  These eyes, alas! may never see,
But even dying, faint, and maimed,
  I still would think of thee.

And then, in coming years, that roll,
  When scenes of peace and brightness throng,
And round each happy hour is twined
  The wreath of friendship, love and song,
Go to his grave, whose heart was thine,
  And by that spot a mourner be,
One tear for him, thy loved and lost,
  Whose last thought clung to thee.

A PRISON SCENE.

BY COL. HAWKINS, C. S A.

Last night a comrade sent in haste
  For me to soothe his fearful pain;
He felt Death's power advancing fast,
  He knew that hope was vain.
God's promises I read again,
  Till Faith's sweet light shone from his eye;
Sole gleam—for sorrow filled me then,
  As shadows fill the sky.

A dreary place that hospital—
  Where dim lamps break the solemn gloom,
And nurses move with slow footfall,
  Like spectres, through the room.
Above those cots all miseries blend,
  On each some form of suffering lies;
Some groan—some sleep—but here one friend
  Puts on the angel's guise.

Scarcely I heard the bugle's call,
  Scarce felt the night-wind's heavy breath,
I only saw the shadows fall,
  And the ghastly chill of death,
Save where a pallid splendor lay
  Upon his brow, like martyr's crown,
The sweet foreshadowing of the day
  In which life's star goes down.

I hear his piteous tones implore
  And heed his hand's hot clinging grasp—
Pale hands, alas—that nevermore
  Shall feel love's answering clasp.
His frenzied spirit flies from pain,
  He thinks himself once more at home:
"Dear wife—dear child—I'm here again,
  Close to me—closer come.

"I could not lag where country led—
  The voice of wrong could not beguile;
You would not have me stay, you said,
  If honor ceased to smile.
Ah! many fall in this wild strife!
  But freedom holds their memories dear,
And makes a gem of every life—
  For the crown *she* yet shall wear.

"And many a time when raged the fight
  I've seemed to see *her* through the smoke,
With smiles that shone in tearful light,
  Bless every valiant stroke.

I'm hurt and tired now—so place
  Our little darling by my bed!
One hand, my own, to your embrace,
  And one on Baby's head."

His voice was hushed—short grew his breath,
  The glazing eyes closed slowly o'er,
The bloodless lips were kissed by Death—
  They'll speak of love no more.
One clammy hand I held in mine
  And o'er it breathed my fervent prayer—
Beneath the other seemed to shine
  His Baby's golden hair.

LINES ON CAPTAIN BEALL.

Lines written on the wish expressed by Capt Beall, that his body
should not be carried to the Valley until his mother could write
upon his tomb "He died in defense of his country."

BY COL. HAWKINS, C. S. A.

Make not my grave in the valley yet,
  'Neath the sod of an alien let it be,
Till· my mother can write with tears of pride,
On my tomb these simple words, "He died
  Dear land, defending thee!"

Not there where the blackened homesteads are,
  And the tokens of deathless wrong,
Not the place where a pall is upon the land,
All scourged by sword and scarred by brand,
  And hushed is every song.

Not there where the church-yard's turf is torn,
  By the hoof of a vile and ruthless foe
Shall his grave be made; for a Northerner's hate
That sacred spot would desecrate,
  A fiendish wrath to show.

In days of Rome as dangers fled,
  When friendly Curtius leaped to save,
The eager votaries sought to share,
And blessed with garlands rich and fair,
  The hero's honored grave.

But he more grand and noble still,
  Uncheered by any loud acclaim,
In the might of his undaunted soul
Drank freely sorrows keenest dole,
  And faced the brink of shame.

Yet ere he plunged, the angels swift
  Along their earthly pathway trod,
They smote away the bitter cup
And bore the star-crowned martyr up,
  On their pinions back to God.

And nature mourns that valiant heart,
  For there, upon his Northern tomb,
The flowers of spring shall wave above
  His ashes in their bloom.

THE HERO WITHOUT A NAME.

BY COL. W. S. HAWKINS, C. S. A., PRISONER OF WAR.°

I loved, when a child, to seek the page
  Where war's proud tales are grandly told,
And to read of the might of that former age,
  In the brave, good days of old ;
When men for Virtue and Honor fought
  In serried ranks, 'neath their banners bright,
By the fairy hands of beauty wrought,
  And broidered with *"God and Right !"*

'Twas there I read of Sir Launcelot true,
  Whose deeds have been sung in a nobler strain ;
And of Roderic, the Bold, who his falchion drew,
  In the cause of his native Spain ;
And, in thought, I beheld gay Sidney ride,
  His white plume dotting the field's expanse ;
And Bayard, who came like the swirl of the tide,
  As he struck for the lilies of France.

On the crags of Scotland then I saw,
  With his hair of golden hue, Montrose ;
And the swarthy Douglas, whose name was law
  In the homes of his English foes.

* By the close of the war Colonel Hawkins was liberated from prison and
ed home o die.

There was Winkelried, in the Swiss-land famed;
   And the mountaineers' boast—devoted Tell—
Before whose patriot shaft, well-aimed,
   His country's tyrant fell.

'Neath Erin's flag, with its glad sunburst,
   Was Emmett, the first in that martyr van,
Whose blood makes sacred the gibbet accursed,
   Where they died for the rights of man.
There was Light-Horse Harry, the first in the fray,
   There was Marion leading his cavaliers,
And Washington, too, whose grave to-day,
   Is the shrine of patriot tears.

These splendid forms were part of the throng
   That delighted me, moving in pageant grand,
Through the wastes of time and the fields of song,
   From the legends of every land.
But little I hoped myself to see
   A spirit akin to these stately men;
Or dreamed that great hearts, like theirs, could be
   In a prison's crowded pen.

Yet, I've seen in the wards of the hospital there,
   A hero, I fancy, as peerless of soul;
A pale-faced boy, whose home is fair,
   Where the waters of Cumberland roll.
On his narrow cot, in that narrow room,
   Where the music he hears is the sigh and the groan,
He lies through the day's long pain and gloom,
   But he never makes a moan!

They hewed him down with their blades of steel,
  Where the troopers charged from the camp of the
     foe ;
But he was not killed—although I feel,
  It would have been better so ;
For my heart within me is very sad,
  As I sit and hold his wasted hand,
And hear him tell of the days that were glad,
  In our own dear, sunny land.

There are hours, again, in his fever's heat,
  When his restless fancies fly to his home :
And he talks of the scythe in the falling wheat,
  And the reapers that go and come ;
Of his boyish mates, in their frolicsome glee,
  In the cedar glades and the woodlawns dim ;
And how he carved there on many a tree,
  A name that was dear to him ;

Of the sweet wild roses that scatter the light,
  Through the open door and the window-pane ;
And October's haze, on the far-off height,
  And the quiet country lane ;
Of the rivulet's plash, and the song of birds,
  And the corn rows, standing like men with spears ;
Of his mother's tones, and her loving words—
  And his cheeks are wet with tears.

And I seem to see her, as autumn leaves
  Like shadows fall in the lonely glen,
And the swallows come home to those silent eaves,
  Where *he* shall not come again.
    16*

And then I rejoice that she can not see,
　How the blight has stained her fairest bloom;
I am glad her footstep will never be
　Beside his northern tomb.

And I think of another who watches too,
　When the early stars are bright on the hill,
Nor dreams that his heart, so confiding and true,
　Will soon be forever still.
Ah! many, in vain, to their hopes shall cling,
　Through the dreamy morn and the mournful eve;
And memory alone shall its solace bring,
　To a thousand hearts that grieve.

My comrade will last but a little while;
　For I see on every succeeding day,
A fainter flush, but a sweeter smile,
　Over his features play.
And he knows that until he is under the sod,
　These walls, little better, shall shut him in;
But his soul puts trust in the Lamb of God,
　That taketh away all sin!

And somehow I think, when our lives are done,
　That this humble hero, without a name,
Will be greater up there, than many a one
　Of the high-born men of fame.
And I know I would rather wear to-day,
　The crown that is his, with its fadeless bloom.
Than Roderic's helm, so golden and gay,
　Or Sidney's snow-white plume!

O prisoner boy! that I were as near,
   As you are now to that "shining shore,"
Where the waters of life and of love are clear,
   And weeping shall come no more.
It can not be now; yet, in God's own time,
   When he calls his weary ones home to rest,
May I join with you in the angel chime—
   Like you, be a welcome guest!

THE CHIMES OF ST. PAULS.

BY TENELLA.

The chimes of St. Paul's Church, Petersburg, Va., were presented by Miss Nannie May when on her death-bed, and though uninjured by the shells which struck the church, were not rung during the bombardment of the place, except at the funeral of the Militiamen who fell at the beginning of the siege.

When first, St. Paul's, your sweet-toned chimes
   Shed music on the air,
They seemed an angel's pleading voice
   Which called us unto prayer;
An angel who had left this earth
   To sing a Heavenly strain,
But in the music of your bells
   Spoke unto us again.
Now loud and clear, then low and sweet,
   You touched each listener's heart,
Till every rising, falling note
   Seemed of its life a part.

You rang a clear, a joyous peal
　　The blushing bride to meet,
Then let your softest, sweetest note,
　　The baptized infant greet.　＇
You rang, alas! a solemn dirge
　　The. mourner's grief to tell,
Then let the ransomed spirit's joy
　　A glorious anthem swell,
That while you bore aloft the wail
　　Of those who wept below,
Sweet comfort to their bleeding hearts
　　Might from your music flow.
Alas! your bells were silenced all,
　　Hushed by relentless foes,
Though once above the battle's din
　　Your solemn protest rose.
You tolled amid ihe cannon's peal
　　When to our doors the tiger crept,
And mothers mourned their half-grown sons,
　　While babes their grand-sires wept.
Yes! let the foe in scorn exclaim
　　We robbed the cradle and the grave,
All! all that woman's heart could give
　　Old Blandford's daughters freely gave.
And now, when every hope is crushed,
　　With bleeding hearts they kneel,
And fancy that your chimes, St. Paul's,
　　Can only requiems peal!

LINES TO LEE.

(Written at the time of Hooker's invasion.)

BY MRS. C. A. WARFIELD, OF KY.

They are pouring down upon you—
    Gallant Lee—
As streams from mountain sources
    Seek the sea.
Four serried lines advancing,
With swords and banners glancing,
With horses plumed and prancing
    Fast and free—
Bugles blowing—banner's flowing,
For a nation's overthrowing,
'Tis a wonderful *out* going
    Jubilee !

As came the haughty Persian,
    Press they on !
But we have not yet forgotten
    Marathon !
And through the memory passes,
With all its mighty masses,
The battle of Manassas
    Lost and won !
Bugles blowing—banners flowing,
For a nation's overthrowing,
All the North to battle going
    Back to run !

Now God in Heaven be with you,
    Noble chief,
For the time of your probation
    Waxes brief—
Your foemen thrice outnumber
The army clad in umber,
Whom no pomps of war encumber,
    " Light and Lief " —
Bugles blowing—banners flowing,
We take comfort in the knowing
Sometimes after great cock-crowing
    Come to grief!

May you turn the tide of battle,
    Dauntless Lee!
Hurling back the wreck of armies,
    Like the sea.
Your force is scant and meagre,
Compared to the beleaguer,
But every heart is eager
    To be free!
" Bugles blowing—banners flowing "
Can make no braver showing
Than the South to battle going
    Under thee!
Than the South the North repelling,.
While her mighty heart is swelling,
And every pulse is glowing
With the fame of thy bestowing
    Robert Lee!

·LEE TO THE· REAR.

The following poetic version of a remarkab'e and well remembered
incident in one of the Wilderness fights, is from the pen of John
R. Thompson, formerly editor of the *Southern Literary Messenger*,
Richmond, Va. It was written for, and appears in *The Crescent
Monthly* :

Dawn of a pleasant morning in May
Broke through the Wilderness cool and gray,
While perched in the tallest tree-tops, the birds
Were carolling Mendelssohn's "Songs without words."

Far from the haunts of men remote,
The brook brawled on with a liquid note, .
And nature, all tranquil and lovely, wore
The smile of the spring, as in Eden of yore.

Little by little as daylight increased,
And deepened the roseate flush in the East—
Little by little, did morning reveal
Two long glittering lines of steel ;

Where two hundred thousand bayonets gleam,
Tipped with the light of the earliest beam,
And the faces are sullen and grim to see,
In the hostile armies of Grant and Lee.

All of a sudden ere rose the sun,
Pealed on the silence the opening gun—.
A little white puff of smoke there came,
And anon the valley was wreathed in flame.

Down on the left of the rebel lines,
Where a breastwork stands in a copse of pines,
Before the rebels their ranks can form,
The Yankees have carried the place by storm.

Stars and Stripes o'er the salient wave,
Where many a hero has found a grave,
And the gallant Confederates strive in vain
The ground they have drenched with their blood to
    regain!

Yet louder the thunder of battle roared—
Yet a deadlier fire on their columns poured—
Slaughter infernal rode with despair,
Furies twain, through the smoky air.

Not far off in the saddle there sat,
A grey-bearded man in a black slouched hat;
Not much moved by the fire was he
Calm and resolute Robert Lee.

Quick and watchful, he kept his eye
On two bold rebel brigades close by—
Reserves, that were standing (and dying) at ease,
While the tempest of wrath toppled over the trees.

For still with their loud, deep, bull-dog bay,
The Yankee batteries blazed away,
And with every murderous second that sped
A dozen brave fellows, alas! fell dead.

The grand old grey-beard rode to the space,
Where death and his victims stood face to face,
And silently waved his old slouched hat—
A world of meaning there was in that!

"Follow me ! Steady ! We'll save the day !"
This was what he seemed to say ;
And to the light of his glorious eye
The bold brigades thus made reply—

"We'll go forward, but you must go back "—
And they moved not an inch in the perilous track :
"Go to the rear, and we'll send them to h—!"
And the sound of the battle was lost in their yell.

Turning his bridle, Robert Lee
Rode to the rear. Like the waves of the sea,
Bursting their dikes in their overflow,
Madly his veterans dashed on the foe.

And backward in terror that foe was driven,
Their banners rent and their columns riven,
Wherever the tide of battle rolled
Over the Wilderness, wood and wold.

Sunset out of a crimson sky,
Steamed o'er a field of ruddier dye,
And the brook ran on with a purple stain,
From the blood of ten thousand foemen slain.

Seasons have passed since that day and year—
Again o'er its pebbles the brook runs clear,
And the field in a richer green is drest
Where the dead of the terrible conflict rest.

Hushed is the roll of the rebel drum,
The sabres are sheathed, and the cannon are dumb,
And Fate, with pitiless hand, has furled
The flag that once challenged the gaze of the world ;

But the fame of the Wilderness fight abides ;
And down into history grandly rides,
Calm and unmoved as in battle he sat,
The Grey-bearded Man in the black slouch hat.

GENERAL LEE AT THE BATTLE OF THE WILDERNESS.

BY TENELLA.

There he stood, the grand old hero, great Virginia's
    god-like son,
Second unto none in glory ; equal of her Washington :
Gazing on his line of battle, as it wavered to and fro,
'Neath the front and flank advances of the almost con-
    quering foe :
Calm as was that clear May morning, ere the furious
    death-roar broke
From the iron-throated war lions crouching 'neath the
    clouds of smoke ;
Cool, as though the battle raging was but mimicry of
    fight,
Each brigade an ivory castle, and each regiment a
    knight,
Chafing in reserve beside him, two brigades of Texans
    lay,
All impatient for their portion in the fortune of the
    day.
Shot and shell are 'mong them falling, yet unmoved
    they silent stand,
Longing—eager for the battle, but awaiting his com-
    mand.
Suddenly he rode before them, as the forward line gave
    way,
Raised his hat with courtly gesture, "Follow me and
    save the day !"
But, as though by terror stricken, still and silent stood
    that troop,
Who were wont to rush to battle with a fierce aveng-
    ing whoop :

It was but a single moment, then a murmur through
    them ran
Heard above the cannon's roaring, as it passed from
    man to man,
"You go back, and we'll go forward!" now the wait-
    ing leader hears,
Mixed with deep, impatient, sobbing, as of strong men
    moved to tears.
Once again he gives the order, "I will lead you on
    the foe,"—
Then, through all the line of battle rang a loud de-
    termined "No!"
Quick as thought a gallant Major, with a firm and
    vice-like grasp,
Seized the General's bridle shouting, "Forward, boys!
    I'll hold him fast."
Then again the hat was lifted, "Sir, I am the older
    man,
Loose my bridle, I will lead them," in a measured
    tone and calm.
Trembling with suppressed emotion, with intense ex-
    citement hot,
In a quivering voice the Texan, "No, by God, Sir, you
    shall not!"
By them swept the charging squadron, with a loud
    exultant cheer,
"We'll retake the salient, General, if you'll watch us
    from the rear."
And they kept their word right nobly, sweeping every
    foe away,
With that grand grey-head uncovered, watching how
    they saved the day,
But the god-like calm was shaken, which no battle
    shock could move,
By this true, spontaneous token of his soldiers' child-
    like love.

"THE CAVALIER'S GLEE."

BY CAPT. BLACKFORD, OF GEN. STUART'S STAFF.

AIR—The Pirate's Glee.

Spur on! spur on! we love the bounding
  Of barbs that bear us to the fray;
" The charge " our bugles now are sounding,
  And our bold Stuart leads the way.
    The path to honor lies before us,
      Our hated foemen gather fast;
      At home bright eyes are sparkling for us,
      And we'll defend them to the last.

Spur on! spur on! we love the rushing
  Of steeds that spurn the turf they tread;
We'll through the Northern ranks go crushing,
  With our proud battle flag o'erhead.
    The path of honor lies before us,
      Our hated foemen gather fast;
      At home bright eyes are sparkling for us,
      And we'll defend them to the last.

Spur on! spur on! we love the flashing,
  Of blades that battle to be free;
'Tis for our Sunny South they're clashing—
  For household gods and liberty.
    The path of honor lies before us,
      Our hated foemen gather fast;
      At home bright eyes are sparkling for us,
      And we'll defend them to the last.

STUART.

BY W. WINSTON FONTAINE, OF VIRGINIA.

Mourn, mourn along thy mountains high!
Mourn, mourn along thine ocean wave!
Virginia, mourn! thy bravest brave
    Has struck for thee his last good blow!
O, south wind, breathe thy softest sigh,
O, young moon, shed thy gentlest light,
Ye silver dews, come weep to-night,
    To honor Stuart—lying low!

The princeliest scion of a royal race, *
The knightliest of his knightly name,
The imperial brow encrowned by Fame,
    Lies pallid on his mother's breast!
How sadly tender is her face.
Virginia dearly loved this son,
And now his glorious course is run!
    Tearful she bows her martial crest.

She bows her head in the midst of war,
With booming cannon rumbling 'round,
'Mid crash of musket and the sound
    Of drum and trumpet clanging wild.
Fierce cries of fight rise near and far;
But "*dulce et decorum est,*"
For him, who nobly falls to rest—
    Virginia mourns her peerless child.

---

* Gen. J. E. B. Stuart sprung from the Royal House of Scotland.

The fair young wife bewails her lord,
The blooming maidens weep for him,
Fierce troopers' eyes with tears grow dim,
   And all, all mourn the chieftain dead!
Place by his side his trusty sword,
Now cross his hands upon his breast!
And let the glorious warrior rest,
   Enshrouded in his banner red!

No more our courtly cavalier
Shall lead his squadrons to the fight!
No more! no more! his sabre bright
   Shall dazzling flash in foeman's eyes.
No more! no more! his ringing cheer
Shall fright the Northman in his tent.
Nor, swift as eagle in descent,
   Shall he the boastful foe surprise.

But when his legions meet the foe,
With gleaming sabre lifted high,
His name shall be their battle cry,
   His name shall steel them in the fray!
And many a Northman 'neath the blow
Of Southern brand shall strew the ground,
While on the breeze the slogan sound
   "Stuart! Stuart!" shall ring dismay.

Mourn, mourn along thy mountains high!
Mourn, mourn along thine ocean wave!
Virginia, mourn! thy bravest brave
   Has struck for thee his last good blow!
O, south wind, breathe thy softest sigh,
O, young moon, shed thy tenderest light,
Ye silver dews, come weep to-night,
   To honor Stuart, lying low!

May. 1864.

GEN. J. E. B. STUART.

BY JNO. R. THOMPSON.

We could not pause, while yet the noontide air
  Shook with the cannonade's incessant pealing,
The funeral pageant fitly to prepare—
  A nation's grief revealing.

The smoke, above the glimmering woodland wide
  That skirts our southward border, in its beauty,
Marked where our heroes stood and fought and died
  For love and faith and duty.

And still, what time the doubtful strife went on,
  We might not find expression for our sorrow;
We could but lay our dear, dumb warrior down,
  And gird us for the morrow.

One weary year agone, when came a lull,
  With victory, in the conflict's stormy closes,
When the glad Spring, all flushed and beautiful,
  First mocked us with her roses—

With dirge and bell and minute gun, we paid
  Some few poor rites—an inexpressive token
Of a great people's pain—to JACKSON's shade,
  In agony unspoken.

No wailing trumpet and no tolling bell,
  No cannon, save the battle's boom receding,
When STUART to the grave we bore might tell,
  With hearts all crushed and bleeding.

The crisis suited not with pomp, and she,
  Whose anguish bears the seal of consecration,
Had wished his Christian obsequies should be
  Thus void of ostentation.

Only the maidens came, sweet flow'rs to twine
  Above his form so still and cold and painless,
Whose deeds upon our brightest record shine,
  Whose life and sword were stainless.

They well remembered how he loved to dash
  Into the fight, festooned from summer bowers;
How like a fountain's spray his sabre's flash
  Leaped from a mass of flowers.

And so we carried to his place of rest
  All that of our great Paladin was mortal:
The cross, and not the sabre, on his breast,
  That opes the heavenly portal.

No more of tribute might to us remain—
  But there will come a time when Freedom's martyrs
A richer guerdon of renown shall gain,
  Than gleams in stars and garters.

I claim no prophet's vision, but I see
  Through coming years—now near at hand, now dis-
      tant—
My rescued country, glorious and free,
  And strong and self-existent.

I hear from out that sunlit land, which lies
  Beyond these clouds that gather darkly o'er us,
The happy sounds of industry arise
  In swelling, peaceful chorus.

And, mingling with these sounds, the glad acclaim
   Of millions, undisturbed by war's afflictions,
Crowning each martyr's never-dying name
   With grateful benedictions.

In some fair future garden of delights,
   Where flowers shall bloom and song-birds sweetly
      warble,
Art shall erect the statues of our knights
   In living bronze and marble:

And none of all that bright, heroic throng,
   Shall wear to far-off time a semblance grander—
Shall still be decked with fresher wreaths of song,
   Than this beloved commander.

The Spanish legend tells us of the Cid,
   That after death he rode erect, sedately,
Along his lines, even as in life he did,
   In presence yet more stately:

And thus our STUART, at this moment, seems
   To ride out of our dark and troubled story
Into the region of romance and dreams,
   A realm of light and glory—

And sometimes, when the silver bugles blow,
   That ghostly form, in battle re-appearing,
Shall lead his horsemen headlong on the foe,
   In victory careering!

17

SEMMES' SWORD.

"Shame, " cried Amyas, hurling his sword far into the sea. "To lose my right—my right, when it was in my very grasp. Unmerciful!"—*Amyas Leigh, Kingsley.*

Into the sea he hurled it,
  Into the weltering sea,
The sword that had led so often
  The onset of the free;
And like a meteor cleaving
  Its pathway through the watery way,
Went down the gory falchion,
  To lie in the depths for aye.

Go sword! no hand of foeman
  Shall grasp thy peerless blade;
On thy path of fire I follow,
  With a spirit undismayed,
Even in the hour of anguish,
  With my gallant ship a wreck,
The comfort that no captor
  Shall ever tread her deck.

'Tis comfort that in freedom
  I draw my latest breath,
And that with ye my brethren,
  I drink the cup of death;
We have roved the sea together,
  We have proved our country's might,
And we leave to the God of battles
  The rescuing of the right.

The noble Alabama
    Was sinking ·as he stood,
Her cross and stars still flying,*
    Her bulwarks stained with blood,
Down with her band of martyrs,
    She settled to her doom,
While the coward cannon thundered†
    Above her living tomb.

But as a desert courser
    Bears his master from the fray,
So the billows bore their hero
    On their foaming crest that day,
Forth plunged the gallant Deerhound,
    To snatch him from the wave,
For the hand that ruled the tempest,
    Was stretched above the brave.

BEECHMORE, 1866.

---

* It is acknowledged that she sunk without striking her flag.

† The Alabama was fired on while sinking.

OH! NO, HE'LL NOT NEED THEM AGAIN.

To Rev. A. J. Ryan, Knoxville, Tenn., the following stanzas are
affectionately inscribed by his friend, J. D. Sullivan:

These stanzas are founded upon the following facts, related to me
by a gentleman whose veracity is unquestionable. On the morning of the battle of Franklin, Tenn., Maj.-Gen. Patrick Cleburne,
C. S. A., while riding along the line encouraging his men, beheld an old friend—a Captain in his command—his feet bleeding
from cold and other causes. Alighting from his horse, he asked
the Captain to "please" pull off his boots. The Captain did so,
when Gen. Cleburne then told him to try them on; this the Captain also did. Gen. Cleburne then mounted his horse, told the
Captain he was tired of wearing them, and could do very well
without them. He would hear of no remonstrance, and bidding
the Captain good bye, rode away. In this condition he was
killed, and in this condition he was found.

Oh! no, he'll not need them again,
　No more will he wake to behold·
The splendor and fame of his men,
　The tale of their vict'ries is told!
No more will he wake from that sleep
　Which he sleeps in his glory and fame,
While his comrades are left here to weep
　O'er *Cleburne*, his grave and his name.

Oh! no, he'll not need them again,
　No more will his banner be spread
O'er the fields of his gallantry's fame;
　The soldier's proud spirit is fled.
The soldier who rose 'mid applause
　From the humble-most place in the van—
I sing not in praise of the cause,
　But rather in praise of the man.

Oh! no, he'll not need them again,
  He has fought the last battle without them,
For barefoot he too must go in,
  While barefoot stood comrades about him.
And barefoot they proudly marched on
  With blood flowing fast from their feet;
They thought of the past vict'ries won,
  And the foes that they now were to meet.

Oh! no, he'll not need them again,
  He is leading his men to the charge—
Unheeding the shells or the slain,
  Or the shower of bullets at large.
On the right, on the left, on the flanks,
  He dashingly pushes his way,
While with cheers, double-quick and in ranks,
  His soldiers all followed that day.

Oh! no, he'll not need them again,
  He falls from his horse to the ground,
Oh anguish! oh sorrow! oh pain!
  In the brave hearts that gathered around.
He breathes not of grief, nor a sigh
  On the breast where he pillowed his head,
Ere he fixed his last gaze upon high,
  "*I'm* gone, but fight on boys!" he said.*

Oh! no, he'll not need them again,
  But treasure them up for his sake;
And oh, should you sing a refrain
  Of the memories they still must awake!
Sing it soft as the summer eve-breeze,
  Let it sound as refreshing and clear,.
Though grief-born, there's that which can please
  In thoughts that are gemmed with a tear!

---

* A Confederate officer, within a few feet of Cleburne when he fell, says his last words were: "*I'm* killed, boys, but fight it out!" · ·

SUMTER IN RUINS.

BY W. GILMORE SIMMS, ESQ.

Ye batter down the lion's den,
  But yet the lordly beast goes free;
And ye shall hear his roar again,
From mountain height, from lowland glen,
From sandy shore and reedy fen,—
Where'er a band of freeborn men,
  Rears sacred shrines to liberty.

The serpent scales the eagle's nest,
  And yet the royal bird, in air,
Triumphant wins the mountain's crest,
And sworn for strife, yet takes his rest,
And plumes to calm his ruffled breast,
Till, like a storm-bolt from the west,
  He strikes the invader in his lair.

What's loss of den, or nest, or home,
  If, like the lion, free to go ;—
If, like the eagle, winged to roam,
We span the rock and breast the foam,
Still watchful for the hour of doom,
When, with the knell of thunder-boom,
  We bound upon the serpent foe !

Oh! noble sons of lion heart!
  Oh! gallant hearts of eagle wing!
What though your batter'd bulwarks part,
Your nest be spoiled by reptile art,—
Your souls on wings of hate, shall start
For vengeance, and with lightning dart,
  Rend the foul serpent ere he sting !

Your battered den, your shattered nest,
　Was but the lion's crouching place ;—
It heard his roar, and bore his crest,
His, or the eagle's place of rest ;—
But not the soul in either breast !—
This arms the twain, by freedom bless'd,
　To save and to avenge their race !

————————

POLK.

BY H. L. FLASH.

A flash from the edge of a hostile trench,
　A puff of smoke, a roar,
Whose echo shall roll from the Kennesaw hills
　To the farthermost Christian shore,
Proclaims to the world that the warrior-priest
　Will battle for right no more !

And that for a cause which is sanctified,
　By the blood of martyrs unknown—
A cause for which they gave their lives,
　And for which he gave his own—
He kneels, a meek ambassador,
　At the foot of the Father's Throne.

And up to the courts of another world
　That angels alone have trod,
He lives, away from the din and strife
　Of this blood-besprinkled sod—
Crowned with the amaranthine wreath
　That is worn by the blest of God.

JOHN PEGRAM.

Fell at the head of his Division, February 6, 1865.—Aged 33.

BY W. GORDON M'CABE.

What shall we say now of our gentle knight,
  Or how express the measure of our woe
For him who rode the foremost in the fight,
  Whose good blade flashed so far amid the foe?

Of all his knightly deeds what need to tell—
  That good blade now lies fast within its sheath;
What can we do but point to where he fell,
  And like a soldier, met a soldier's death?

We sorrow not as those who have no hope;
  For he was pure in heart as brave in deed—
God pardon us, if blind with tears we grope,
  And love be questioned by the hearts that bleed.

And yet—oh! foolish and of little faith!
  We cannot choose but weep our useless tears;
We loved him so! we never dreamed that death
  Would dare to touch him in his brave young years!

Ah! dear, browned face, so fearless and so bright!
  As kind to friend as thou wast stern to foe—
No more we'll see thee radiant in the fight,
  The eager eyes—the flush on cheek and brow!

No more we'll greet the lithe familiar form
  Amid the surging smoke with deaf'ning cheer ;
No more shall soar above the iron storm
  Thy ringing voice in accents sweet and clear.

Aye ! he has fought the fight and pass'd away—
  Our grand young leader smitten in the strife ;
So swift to seize the chances of the fray,
  And careless only of his noble life.

He is not dead but sleepeth ! Well we know
  The form that lies to-day beneath the sod
Shall rise that time the golden bugles blow
  And pour their music through the courts of God.

And there amid our great heroic dead,
  The war-worn sons of God whose work is done,
His face shall shine, as they, with stately tread,
  In grand review sweep past the jasper throne.

Let not our hearts be troubled ! Few and brief
  His days were here, yet rich in love and faith !
Lord, we believe, help Thou our unbelief,
  And grant Thy servants such a life and death !

17*

A PRAYER FOR PEACE.

BY S. T. WALLIS.

Peace ! Peace ! God of our fathers, grant us Peace !
Unto our cry of anguish and despair
Give ear and pity ! From the lonely homes,
Where widowed beggary and orphaned woe
Fill their poor urns with tears—from trampled plains,
Where the bright harvest Thou hast sent us, rots—
The blood of them who should have garnered it
Calling to Thee—from fields of carnage, where
The foul-beaked vultures, sated, flap their wings
O'er crowded corpses, that but yesterday
Bore hearts of brothers, beating high with love
And common hopes and pride, all blasted now—
Father of Mercies ! not alone from these
Our prayer and wail are lifted. Not alone
Upon the battle's seared and desolate track,
Nor with the sword and flame, is it, O God,
That Thou hast smitten us. Around our hearths,
And in the crowded streets and busy marts,
Where echo whispers not the far-off strife
That slays our loved ones ; in the solemn halls
Of safe and quiet counsel—nay, beneath
The temple-roofs that we have reared to Thee,
And 'mid their rising incense—God of Peace !
The curse of war is on us. Greed and hate
Hungering for gold and blood : Ambition, bred
Of passionate vanity and sordid lusts,

Mad with the base desire of tyrannous sway
Over men's souls and thoughts; have set their price
On human hecatombs, and sell and buy
Their sons and brothers for the shambles. Priests,
With white, anointed, supplicating hands,
From Sabbath unto Sabbath clasped to Thee,
Burn, in their tingling pulses, to fling down
Thy censers and thy cross, to clutch the throats
Of kinsmen by whose cradles they were born,
Or grasp the brand of Herod, and go forth
Till Rachel hath no children left to slay.
The very name of Jesus, writ upon
Thy shrines, beneath the spotless, outstretched wings
Of Thine Almighty Dove, is wrapt and hid
With bloody battle-flags, and from the spires
That rise above them, angry banners flout
The skies to which they point, amid the clang
Of rolling war-songs tuned to mock Thy praise.

All things once prized and honored are forgot.
The Freedom that we worshipped, next to Thee;
The manhood that was Freedom's spear and shield;
The proud, true heart; the brave, outspoken word,
Which might be stifled, but could never wear
The guise, whate'er the profit, of a lie;—
All these are gone, and in their stead have come
The vices of the miser and the slave,
Scorning no shame that bringeth gold or power,
Knowing no love, or faith, or reverence,
Or sympathy, or tie, or aim, or hope,
Save as begun in self, and ending there.
With vipers like to these, O blessed God,

Scourge us no longer! Send us down, once more,
Some shining seraph in Thy glory clad,
To wake the midnight of our sorrowing
With tidings of Good Will and Peace to men:
And if the star that through the darkness led
Earth's wisdom then, guide not our folly now,
Oh, be the lightning Thine Evangelist,
With all its fiery, forked tongues, to speak
The unanswerable message of Thy will.

    Peace! Peace! God of our fathers, grant us Peace!
Peace in our hearts and at Thine altars; Peace
On the red waters and their blighted shores;
Peace for the leaguered cities, and the hosts
That watch and bleed, around them and within;
Peace for the homeless and the fatherless;
Peace for the captive on his weary way,
And the mad crowds who jeer his helplessness.
For them that suffer, them that do the wrong—
Sinning and sinned against—O, God! for all—
For a distracted, torn, and bleeding land—
Speed the glad tidings! Give us, give us Peace!

"SHERMANIZED."

BY L. VIRGINIA FRENCH.

In this city of Atlanta, on a dire and dreadful day,
'Mid the raging of the conflict, 'mid the thunder of the
    fray,
In the blaze of burning roof-trees, under clouds of
    smoke and flame,
Sprang a new word into being from a stern and dreaded
    name;
Gaunt and grim and like a spectre, rose that *word* before
    the world,
From a land of bloom and beauty into ruin rudely
    hurled,

From a people scourged by exile, from a city ostracised,
Pallas-like it sprang to being, and that *word* is—*Shermanized.*

And forevermore hereafter, where the fierce Destroyer
reigns,
- Where Destruction pours her lava over cultivated
plains,
Where want and woe hold carnival—where bitter blight
and blood
Sweep over prosperous nations in a strong relentless
flood ;
Where the golden crown of harvest trodden into ashes
lies,
And Desolation stares abroad with famine-phrenzied
eyes ;
Where the wrong with iron-sceptre crushes every right
we prized,
There shall people groan in anguish—*"God! the right,
is Shermanized!"*

Man may rule the raids of ruin, lead the legions that
despoil,
From the lips of honest labor dash the guerdon of his
toil,
" Sow with salt" the smiling valleys, and on every
breezy height
Kindle bale-fires of destruction, lurid on the solemn
night ;
He may sacrifice the aged, and exult when woman
stands
'Mid the sunken, sodden ashes of her home, with palsied
hands

Drooping over hungered children—man may thus immortalize
His name with haggard infamy—his watchword—"*Shermanize !* "

Nobler deeds are Woman's province—she must not destroy, but build, .
She must bring the urns of Plenty, with the wine of Pleasure filled ;
She must be the " sweet restorer " of this sunny Southern land,
Fill our schools, rebuild our churches, take the feeble by the hand,
Aid the press, befriend the teacher, give to Want its daily bread,
And never, *never* fail to weave above our "noble dead "
The laurel garland due to deeds of Valor's high emprise,
And won by men whom *failure* could not sink, or— *Shermanize !*

With her wakened love of labor, let her labor on in love,
Still, in softness and in stillness, as the starry circles move,
Bearing light, and bringing gladness, from the leaden clouds unfurled,
As the soft rise of the sunlight bringeth morning to the world ;
Grandly urging on Endeavor, as the gates of Day unclose,
Till the " solitary place again shall blossom as the rose,"
And *Woman, the rebuilder*, shall be freely eulogized
By the triumph of her people, then no longer *Shermanized !*

God bless our noble Georgia! though her soil was over-
    run,
And her lands in desolation laid, beneath an autumn's
    sun ;
With her signal shout " To action!" like the boom of
    signal guns,
She has roused the lion mettle of her strong and stal-
    wart sons,
May her daughters aid that effort to rebuild and to
    restore,
Working on for *Southern freedom* as they never worked
    before !
May Georgia as a laggard never once be stigmatized,
And her *people, press* or *pulpit,* never more be—*Sher-
    manized !*

THE SURRENDER OF THE ARMY OF NORTH-
ERN VIRGINIA—APRIL 10, 1865.

BY FLORENCE ANDERSON, OF KY.

Have we wept till our eyes were dim with tears,
Have we borne the sorrows of four long years,
    Only to meet this sight?
Oh! merciful God! can it really be,
This downfall awaits our gallant Lee,
    And the cause we counted right?

Have we known this bitter, bitter pain,
Have all our dear ones died in vain?
    Has God forsaken quite?

Is this the answer to every prayer,
This anguish of untold despair,
    This spirit-scathing blight?

Heart-broken we kneel on the bloody sod,
We hide from the wrath of our angry God,
    Who bows us in the dust!
We heed not the sneer of the insolent foe,
But that Thou, O, God, should forsake us so,
    In whom was our only trust!

Even strong men weep! the men who stand
Fast in defense of our native land,
    These gallant hearts and brave,
They wept not the souls who fighting fell,
For the hero's death became them well,
    And they feared not the hero's grave!

They have marched through long and stormy nights,
They have borne the brunt of a hundred fights,
    And their courage never failed!
Hunger and cold, and the summer heat,
They have felt on the march and the long retreat,
    Yet their brave hearts never quailed!

Now all these hardships seem real bliss,
Compared with the grief of a scene like this,
    This speechless, this wordless woe!
That Lee at the head of his faithful band,
The flower and pride of our Southern land,
    Must yield to the hated foe!

The conquered foe of a hundred fields!
The foe that conquering, the laurel yields,
    Lee's sad, stern brow to grace!

For he with the pain of defeat in his heart,
Will bear in history the nobler part,
    And fill the loftier place!

Scatter the dust on each bowed head,
Happy, thrice happy the honored dead,
    Who sleep their last, long sleep!
For we who live in the coming years,
Beholding days ghastly with phantom fears,
    What can we do but weep?

THE SWORD OF ROBERT LEE.

BY MOINA.°

Forth from its scabbard, pure and bright,
    Flashed the sword of Lee!
Far in the front of the deadly fight,
High o'er the brave, in the cause of right,
Its stainless sheen, like a beacon-light,
    Led us to victory.

Out of its scabbard, where full long,
    It slumbered peacefully—
Roused from its rest by the battle-song,
Shielding the feeble, smiting the strong,
Guarding the right, and avenging the wrong—
    Gleamed the sword of Lee!

* Author of the "Conquered Banner."

Forth from its scabbard, high in air,
　　Beneath Virginia's sky—
And they who saw it gleaming there,
And knew who bore it, knelt to swear,
That where that sword led they would dare
　　To follow and to die.

Out of its scabbard! Never hand
　　Waved sword from stain as free,
Nor purer sword led braver band,
Nor braver bled for a brighter land, .
Nor brighter land had a cause as grand,
　Nor cause, a chief like Lee!

Forth from its scabbard! how we prayed
　　That sword might victor be!
And when our triumph was delayed,
And many a heart grew sore afraid,
We still hoped on, while gleamed the blade
　　Of noble Robert Lee!

Forth from its scabbard! all in vain!
　　Forth flashed the sword of Lee!
'Tis shrouded now in its sheath again,
It sleeps the sleep of our noble slain,
Defeated, yet without a stain,
　　Proudly and peacefully.

GENERAL ROBERT E. LEE.

BY TEXELLA.

As went the knight with sword and shield,
To tournay or to battle field,
Pledged to the lady fair and true,
For whom his knightly sword he drew;
You offered at your country's call,
"Your life, your fortune and your all;"
Pledging your sacred honor high
For her to live, for her to die.
With her you cast your future lot,
And now, without one single spot
To dim the brightness of your fame,
Or cast a shadow o'er your name,
You lay your sword with honor down,
And wear defeat as 'twere a crown;
Nor sit, like Marius, brooding o'er
A ruin which can rise no more,
But from your Pavia bear away
A glory brightening every day.
Above the wreck which round you lies,
Calm and serene I see you rise,
A grand embodiment of Pride,
Chastened by sorrow and allied
To disappointment, but to show
How bright your virtues 'neath it glow;
But who may tell how deep its dart
Is rankling in your noble heart,
Or dare to pull the robe aside,
Which Cæsar draws his wounds to hide!

APRIL TWENTY-SIXTH.

BY ANNIE KETCHUM CHAMBERS.

Dreams of a stately land,
  Where rose and lotus open to the sun,
Where green ravine and misty mountains stand,
  By lordly valor won.

Dreams of the earnest-browed
  And eagle-eyed, who late with banners bright,
Rode forth in knightly errantry, to do
  Devoir for God and right.

Shoulder to shoulder, see
  The crowding columns file through pass and glen!
Hear the shrill bugle! List the rolling drum,
  Mustering the gallant men!

Resolute, year by year,
  They keep at bay the cohorts of the world;
Hemmed in, yet trusting in the Lord of Hosts,
  The cross is still unfurled.

Patient, heroic, true,
  And counting tens where hundreds stood at first;
Dauntless for truth, they dare the sabre's edge,
  The bombshell's deadly burst.

While we, with hearts made brave
  By their proud manhood, work, and watch, and pray,
'Till, conquering fate, we greet with smiles and tears
  The conquering ranks of grey!

Oh, God of dreams and sleep,
   Dreamless they sleep—'tis we, the sleepless, dream,
Defend us while our vigil dark we keep,
   Which knows no morning beam!

Bloom, gentle spring-tide flowers—
   Sing, gentle winds, above each holy grave,
While we, the women of a desolate land,
   Weep for the true and brave.

MEMPHIS, Tenn.

DIXIE.*

BY ROSA VERTNER JEFFREY.

Dixie, home of love and beauty; in the past supremely
   blest,
Now athwart thee, falling darkly, see, a funeral shadow
   rest!
Joy is quenched, where e'er it gathers, e'en as flocks of
   vultures brood,
Where the battle pageant's ended, and there's nothing
   left but blood.

Erst thy halls were lit with gladness, and thy homes with
   love and mirth,
Thou wert crowned with peace and plenty, 'mid the
   fairest lands of earth;
But that crown is crushed and broken: mourning sadly
   veils thy brow,
And among all sorrowing nations, lo! *thou* art the
   dearest now.

   * "Dixie" means *beloved, sweetheart, dearest.*

Songs of joy are lost in dirges, music dies in doleful knells,
And where clustered rose and myrtle, now are wreaths of
    asphodels!
Husbands, fathers, lovers fallen, stately homes in ruins laid,
Lone and poor, thy fairest daughters, suffering proudly,
    droop and fade.

Gently nurtured, fondly tended, reared to luxury and ease,
Graceful, tender, and as shrinking as the young mimosa
    trees;
Loved of heroes! your endurance through the strife
    transcendent shines,
Born of sunlight! 'mid the tempest stood ye, firm as
    mountain pines.

History tells us of a maiden, pure, and beautiful and brave,
Drinking gore of murdered kinsmen, her loved father's
    life to save:
Who amid relentless judges, sick with horrors, firmly stood,
Saw it poured, and, death preferring, drained a goblet
    brimmed with blood! *

Ye have quaffed long draughts of sorrow, bitter as that
    cup of gore;
The cause is lost for which *ye* suffered, and your loved
    ones are no more!
Daughters of a stricken country, with your high hopes in
    the dust,
Gather strength for earnest labor, fortified by *faith* and trust.

Rend the gloom and look beyond it! God is there, and
    "God is love!"
Overwhelmed, yet brave and constant — mourning Dixie,
    look above.
Harvest fields, and homes and cities, ruthless armies may
    despoil,
But they cannot break your spirit, or destroy your teem-
    ing soil.

* Lamartine's History of the Girondists "Reign of terror."

Loved ones who have passed in battles, bid ye rise in
    strength and might :
Southern hearts are full of fire, as eastern opals are of
    light !
Forests fall, but acorns springing leave us not of shade
    bereft ;
Nations fall—but not to perish, with a race of heroes left !

WEEP ! WEEP !

Weep ! for a fallen land,
    For an unstained flag laid low ;
Freedom is lost ! let every heart
    Echo the note of woe.
Yes, weep ! ye soldiers weep !
    'Twill not your manhood stain
To mourn with grievous bitterness
    Honor and valor slain !

Weep ! friendless woman, weep
    For golden days of yore,
For ruined homes, for aching hearts,
    For loved ones now no more !
Bravely they fought, and well,
    That noble, hero band ;
Bravely they fought, and bravely died,
    To save a suffering land.

Our southern soil is red
    With the blood of many slain ;
Like sacrificial wine it fell,
    But the offering was in vain.

Peace smiles upon our land,
  (A land no longer free);
That peace should smile o'er freedom's grave,
  And we the smile should see!

Let southern men now take
  A long farewell of fame;
Let southern men bow meekly down
  To tyranny and shame.
Great God! that such should live
  To hail the fatal hour
That crushes *freedom* in the dust,
  'Neath northern hate and power!

But many a patriot's heart
  Yet thrills to the war-god's breath;
And many still would battle on
  For freedom, 'till the death.
Weep! weep! but not for those
  That lie beneath the sod:
For they eternal peace have found,
  Around the throne of God.

"Peace!" "peace!"   'Tis but a word—
  A mockery in a name.
Alas! oh God, 'tis but the wreath
  That hides the tyrant's chain!
But, if it thus must be,
  And freedom ne'er be won,
Then, Father, give us strength to say,
  "Thy will on earth be done!"

PEACE.

BY L. BURROUGHS, OF SAVANNAH, GA.

They are ringing Peace on my weary car,
　No Peace to this heavy heart,
They are ringing Peace, I hear! I hear!
　Oh! God! how my hopes depart.

They are ringing Peace from the mountain side,
　With a hollow sound it comes;
They are ringing Peace o'er the swelling tide,
　While the billows sweep our homes.

They are ringing Peace, and the spring-tide blooms
　Like a garden fresh and fair,
But our martyrs sleep in their silent tombs,
　Do they hear! O God! *do they hear!*

They are ringing Peace, and the battle cry,
　And the bayonet's work are done,
And the armour bright they are laying by,
　From the brave sire to the son.

And the musket's clang, and the soldier's drill,
　And the tattoo's nightly sound,
We shall hear no more with a joyous thrill,
　Peace, Peace, they are ringing around.

18

There are women still as the stifled air
  On the burning desert's track,
Not a cry of joy, not a welcome cheer,
  And their brave sons coming back.

There are fair young heads in their morning pride,
  Like the lilies pale they bow,
Just a memory left to the soldier's bride,
  God help, God help them now!

There are martial steps that we may not hear,
  There are forms that we may not see,
Death's muster-roll they have answered clear,
  They are *free*—thank God, *some are free!*

Not a fetter fast, not a prisoner's chain
  For the noble army gone,
No conqueror comes in the heavenly plain,
  Peace, Peace to the dead alone!

They are ringing Peace, but strangers tread
  O'er the land where our fathers trod,
And our birthright joys like a dream are fled,
  And thou, where art thou, oh, God!

They are ringing Peace. Not here, not here,
  Where the victor's march is set,
Roll back to the North its mocking cheer,
  No Peace to the Southland yet.

April, 1865,

THE PRICE OF PEACE.

BY " LUCLA."

A woman paced with hurried step, her lone and dreary
 cell—
The setting sun with golden ray, upon her dark hair
 fell,
Which lay dishevelled on her breast—and many a shred
 of grey
Wound 'midst those tresses, sorrow's gift, while on her
 breast they lay.

She murmured disconnected strains, as to and fro she
 passed,
And wildly beamed her piercing eye, and on her wasted
 face
A burning flush of fever glowed. Then rolled the lava
 tide
Of thought from those thin, coral lips, as passionate she
 cried :

"Peace ! Peace, they tell me, Peace has come; they say
 the war is o'er—
The battle cry, the shriek of death shall fill the land no
 more.
They bid my heart rejoice—be glad, they bid my tears
 to cease,
Yes, yes, my heart, thou *shouldst* rejoice, for thou hast
 paid for Peace !

"Ah, let me count the price once more, for fear my lips
    restrain
The faintest note that they should give to the rejoicing
    strain!
I had a son, a noble boy, just entered manhood's bloom,
But he forgot his mother's tears when first the cannon's
    boom
Was heard upon our southern shore. Ah! 'twas a magic
    spell,
And gallantly he bore our flag, and gallantly he fell—
I never saw my boy again—they say my tears must
    cease,
But, Herbert, *drop for drop*, with *thine*, my heart paid
    blood for Peace!

"Another son—a stripling boy—who always by my side,
Frail as a lily, was content forever to abide;
Not eighteen summers had I nursed, with all a mother's
    care,
This tender plant, when orders came, my only child to
    tear
From mine embrace. I knew he'd die, and on my bended
    knee
I begged his life—besought and wept; but no, it could
    not be!
They bore him off. He never met the foe on hill or
    plain,
But drooped and died, I know not where—we never met
    again!
Oh, Willie, with thy soft blue eyes!—hush, hush, my tears
    must cease—
Yet darling, with thy dying groans, *I paid in part for
    Peace!*

"Now *both* are gone, whom have I left? None but the
    fond, true heart
Who'd mingled tear for tear with mine; he who had
    borne a part
In every throb of anguish wild which still my bosom
    rent,
Whose eyes were dim, whose hair was grey with nights
    of weeping spent
For these *our* sons. I thought that we, through all the
    midnight gloom,
Would hand in hand, walk mournfully together to the
    tomb.

"But war, insatiate, claimed *him* too. I saw him too
    depart,
And something made of stone I think, was given me for
    a heart:
I could not weep for many a day; I was alone — alone
With that cold weight within my breast — that heavy
    heart of stone!

"Tears came and melted it at last. In prison far
    away,
Heavy and worn, uncared for, too, he languished day by
    day;
But Herbert and our Willie came, and bade the captive
    go;
They broke his chains! I know they did — the angels
    told me so!
And when they bore his soul aloft, and bade his suffer-
    ings cease,
*I paid in spirit on his grave all that I owed for
    Peace!*

"Must I rejoice? perchance I might; but was this all
    the price?
Ah! did *my* jewels, did *my* tears, *my* broken heart
    suffice?
No! count upon the battle-field ten thousand nameless
    graves;
Call on the winds for sighs and groans; go tell the ocean
    waves
To bring their dead, the prison walls to shriek their
    sickening tales!
Concentrate, if you've power, to-night, widows and orph-
    ans' wails,
Heap broken hearts on broken hearts, till Pity bids you
    cease,
And you'll have *not half the price that we have paid
    for Peace!*

"They say I'm mad. It may be so. The've bound me
    in this cell;
I know not when they brought me here, and nothing can
    I tell
Of Heaven above or earth beneath; but oh! 'till life
    shall cease,
Though reason's gone, *the price I'll know which I have
    paid for Peace!*"

ACCEPTATION.

BY MRS. MARGARET J. PRESTON.

We do accept thee, heavenly Peace!
   Albeit thou comest in a guise
   Unlooked for—undesired, our eyes
Welcome, thro' tears, the kind release
From war, and woe, and want—surcease
For which we bless thee, holy Peace!

We lift our foreheads from the dust;
   And as we meet thy brow's clear calm,
   There falls a freshening sense of balm
Upon our spirits. Fear—distrust—
The hopeless present on us thrust—
We'll front them as we can, and *must.*

War has not wholly wrecked us: still
   Strong hands, grand hearts, stern souls are our's—
   Proud consciousness of quenchless powers—
A Past, whose memory makes us thrill—
Futures uncharactered—to fill
With heroisms—if we will!

Then courage, brothers! Tho' our breast
   Ache with that rankling thorn, despair,
   That failure plants so sharply there—
No pang, no pain shall be confessed:
We'll work and watch the brightening west,
And leave to God and heaven, the rest!

VIRGINIA CAPTA.

BY MRS. MARGARET J. PRESTON.

Unconquered captive close thine eye,
    And draw the ashen sackcloth o'er,
    And in thy speechless woe deplore,
The fate that would not let thee die!

The arm that wore the shield, strip bare;
    The hand that held the martial rein,
    And hurled the spear on many a plain—
Stretch—till they clasp the shackles there!

The foot that once could crush the crown,
    Must drag the fetters 'till it bleed
    Beneath their weight:—thou dost not need
It now, to tread the tyrant down.

Thou thought'st him vanquished—boastful trust,
    His lance in twain, his sword a wreck,
    But with his heel upon thy neck,
He holds *thee* prostrate in the dust!

Bend, though thou must, beneath his will,
    Let no one abject moan have place;
    But with majestic silent grace,
Maintain thy regal bearing still!

Look back through all thy storied past,
    And sit erect in conscious pride,
    No grander heroes ever died—
No sterner, battled to the last!

Weep, if thou wilt, with proud, sad mien,
  Thy blasted hopes—thy peace undone;
  Yet brave, live on—nor seek to shun
Thy fate, like Egypt's conquered Queen.

Though forced a captive's place to fill,
  In the triumphal train—yet there,
  Superbly, like Zenobia, wear
Thy chains—*Virginia victrix* still !

April 9th, 1866.

THE CONQUERED BANNER.

BY " MOINA."

The Rev. J. A. RYAN, Catholic Priest of Knoxville, Diocese of Nashville, Tenn.

Furl that Banner, for 'tis *weary*,
Round its staff 'tis drooping dreary;
    Furl it, fold it, it is best:
For there's not a man to wave it,
And there's not a sword to save it,
And there's not one left to lave it
In the blood which heroes gave it;
And its foes now scorn and brave it;
    Furl it, *hide* it—let it *rest*.

Take that Banner down, 'tis tattered,
Broken is its staff and shattered,
And the valiant hosts are scattered,
    Over whom it floated high;
Oh ! 'tis hard for us to fold it,
Hard to think there's none to hold it,
Hard that those who once unrolled it,
    Now must furl it with a sigh.

18*

Furl that Banner—furl it sadly—
Once ten thousands hailed it gladly,
And ten thousands wildly, madly,
    Swore it would forever wave—
Swore that foeman's sword could never
Hearts like theirs entwined dissever,
'Till that flag would float forever
    O'er their freedom or their grave.

Furl it, for the hands that grasped it,
And the hearts that fondly clasped it,
    Cold and dead are lying low;
And the Banner, it is trailing,
While around it sounds the wailing
    Of its people in their woe;
For though conquered, they adore it,
Low the cold, dead hands that bore it,
Weep for those who fell before it,
Pardon those who trailed and tore it,
And oh! wildly they deplore it,
    Now to furl and fold it so.

Furl that Banner, true 'tis gory,
Yet 'tis wreathed around with glory,
And 'twill live in song and story,
    Though its folds are in the dust:
For its fame on brightest pages,
Penned by poets and by sages,
Shall go sounding down the ages—
    Furl its folds though now we must.

Furl that Banner, softly, slowly,
Treat it gently—it is holy—
    For it droops above the dead;
Touch it not—unfold it never,
Let it droop there *furled* forever,
    For its people's *hopes* are dead.

From the "Freeman's Journal," June 24th, 1865.

"FOLD IT UP CAREFULLY."

A REPLY TO THE LINES ENTITLED "THE CONQUERED BANNER."

BY SIR HENRY HOUGHTON, BART.

The beautiful lines entitled "The Conquered Banner," have been exten-
sively copied by the Southern Press, and are now classed among the
favorite poems of that section. The following reply, written in England,
comes to us from a friend in Virginia, who says it was sent by the author
to a gentleman in that State, and that it has not yet appeared in print:

Gallant nation, foiled by numbers,
  Say not that your hopes are fled;
Keep that glorious flag which slumbers,
  One day to avenge your dead.
Keep it, widowed, sonless mothers,
Keep it, sisters, mourning brothers,
Furl it with an iron will;
Furl it now, but—keep it still,
  Think not that its work is done.
Keep it 'till your children take it,
Once again to hail and make it
All their sires have bled and fought for,
All their noble hearts have sought for,
  Bled and fought for all alone.
All alone! aye shame the story,
  Millions here deplore the stain,
Shame, alas! for England's glory,
  Freedom called, and called in vain.
Furl that banner, sadly, slowly,
Treat it gently, for 'tis holy.
'Till that day—yes, furl it sadly,
Then once more unfurl it gladly—
  Conquered Banner—keep it still!

ENGLAND, *October,* 1865.

CRUCI DUM SPIRO, FIDO.

BY J. C. M.

You may furl the gleaming star-cross,
　That lit a hundred fields;
And sing your triumphs o'er its loss;
　'Tis all your power yields!
Aye, tear the buttons from the grey,
　" Confederate " from our scroll;
The heart will sear its own decay,
　Ere ye can chain the soul!

Furl the red banner—scribe its tale,
　And shroud with regal pall!
Thrill the requiem's surging wail,
　While ye sound our thrall.
A dauntless race has owned its sway,
　That cross baptized in flame,
That shone on Jackson's deathless way,
　The Valley-march of Fame!

Aye live the years that hailed thy light—
　Flash immortality!
Labarum waving for the Right,
　Claims yet our fealty!
Cruci dum spiro, fido,
　Echoes each fiery soul—
The dead yet crown their thousand hills,
　And point their hero-roll.

" Subdued ! " ye whisper; catch the gleam
　That flashes from the West;
From the staunch heart of Donelson,
　From Shiloh's gory breast!
Mansfield, Belmont, mem'ries bring—
　Olustee and her glades—
And boldly Cleburne's echoes ring
　From the kingly realm of shades;

And Charleston, prouder in her pride,
  More haughty in her fall,
Than when upon the stormy tide
  She rang th' evangel call!
And last, those faces gaunt and grim,
  That caught that April light;
'Neath that array, with war-smoke dim,
  Smouldered heart-fires of might.

Then furl our banner'd glory
  That erst flamed in the fight,
Ye cannot tomb the story
  Burned on its stainless white!
From Sumter's battlements it calls,
  When Elliot guarded there,
And each proud fold a hero palls
  Whose life nerves our despair!

NEW YORK, *March* 20, 1866.

LINES WRITTEN JULY 15, 1865.

The day that the Confederate soldiers in North Carolina were ordered to take off their uniforms.

BY A. L. D.

Let others sing of conquerors great,
  Far famed in minstrel story,
Another, humbler theme I'll take,
  But not less full of glory.

Their hireling troops let others boast,
  Who fought for spoil and prey,
Our southern lads we love the most,
  In a private's suit of grey.

In vain before our eyes they flaunt
  Their rich equipments gay;
'Tis bright and costly, we must grant,
  But still, 'tis not the grey!

Ah! who are like our southern boys?
  And who can match them, say?
Who gladly left their peaceful joys
  To don the private's grey.

Who faced the dangers, toils and strife
  Which veterans oft would shun,
And gladly gave their young, bright life,
  Nor thought 'twas nobly done.

No meed of praise they asked, nor thought
  A hero's name to gain;
'Twas for their land alone they fought,
  And not for praise or fame!

What honor is in purple pall,
  Or gold and diamonds gay?
Can they arouse the hearts of all,
  Like a tattered suit of grey?

Aye! poor and conquered though we be,
  May we never know the day,
When we can look unmoved and see,
  The soldier's suit of grey!

And they may force our boys to part
  With the dress they so much fear;
But ne'er can change our patriot heart,
  Or make the grey less dear!

And still each morn and even-tide,
  The southern women pray,
"In mercy, Lord, remember us,
  And bless our boys in grey!"

RALEIGH, N. C.

OFF WITH YOUR GREY SUITS, BOYS!

Off with your grey suits, boys!
   Off with your rebel gear!
It smacks too much of the cannon's peal,
The lightning flash of your deadly steel,
   And fills our hearts with fear.

The color is like the smoke
   That curled o'er your battle line;
It calls to mind the yell that woke,
When the dastard columns before you broke,
   And their dead wore your fatal sign!

Off with your starry wreaths,
   Ye who have led our van!
For you 'twas the pledge of a glorious death,
As we followed you over the glorious heath,
   Where we whipped them man to man!

Down with the cross of stars!
   Too long has it waved on high;
'Tis covered all over with battle scars,
But its gleam the hated banner mars—
   'Tis time to lay it by.

Down with the vows we had made!
   Down with each memory!
Down with the thoughts of our noble dead!
Down, down to the dust where their forms are laid,
   And down with liberty!

WEARING OF THE GREY.

BY A MISSISSIPPIAN.

The editor of the *Citizen,* introducing the following to his readers, re-
marked that it "has never before been published," but that it "is now
being set to music in Louisville, and. will make its appearance in a
short time."

Oh, have you heard the cruel news? Alas! it is too true:
Upon the Appomattox down went our cross of blue—
Our armies have surrendered—we bow to northern sway,
And forevermore forbidden is the wearing of the grey!

No more on fields of battle waves the banner of our pride,
In vain beneath its crimson folds, our Stewart and Jackson
      died;
Like a meteor of evening, that flag has passed away,
And low are they who guarded it, the wearers of the grey.

I met a Mississippian, right hard my hand he wrung,
The tear was in his dauntless eye, and faltering was his tongue,
As in broken words he told me of that disastrous day,
Which made a badge of infamy the wearing of the grey.

Now, honor to the soldier who still is firm and true,
And shame upon the southern beast that wears the foe-
      man's blue!
While 'round the Blue Ridge rocky peak the evening
      mist shall play,
We'll, like our mountains, never leave the wearing of the grey.

Remember how we scattered them, beneath those moun-
      tains old—
How we tamed the powers of the strong, the valor of the
      bold,
When thund'ring through the bloody gap, old Longstreet
      thrust his way!
Remember this, and ne'er forsake the wearing of the grey.

We have lost all but honor—our banner bears no shame;
Though beaten down by numbers, we keep our ancient
    fame;
And though exiles from our country, in foreign lands we
    stray,
We'll not forget our early love, but proudly wear the grey.

Now, here's to our companions—the comrades true who
    died,
In fore front of the battle, closely fighting by our side!
Though our lips are little used to prayer, yet for their
    souls we'll pray,
For they fell beneath our banner, for wearing of the
    grey.

But a day may yet be coming, boys, in future rolling
    years,
Which may bring revenge and triumph—may wipe away
    our tears—
When the azure cross shall float again, no more to pass
    away,
And the token of our victory be—the wearing of the
    grey.

OUR FAILURE.

BY THE AUTHOR OF "SOUTHRONS."

Yes, we have failed ! That iron word
    Drove never home its bolt of fate
More ruthlessly, than when it barred
    All egress from the prison gate
    That closed upon our sad estate,
And left us powerless—in the dark,
A world's reproach, a nation's mark.

Failed ?   Aye, so grievously that pain
  Is put aside in pure amaze,
As, at our weary length of chain
  And steel-girt path we stand, and gaze
  With dark distrust of coming days,
And marvel if we be the same,
Who lit the Christian world to flame.

The same who owned this lovely land
  Now lying waste—a tyrant's spoil—
And saw its stately dwellings stand
  'Mid waving fields of fertile soil,
  Enriched by swarthy sons of toil—
The princes of a proud estate—
Now stricken, sterile, desolate !

The same !   Where be our legions now ?
  Where stand our homes so fair and proud ?
Where rings each step, where beams each brow
  Of those we loved—our martyr crowd,
  To home and country nobly vowed ?
Of sons and brothers, where the hope
That wreathed our splendid horoscope ?

And where the banner, which on high
  We flung, with all the pride of race,
An emblem from our southern sky,
  Snatched from its sovereign dwelling place
  Our deeds of arms to gild and grace—
The flag our breezes loved to toss,
Our ark of strength—our Southern Cross ?

All buried in one common grave
 . Are these, the glories of the past ;
Let the swamp cypress o'er it wave,
The bittern sail, the eagle rave,
  The simoom sweep, the midnight blast
  Make requiem meet !   The die is cast,
And we—who counted ill the cost,
Who ventured all—have staked and lost !

What marvel, then, if in the burst
  Of an incredulous despair,
When fate has seemed to do its worst,
  And all proves false that seemed so fair,
  Such words as these should mock the air?
And that, mistrusting fate and fame,
We question, "Are we still the same?"

Oh, morbid doubt! Oh, words of wind!
  I cast ye forth as little worth.
Forgive them, Omnipresent Mind!
  Forgive them, brothers, bound on earth
  To one poor heritage of dearth,
And hear conviction's voice proclaim
The potent truth, "We are the same!"

The same who faced the northern hosts
  With dauntless hearts and shining spears;
The same who laughed to scorn their boasts,
  And proved the few the many's peers,
  And did in days the work of years!
O'erwhelmed—not conquered—overrun,
And desolated, and undone.

Yet still the same—the very same!
  Believe it—tremble and believe,
Oh, tyrants, who with sword and flame
  Advanced to slaughter and bereave,
  Then *stayed* to torture and deceive!
And we, who with a faith sublime
Endure our fate, abide our time!

BEECHMORE, KY., *June* 1, 1866.

HERE AND THERE.

A CONTRAST.

I.

There's clashing of arms in the Sunny South,
   There's hurrying to and fro,
And the young men flock to the dauntless chief,
   Who will lead them against the foe.

The ledger is closed on the merchant's desk,
   And the printer has left his case;
The cavalier mounts the horse from the plow,
   The ranks of the squadron to grace.

From the hut of logs in the piny woods,
   Behold there is coming forth,
The rustic, with rifle, trusty and true,
   To do battle against the North.

There is never a quiver upon his lip,
   There is never a tear or a sigh,
And there's pride in the voice from the window
   That cheers while it bids "good bye."

She will till the soil 'till he comes again;
   He can leave her no money to hire
A strong arm to guide the home-made plow,
   Or cut wood for the winter's fire.

II.

Martial music is heard in the busy North,
   Though the battles are far away;
There's a call for five hundred thousand men
   To go forth to the deadly fray.

The "speaker" appeals to the youthful and brave,
   The minister echoes the call;
And the "poster" proclaiming the "bounty,"
   Looks down from each fence and wall.

Then the laborer, pausing in his work,
   The tempting challenge reads,
And cyphering proves, with a stick in the dust,
   That the bounty his hire exceeds.

Exceeds his wages for three weary years
   Of delving with spade and pick,
Of drawing of water and hewing of stone,
   Or of bearing the hod of brick.

So away he speeds to the desk
   Where the mustering officer sets,
And he dons the blue and the knapsack too,
   Then home with the bounty he gets.

From the neat, white house, with his musket,
   Next morning he goeth forth:
There'll be bloody work in the distant South,
   But there's bread in that house in the North.

· III.

The terrible battle is lost and won,
   The dead on the field lie cold,
The strength of the North prevaileth at last,
   And the tale of the South is told.

She may have been just or she may have been wrong
   Yet each soldier· struck for the right;
No matter whether the stripes or the bars
   Waved over him in the fight.

Liberty's wings over all were spread
   As the rivals prepare for battle;
And Liberty wept over *all* the dead
   When the muskets had ceased to rattle.

She smiled on the victor who proudly claimed
   The sulphury, smoke-canopied field;
And she wrote the names of the vanquished braves
   In letters of light on her shield.

IV.

The hut still stood in the piny woods,
   Though the raiders the fence had burned,
They had broken the plow and stolen the horse,
   Ere the farmer from the war returned.

The child that had blessed that lowly cot
   Was cold in the new-made grave;
And the bread that the lowly mother cut,
   Was a boon that charity gave.

The farmer returned—he returned a wreck,
  To the home so cheerful of yore;
And the care-worn wife rushed forth to help
  The cripple that stood at the door.

The yeoman no longer could follow the plow,
  Nor sow in the furrow it cleft;
And the withered arm could not wield an axe,
  If the raiders an axe had left.

They sorrowing thought of the happy past;
  And the future seemed dark and dread,
For the dying wife and the crippled brave,
  Must go forth to beg their bread.

v.

The steamer arrived almost covered by flags;
  There was joy in the Northern port,
And the merry shouts from the crowded decks,
  Replied to the guns from the fort.

A soldier in blue—he was crippled too—
  Was borne by his comrades to shore;
An ambulance waited to bear him away,
  To his little white cottage door.

The wife who received him, though tears were shed,
  Had never known want or care,
For the bounty he left was more than enough,
  And she told him she'd "most of it" there.

He'd many a good months pay yet due;
  And the leg he had lost in the fight,
Would yield him a pension as long as he lived,
  And the cripple's heart beat light.

And happy he was when they gave him a stool
  In the Treasury office next day,
And told him his wages were greater far,
  Than ever the laborer's pay.

   *   *   *   *   *   *

If God ordained that in different climes
  Men different views should take,
Who dare aver they *should* suffer here
  Who struggled for conscience's sakè?

Yet the Southern cripple, who bled for the right
  As "God gave him the right to know,"
If perchance he saved from the wreck a mite,
  Must support his crippled foe!

And yet it were heresy, deadly and damned,
  For him to ask pension too,
Enough that he helps to pay for the crutch
  That supports the maimed veteran in blue.

From the Sunny South.

IN THE LAND WHERE WE WERE DREAMING.

BY DAN. LUCAS, OF JEFFERSON COUNTY, VA.

Fair were our visions! Oh, they were as grand
As ever floated out of Fancy land;—
    Children were we in simple faith,
    But God-like children, whom, nor death,
Nor threat, nor danger drove from Honor's path,
          In the land where we were dreaming.

Proud were our men, as pride of birth could render;
As violets, our women pure and tender;
    And when they spoke, their voice did thrill
    Until at eve, the whip-poor-will,
At morn the mocking-bird, were mute and still
          In the land where we were dreaming.

And we had graves that covered more of glory,
Than ever taxed tradition's ancient story;
    And in our dreams we wove the thread
    Of principles for which had bled,
And suffered long our own immortal dead
          In the land where we were dreaming.

Though in our land we had both bond and free,
Both were content; and so God let them be;—
    'Till envy coveted our sun
    And those fair fields our valor won,
But little recked we, for we still slept on,
          In the land where we were dreaming.

19

Our sleep grew troubled and our dream grew wild—
Red meteors flashed across our Heaven's field;
　　Crimson the moon; between the 'Twins
　　Barbed arrows fly, and then begins
Such strife as when disorder's Chaos reigns
　　　　In the land where we were dreaming.

Down from her sun-lit heights smiled Liberty
And waved her cap in sign of Victory—
　　The world approved, and everywhere
　　Except where growled the Russian bear,
The good, the brave, the just gave us their prayer
　　　　In the land where we were dreaming.

We fancied that a Government was ours—
We challenged place among the world's great powers;
　　We talked in sleep of Rank, Commission,
　　Until so life-like grew our vision,
That he who dared to doubt, but met derision
　　　　In the land where we were dreaming.

We looked on high; a banner there was seen,
Whose field was blanched and spotless in its sheen—
　　Chivalry's cross its Union bears,
　　And vet'rans swearing by their scars
Vowed they would bear it through a hundred wars
　　　　In the land where we were dreaming.

A hero came amongst us as we slept;
At first he lowly knelt—then rose and wept;
　　Then gathering up a thousand spears
　　He swept across the field of Mars;
Then bowed farewell, and walked beyond the stars—
　　　　In the land where we were dreaming.

We looked again : another figure still
Gave hope, and nerved each individual will—
    Full of grandeur, clothed with power,
    Self-poised, erect, he ruled the hour
With stern, majestic sway—of strength a tower
        In the land where we were dreaming.

As, while great Jove, in bronze, a warder God,
Gazed eastward from the Forum where he stood,
    Rome felt herself secure and free,
    So "Richmond's safe," we said, while we
Beheld a bronzed Hero—God-like Lee,
        In the land where we were dreaming.

As wakes the soldier when the alarum calls—
As wakes the mother when her infant falls—
    As starts the traveller when around
    His sleeping couch the fire-bells sound—
So woke our nation with a single bound
        In the land where we were dreaming.

Woe! woe is me! the startled mother cried—
While we have slept our noble sons have died!
    Woe! woe is me! how strange and sad,
    That all our glorious vision's fled,
And left us nothing real but our dead
        In the land where we were dreaming.

And are they really dead, our martyred slain?
No! dreamers! morn shall bid them rise again
    From every vale—from every height
    On which they *seemed* to die for right—
Their gallant spirits shall renew the fight
        In the land where we were dreaming.

Wake! dreamers, wake! none but the sleeping fail!
Our cause being just, must in the end prevail;
    Once this Thyestean banquet o'er,
    Grown strong, the few who bide their hour,
Shall rise and hurl the drunken guests from power
        In the land where we were dreaming.

THE BROKEN MUG.

BY A SOLDIER.

My mug is broken, my heart is sad!
  What woes can fate still hold in store?
The friend I cherished a thousand days
  Is smashed to pieces on the floor!
  Is shattered and to Limbo gone,
    I'll see my mug no more!

Relic it was of joyous hours
  Whose golden memories still allure—
When coffee made of rye we drank,
  And grey was all the dress we wore!
  When we were paid some cents a month,
    But never asked for more!

In marches long, by day and night
  In raids, hot charges, shocks of war;
Strapped on the saddle at my back
  This faithful comrade still I bore—
  This old companion, true and tried,
    I'll never carry more!

Bright days! when young in heart and hope
  The pulse leaped at the words "La Gloire!"
When the grey people cried—"hot fight,"
  Why we have one to four!
When but to see the foeman's face
    Was all they asked—no more.

From Rapidan to Gettysburg—
  "Hard bread" behind, "sour krout" before—
This friend went with the cavalry
  And heard the jarring cannon roar
In front of Cemetery Hill—
    Good heavens! how they'd roar!

Then back again, the foe behind,
  Back to the "Old Virginia Shore"—
Some dead and wounded left—some holes
  In flags the sullen greybacks bore;
This mug had made the great campaign,
    And we'd have gone once more!

Alas! we never went again!
  The red cross banner, slow but sure,
"Fell back"—we bade to sour krout
  (Like the lover of Lenore)
A long, sad, lingering farewell—
    To taste its joys no more.

But still we fought, and ate hard bread,
  Or starved—good friend our woes deplore!
And still this faithful friend remained
  Riding behind me as before—
The friend on march, in bivouac
    When others were no more.

How oft we drove the horsemen blue
    In Summer bright or Winter frore!
How oft before the Southern charge
    Thro' field and wood the blue birds tore!
    I'm "harmonized" to-day, but think
        I'd like to charge once more.

Oh yes! we're all "fraternal" now,
    Purged of our sins, we're clean and pure;
Congress will "reconstruct" us soon—
    But no grey people on *that* floor!
    I'm harmonized—"so called"—but long
        To see those times once more!

Gay days! the sun was brighter then,
    And we were happy, though so poor!
That past comes back as I behold
    My shattered friend upon the floor,
    My splintered, useless, ruined mug
        From which I'll drink no more.

How many lips I'll love for aye,
    While heart and memory endure,
Have touched this broken cup and laughed—
    How they did laugh! in days of yore!
    Those days we'd call "a beauteous dream—
        If they had been no more!"

Dear comrades, dead this many a day—
    I saw you weltering in your gore
After those days, amid the pines
    On Rappahannock shore!
    When the joy of life was much to me
        But your warm hearts were more!

Yours was the grand heroic nerve
  That laughs amid the. storm of war—
Souls that "loved much" your native land,
  Who fought and died therefor !
   You gave your youth, your brains, your arms,
    Your blood—you had no more !

You lived and died true to your flag !
  And now your wounds are healed—but sore
Are many hearts that think of you
  Where you have "gone before."
   Peace, comrade ! God bound up those forms,
    They are " whole " forevermore !

Those lips this broken vessel touched,
  His, too !—the man's we all adore—
That cavalier of cavaliers,
  Whose voice will ring no more—
   Whose plume will float amid the storm
    Of battle never more !

Not on this idle page I write
  That name of names, shrined in the core
Of every heart. Peace ! foolish pen ;
  Hush ! words so cold and poor—
   His sword is rust, the blue eyes dust,
    His bugle sounds no more !

Yet ever here write this : He charged
  As Rupert, in the years before ;
And when his stern, hard work was done,
  His griefs, joys, battles o'er,
   His mighty spirit rode the storm,
    And led his men once more !

He lies beneath his native sod,
  Where violets spring, or frost is hoar;
He recks not! Charging squadrons watch
  His raven plume no more!
    That smile we'll see, that voice we'll hear,
      That hand we'll touch no more!

My foolish mirth is quenched in tears;
  Poor fragments strewed upon the floor,
You are a type of nobler things
  That find their use no more—
    Things glorious once, now trodden down—
      That makes us smile no more!

Of courage, pride, high hopes, stout hearts,
  Hard, stubborn nerve, devotion pure!
Beating his wings against the bars,
  The prisoned eagle tried to soar!
    Outmatched, o'erwhelmed, we struggled still;
      Bread failed—we fought no more!

Lies in the dust the shattered staff
  That bore aloft on sea and shore
That blazing .flag, amid the storm!
  And none are now so poor—
    So poor to do it reverence,
      Now when it flames no more!

But it is glorious in the dust,
  Sacred 'till time shall be no more.
Spare it, fierce editors, your scorn!
  The dread "rebellion's" o'er!
    Furl the great flag, hide cross and star,
    Thrust into darkness star and bar.
    But look! across the ages far,
      It flames forevermore!

LAST REQUEST OF HENRY C. MAGRUDER.

This unfortunate youth, who was executed on Friday, October 20, 1865, in his last moments displayed a firmness and courage unprecedented in the annals of the world's history, save by Marshal Ney himself, whom Napoleon termed the "bravest of the brave." Laying aside the charges preferred against him by the powers who tried and condemned him, he was more "sinned against than sinning;" for, young, ardent and impetuous, he became an easy prey to those follies and temptations for which he atoned with the sacrifice of his life. Poor unfortunate child! weak and feeble, suffering agonies from a mortal wound eight long months within gloomy prison walls, shut off from every hope, yet he never murmured nor complained to the very few friends who would occasionally gain access to his prison cell, who ever found him cheerful and hopeful. In his last moments he addressed himself to two particular friends, upon whom he did ever rely with the utmost confidence, and expressed "his request" in the following beautiful lines.

Oh! wrap me not, when I am dead,
    In the ghastly winding-sheet,
And bind no 'kerchief round my head,
    Nor fetter my active feet;
But let some friend who loves me best
    Comb out my long dark hair,
And part the ringlets round my face,
    In the fashion I loved to wear.

And robe me in my favorite garb,
    And let sweet flowers be pressed
Within my hand and to my heart,
    When you lay me down to rest;
For I would not my friends should turn
    Away with a thrill of fear,
As they give the last fond look and kiss
    To one in life so dear.

And lay me down in a quiet spot,
    Beneath some spreading tree,
Where birds may build their nests, and sing
    Their sweetest songs o'er me;

19*

And let no tears be o'er me shed,
　　But the pearly tears of night,
As the flowers I love weep o'er my bed,
　　In the pale moon's silver light.

And let no chilling marble rest
　　On my heart so warm and true;
But the verdant turf be my winding-sheet,
　　Kept green by the summer dew.
Thus let me sleep—and my glad soul,
　　On wings of hope and love,
Shall haste to meet my loved and lost,
　　In a world of bliss above.

LOUISVILLE, *October 20, 1865.*

FORGET? NEVER!

BY MRS. C. A. BALL.

In answer to the sentiment which has been expressed of late by many,
"we should forget the past."

I.

Can the mother forget the child of her love,
Who was in her tenderest heart-strings wove,
Who lisped his first prayer her knee beside,
And grew to manhood her joy and pride?
Can she look over his early grave,
And forgetting the cause he died to save,
Think of the past as it ne'er had been?
These years in her thoughts are too fresh, I ween.
　　　　　　　　　　　　　Forget? Never!

II.

Can the father forget his first-born son,
Who, ere his boyhood was fairly run,
Shouldered his musket and left his side,
And for love of country fought and died?
Think you oblivion's waves can roll
Over a parent's stricken soul?
Oh, no! the past, with its waves of blood,
Surges his heart like a mighty flood.

Forget? Never!

III.

Can the sister forget the brother beloved,
Who with her through the haunts of childhood roved?
Can she think of the wound on his manly brow,
Which laid his proud form forever low?
And can memory be a thing of nought,
And the years with such fearful anguish fraught,
Be unto her as they ne'er had been?
Oh, no! they will ever be fresh and green.

Forget? Never!

IV.

Can the maiden forget the noble youth
Who had pledged to her his love and truth?
Can the wife forget the husband tried,
Who for the love of his country left her side?
Can the stricken orphan dry her tears,
And think no more of those vanished years—
Dark years of terror, of death and woe?
Their bleeding hearts cry "no! oh, no!"

Forget? Never!

V.

Can any true southern heart forget,
While our land with blood and tears is wet?
While the mother's, the widow's, the orphan's wail,
Is borne to our ears from hill and 'vale?

While our homesteads in ashes round us lie,
And for bread our starving myriads cry?
While he, the head of our fallen cause,
('Gainst mercy's plea, and honor's laws,)
Pines still within his prison walls,
And justice in vain for his freedom calls?

> Forget? Never!

VI.

Time may bring healing upon his wings,
May bind in our hearts the shattered strings;
Forgiveness of injuries yet may come,
Though oppression be felt in each southern home.
But ask no more! The terrible past
Must ever be ours, while life shall last:
Ours, with its memories—ours, with its pain—
Ours, with its best blood shed like rain—
Its sacrifices—all made in vain.

> Forget? Never!

ARLINGTON.

BY MARGARET J. PRESTON.

You stand upon the chasm's brink,
　　That yawns so deadly deep,
Ready to bridge the rift, we think,
　　And dare the noble leap;
So—fill this rent with purpose bold—
　　Right war's red deeds of shame,
And Curtius, with his legend old,
　　Will pale before your name!

We meddle not with questions high;
  The holier office ours,
To follow where man leads, and try
  To hide the flints with flowers.
We sought, thro' all our bloody strife,
  To succor, soothe, sustain;
And not one southern maid nor wife
  Has grudged the cost or pain.

So, now, when might has won the day,
  When every hope is crossed,
We cheer, uphold, as best we may,
  The hearts whose all is lost.
"Rebellious," "outlawed," what you will,
  We yet a boon would crave,
Trusting that calm forbearance still—
  Against such odds—so brave!

For sons, for husbands, not one plea!
  (For *men*, to whom you give,
With unupbraiding leniency,
  Free right, broad room to live!)
But with a tender woman's claim,
  Warm in our souls, we come,
Armed with the spell-word of a name
  That holds denial dumb.

He, in whose more than regal chair
  You sit, supreme, to-day:
Could *he*, unmoved, uncensuring, bear
  That wrong should wrest away

What calmed a dying father's breast,*
  As with rare tear and moan,
Within *his* childless arms he prest
  The babes, thence named "his own?"

His own? Yet she, sole daughter left
  Of all that stately race,
An exile wanders, sad, bereft
  Of certain dwelling place.
Within her old ancestral halls
  The hearths no beams reflect,
And over lawn and garden falls
  The mildew of neglect.

The blood allied to Washington,
  Spurned from the rights *he* gave!
Denied the vaunted justice done
  To every home-born slave!
Tell not the brood of Askelon—
  Let Gath not hear afar,
Lest Kingdoms sneer it, one to one—
  "How base Republics are?"

"You do not war with women!" Good!
  Let such your boast still be;
We do not ask a single rood
  Of ground for Mary *Lee*.
Yet, tho' our hero's wife be banned
  As touched with treason's stain,
For Mary *Custis* we demand
  Her Arlington again!

* See *Irring's Washington.*—Death of Col. Custis.

OUR CHIEF.

BY THE AUTHOR OF "SOUTHRONS."*

No ! not forgotten, though the halls
  Of state no more behold him.
No ! not forsaken, though the walls
  Of dungeon keeps enfold him.
Still dearest to the southern heart,
  Because her priest annointed,
The prophet chosen for his part,
  The man by God appointed.

If dumb, it is that tyrants check
  The words that fain were spoken,
And set the foot upon the neck
  Of the people they have broken;
If still, it is that bond and chain
  Each manly limb encumber,
And men but murmur in their pain,
  As children talk in slumber.

We bow our foreheads to the dust
  In deep humiliation,
Forgetting in our prayerful trust
  Our own dark desolation;
We ask for him who steered our ship,
  Until it met the breakers,
That the cup may pass that meets his lip,
  Through mercy of his Maker's.

* Better known as the "Southern Chaunt of Defiance."

That grace divine may touch the hearts
　Of those who now oppress him,
And tyrants, tired of Draco's parts,
　　Lean from their thrones to bless him!
Thus from the throne of mighty God,
　The cry of love has risen,
For him who groans beneath the rod,
　　Proud, prostrate, and in prison.

BEECHMORE, *Jan.* 10, 1866.

JEFFERSON DAVIS.

BY WM. MUNFORD.

For spirit ever quick
　With sword or rhetoric,
To cleave for right, and dare the sternest brunt!
　For that when Spanish steel
　Bade bristling Texans kneel,
And thy true heart had urged them to the front,
Thy knightly blade leaped from the sheath,
And flashed against the southern sky, a fiery wreath!

For honor pure as ice,
　That spurned low artifice,
And brought no blemish from the forum's brawls!
　For that exalted fame,
　That bore so fair a name
With Cabinets, and in the Senate halls!
For Bayard's knightly pride that charmed,
For Sydney's courtly grace that wooed and warmed!

For that majestic mind,
That towers above its kind
Like some grand peak among the mighty hills !
For that pure wealth of soul
That dignifies the whole
Rare song that Clio's trumpet trills—
A virgin nation at the shrine,
Looked up to thee, and placed her trembling hand in thine !

But while the bridal strains
Pealed o'er her sunny plains
Like Egypt's freighting royal caravans,
With iron notes of war
Came a mighty conqueror,
Forbidding, all too late, those righteous bans.·
The southern blood leaps to its shields,   .
And flaunts the virgin's snowy flag along her fields.

Oh, years of noble toil
That stronger strength to foil,
How flowed our firstling blood of sacrifice !
Oh, spirits that are gone,
Like Abel you have won,
And blood cries from our wasted paradise !
Her places know her now no more,
Her spotless ensign droops upon the other shore.

But thou, our stricken Chief,
As grand in all thy grief
As ever St. Helena's chained king,
Communing with the skies,
Above thyself dost rise ;
And comes that voice, as if an angel's wing,
To whisper from the prison cave,
And bid thy people sternly be still duty's slave.

Great chieftain of our choice,
Albeit that people's voice
No comfort speaks in thy lone granite keep;
Through those harsh iron bars
There come back from the stars
Low echoes of the prayers they nightly weep.
Thy children show their manhood best
That all their fears are circling round thine honored crest!

DERNIER RESORT, MONTGOMERY CO., VA., *Jan.* 22, 1866.

JEFFERSON DAVIS.

BY A SOUTHERN WOMAN.

The cell is lonely, and the night
   Has filled it with a darker gloom;
The little rays of friendly light
   Which through each chink and crack found room
To press in, with their noiseless feet
All merciful and fleet,
And bring, like Noah's trembling dove,
God's silent messages of love,
      These, too, are gone—
      Shut out—and gone,
      And that great heart is left alone!

Alone with darkness and with woe!
   Around him Freedom's temple lies,
Its arches crushed, its columns low,
   The night wind through its ruin sighs.

Rash, cruel hands that temple razed,
(Then stood the world amazed!)
And now those hands—ah, ruthless deeds !—
Their captive pierce ! His brave heart bleeds,
    And yet no groan
    Is heard ! no groan !
    He suffers silently, alone !

For all his bright and happy home,
  He has that cell so drear and dark,
Those narrow walls for heaven's blue dome,
  The clank of chains for song of lark ;
And for the grateful voice of friends—
That voice which ever lends
Its charm where human hearts are found—
He hears the key's dull grating sound.
    No heart is near,
    No kind heart near,
    No sigh of sympathy, no tear !

Oh, dream not thus, thou true and good !
  Unnumbered hearts on thee await,
By thee invisibly have stood,
  Have crowded through thy prison gate,
Nor dungeon bolts, nor dungeon bars,
Nor floating "stripes and stars,"
Nor glittering gun or bayonet,
Can ever cause us to forget
    Our faith to thee,
    Our love to thee,
    Thou glorious soul, thou strong, thou *free !*

AN APPEAL FOR JEFFERSON DAVIS.

BY A LADY OF VIRGINIA.

To His Excellency, Andrew Johnson, President of the United States:

Unheralded, unknown, I come to thee,
Who holdest in thy hands the scales of power;
Assured thou wilt not spurn the suppliant,
Who with frail, helpless hands and burning heart
Lays at thine honored feet *her* simple plea
Of "*Mercy for the Captive.*"

                       Thou hast known
The tempest-tossing of a chequered life,
The chill of adverse winds, the wintry blight
Of hopes too fondly cherished. Thou hast seen
How frail a bubble is the world's applause,
How empty its poor praise. Oh, pity us
On whose life-paths shadows have darkly fallen,
Whose bruised hearts thy clemency may heal!
We plead for one honored, revered, beloved.
Spare him on whose brave head cowards would lay
A nation's penalty! If *he* has sinned,
The humblest champion of our fallen cause
Did just as truly sin; if guilty he,
Our *Jackson* too was guilty, yet who seeks
To brand *his* glorious name? Ah! who so bold
As, with the lash of stern rebuke, to dare
Assail whom God approveth? Jackson's soul
Rests with the *Crucified;* shall *Davis* bear
The penance of his guilt?

Oh, honored Chief,
Be kind, be *just* to him whom Jackson loved,
And proudly honored with his high esteem!
Upon his head blessings unspoken rest; ties
Stronger than hooks of steel circle him round;
Prayers from unnumbered hearts go up for him.
Art thou a *husband?* For his safety now
A wife sits weeping, through the lonely hours
Of long absence. Silent, bitter tears
Well from her burdened heart, while boding fears
Sadden with anxious thoughts her sleepless pillow.
Art thou a *father?* In their stranger home
Young children watch for *him,* and *pause* to hear
The step that comes not. Aye, they often ask,
" *Where is our father? why does he not come?*"
And grave lips blanch, and quiver in reply,
And talk of "*prayer,*" and "*abiding trust*"
In the All-Father, God. Oh! round his neck
Fond arms would gladly circle; prattling lips
Would pour into his ears their music tones
Of simple, guileless love! Say, wouldst thou give
Joy to these *blameless ones?* Then open wide
His dreary prison door!

For this one act
Heaven would smile on thee in that solemn hour
When life is pausing at the Gates of Death,
And *thy* sole hope is *Christ's benificence.*
Aye, for this single act, *so much desired,*
A thousand hearts would pour their prayers for thee
At God's own mercy-seat; a thousand tongues
Would speak thy praise, as that of one who knew
How, with the tempted hand of conscious Power,
To shield the helpless.

Oh, most honored Chief,
Head of a mighty nation, lend thine ear
To this poor, earnest plea for one beloved!
Set the brave captive free! and when at last
Thy soul stands trembling at that judgment-seat
Where prayers avail not, when the written scroll
Of human deeds is opened, and there lies
The record of *thy life*, should aught appear
Which justice would consign to punishment,
May the recording angel *blot it out*,
And o'er thy name, in testimony, write,
" Blessed are the merciful !"

JEFFERSON DAVIS.

BY MOLLIE E. MOORE.

"To err is human—to forgive divine."

Mercy for a fallen chief!
The angel, Peace, hath stilled the mighty storm;
    But a deep and restless grief
Stirs the mute heart, and urges the warm
Lips to plead for that bowed, defenceless form !

    Upon that captive head
Must the strong arm of vengeance wreak its wrath?
    Alas ! if his hands are red,
Ours are not less so ; we trod the path
He trod ; we followed where he led !

We know that blood hath poured,
We know that voices have been stilled, we know
 Among ye the cold sword
Hath made sad havoc, that the golden glow
Hath faded from many a warm hearth and board!

 But have we not bled
And suffered too? Are not those dark fields strewn
 With our unmonumented dead?
Did we not feel the dark clouds overhead,
And the sudden midnight that overtook the moon?

 And if ye call it sin,
The Past—are then our sufferings less? But oh,
 As if had not been   •
That past appears while we with grief and woe
Plead for your captive—he has ceased to be your foe!

 The little child
Robed for his couch at night, lifting his brow
 In supplication mild,
Whispers the honored name; a hallowed glow
Seems to enwrap him as his accents flow!

 The young girl trimming her wreath,
Pauses among her heaps of dewy flowers,
 And reverently breathes
A prayer for that great heart whose weary hours
No love may soothe, for whom there spring no flowers!

 The wintry head
Of the heart-broken sire who has heard the knell
 Of his first-born dead
On the field where his friend and brother fell,
Bows while he names the captive in his cell.

Behold !
Bitter with grief and stung with gnawing pain
      Which never can grow old!
And crossed with many a bloody stain,
A nation's throbbing heart upon the shrine is lain !

      And by the brave red streams
That mingled when the strife was hot and high,
      And by the flashes and the lurid gleams
That shot up from our burning homes, and by
The pleading hearts that mount toward the sky ;

      And by those memories
Common to us all, or friend or foe,
      Yea, by the dear, dear eyes,
Hidden forever 'neath the clods that know
No bond or barrier 'twixt the hearts that sleep below ;

      By the tender hearts that grope
Vainly after the lost, and by the lone
      Proud souls that yield all earthly hope,
By that sad Past o'er which all true hearts moan,
"Mercy" we plead for that loved and honored one !

      Behold!
Shaken with tears, as by the rain a leaf,
      Filled with sad thoughts that never can grow old,
But wreathed with sweet flowers of sympathy and grief,
A fallen Nation's heart pleads for her fallen Chief !

Houston Telegraph.

REGULUS.*

BY MARGARET J. PRESTON.

Have ye no mercy? Punic rage
  Boasted small skill in torture, when
The sternest patriot of his age—
  And Romans all were patriots then—
Was doomed with his unwinking eyes,
To stand beneath the fiery skies,
Until the sun-shafts pierced his brain,
And he grew blind with poignant pain,
  While Carthage jeered and taunted! Yet
When day's slow-moving orb had set,
And pitying Nature—kind to all—
  In dewy darkness bathed her hand,
And laid it on each lidless ball,
  So crazed with gusts of scorching sand—
They yielded,—nor forbade the grace,
  By flashing torches in his face.

Ye flash the torches! Never night
  Brings the blank dark to that worn eye:
In pitiless, perpetual light,
Our tortured Regulus must lie!
  The tropic suns seemed tender; they
Eyed not with purpose to betray:
No human vengeance like a spear
Whetted to sharpness, keen and clear,

*See Craven's Prison Life of Jefferson Davis, p. 166.

20

By settled hatred—pricked its way
Right thro' the bloodshot iris! Nay,
Ye are refined tormentors! Glare
    A little longer thro' the bars,
At the bay'd lion in his lair—
    And God's dear hand from out the stars,
To shame inhuman man, may cast
Its shadow o'er those lids at last,
And end their aching with the blest
Signet and seal of perfect rest!

THE BATTLE OF BUENA VISTA.

INSCRIBED TO JEFFERSON DAVIS.

BY A MISSISSIPPIAN.

It was upon the battle field,
    Where lay the dead and dying,
And many a gallant hero fell,
    While routed friends were flying.

On rolled the overwhelming tide,
    The haughty foes confiding,
Rushed o'er the dead and wounded forms,
    Their furious chargers riding.

Here lay Kentucky's chief in dust,
    Her younger hero dying,
And there Arkansas pierced to death,
    With many a horseman lying.*

* Colonel McKee was killed, Lieutenant Colonel Clay was left mortally wounded upon the field, and Col. Yell was killed with a lance while heading a cavalry charge.

On rolled the raging tide of war,
  In serried lines of battle,
The gaudy pennants flaunt in air,
  The shining armors rattle.

On, on the furious horsemen pour
  Like the resistless river,
The hills beneath the heavy tread
  Of rushing squadrons quiver.

A nation's fate and honor lie
  Poised in the balance now,
Lo, where *he* stands, his little band
  Upon the mountain's brow.

Must they before the avalanche
  Of the advancing foe,
Be swept like chaff before the wind,
  Or on the field laid low?

They move not, stir not—still they stand,
  Firm as the mountain rock,
Defiant wait the exulting foe,
  And brave the coming shock.

They stand, and still as death—
  No murmur whispers there,
Lo! there the smoke! the flash!
  Their volleys rend the air.

Down horse and rider roll in dust,
  Their melting ranks give way,
Their broken columns back recoil,
  And Davis saves the day.

But still the hills re-echo back
  The cannon's thundering roar,
Where gallant Bragg stills holds in check,
  The foemen as they pour.

'Tis there beneath the canopy
   Of sulphury clouds that rise,
'Mid lurid flames and reeking gore,
   A bloody sacrifice.

'Tis there converge the inveterate foes,
   And centre all their force,
There "Rough and Ready" gives his care,
   And marks the battle's course.

Lo, o'er the field with hurried stride,
   They hasten to the strife,
Who staked upon the mountain brow,
   Their honor and their life.

Again they rush where fate impends,
   To give the welcome aid —
Their deeds have on their country's page
   Their names immortal made.

Before the unerring rifle's flash,
   The storm of shot and shell,
Fierce as the raging tempest's wrath,
   The slaughtered foemen fell.

And then again in triumph rose
   The loud exulting cry,
As back recoiled the baffled foe,
   The shout of victory.

And Buena Vista's field was won —
   A nation's honor saved,
Its banner all unstained on high,
   In glorious triumph waved.

Louisville Courier. April, 1866.

THE CONFEDERATE NOTE.

The following lines were written upon the back of a five hundred dollar
Confederate note, by Major S. A. Jonas, subsequent to the surrender:

Representing nothing on God's earth now,
   And naught in the water below it;
As a pledge of a nation that's dead and gone,
   Keep it, dear Captain, and show it.
      Show it to those that will lend an ear,
       To the tale this paper can tell
      Of liberty born, of the patriot's dream,
       Of a storm-cradled nation that fell.

Too poor to possess the precious ore,
   And too much a stranger to borrow,
We issue to-day, our "promise to pay,"
   And hope to redeem on the morrow.
      Days rolled by, and weeks became years,
       But our coffers were empty still,
      Coin was so rare that the treasurer quakes
       If a dollar should drop in the till.

But the faith that was in us was strong indeed,
   And our poverty well we discerned,
And these little checks represented the pay
   That our suffering veterans earned.
      We knew it had hardly a value in gold,
       Yet as gold the soldiers received it,
      It gazed in our eyes with a promise to pay,
       And each patriot soldier believed it.

But our boys thought little of price or pay,
  Or of bills that were over-due,
We knew if it bought our bread to-day,
  'Twas the best our country could do.
      Keep it! it tells all our history over,
        From the birth of the dream to its last;
      Modest, and born of the angel, Hope,
        Like our hope of success it passed!

GIVE THEM BREAD!

BY G. L. R.

Have you heard the calls for succor,
  Cries of hunger that have come,
From the land where want and sorrow,
  Shadow every stricken home?

From the land where blasted deserts
  Reign, where once the rose has bloomed,
Where ten thousands of her noblest,
  Bravest warriors lie entombed!

Where the wild tide of the battle,
  Like a fiery billow swept —
Where the flames from burning homesteads,
  High into the midnight leapt.

Where the streaming blood of heroes,
  Sinking 'neath the waves of fight,
Stained the earth so deep a crimson,
  That it changed the hue of night.

Have you heard them? then, oh hearken
  To the cries that swell to heaven!
Let a bounteous stream of mercies,
  To that stricken land be given.

Listen to the sad appealings,
  Listen to the cry for bread,
Listen to the widow-praying
  That her orphans may be fed!

Oh! by all the woe and suffering
  That a noble people bear—
By their anguish and their misery,
  By their weight of dark despair;

By their bright hopes, dead and withered,
  By the glories of their past,
By their drear and hopeless future,
  Where no cheering light   t;

By the ashes of their warriors,
  By each gallant life cut short,
By the white bones that are bleaching,
  Where the thousand fights were fought;

By the courage of their matrons,
  Proudly arming for the field,
E'en their youngest, there to conquer
  Or be borne back on his shield!

By the smiles that hid the breaking
  Heart of each chivalric maid,
When she bid her lover go forth,
  Bravely belting on his blade;

By the mourning for the fallen,
  By the mother's heart in grief,
By the wife's—the maiden's anguish,
  Deathless pain without relief;

By the graves of all their dearest,
  'Neath the distant battle plain,
Where in nameless charnel trenches,
  Sleeps the foeman with his slain ;

By their desolated hearth-stones,
  By each ruined fireside,
By the hovels where in hunger
  All the proudest now abide ;

By their courage in their sorrow,
  By their woe so grandly borne,
By their majesty—though conquered,
  By their chains so sternly worn ;

By the greatness of the living,
  By the memories of the dead,
Stretch the   th the hand of helping !
  By God   ve, oh, give them bread !

A WIND FROM THE SOUTH.

(Written for the Fair Journal.)

BY C. C.

  I sing of the South !
Not as she sat in her pride of yore,
Peace encircled from the gulf to shore,
Golden throned in her dreamful ease,
Lulled by a wandering tropic breeze—
Rich in fruitage, and rare in flowers,
Under the shelving orange bowers.

But in days that came,
When hand to hilt for her honor's sake,
Dearer far than the lives at stake,
Sweeping on to the battle's fore,
She flashed on, a bright Escalibore,
Where surging hosts made the deadliest fight,
She dared a world in her single might.

'Twas a form inspired,
That lion-like, as the struggle wore,
Starved, and bleeding at every pore,
Weak with famine, and faint for blood,
Brave in sinking, as when she stood,
Hunted, fell, in her own green glades,
Hacked and hewn by a hundred blades.

It is not for her!
This cry that echoes across the seas,
Of a nation's welfare, and peace and ease,
Nor the haughty banner that floats unfurled,
In the face of the startled Mother-world,
This roll of drums, and the trumpet's blare,
Mock the silence of her despair.

She is bereaved.
Her best and bravest are scattered far,
Fallen in conflict, and worn of war,
She has piled her sacrificial heaps,
Out in the voiceless ocean deeps,
In the dreary marsh, in the serpent's lair,
Her dead are sleeping—everywhere.

She loved them so!
God knows,—for He has given His own,
How closely knitted to flesh and bone,
The human ties that lie shattered here,
Watered by many a blinding tear.
He knows and cares—and there's one star's light,
In the blackest cloud of the blackest night.

20*

A wind from the South.
It has swept afar o'er a lonely plain,
And gathered strength for its sad refrain,
From the widow's wail for her hero dead,—
From the orphan's sharp, shrill cry for bread,—
From the exile's sigh, and the prison moan,
'Lost and gone,' is the monotone.

It is not in vain!
Ah! gentle women of Baltimore,
True ye are to the warm heart's core—
True ye are to the name ye bore,
When a suffering sister's lack was sore,
When ye sent your striplings at our need,
With a cheerful trust, and a stout God-speed.
True and tender, and often tried,
It is not now that ye turn aside.
'Tis pure religion and undefiled,
To feed the mouth of the starving child,
To kindle hope in the fainting breast,
To guide the homeless into rest,
And when a dire Apocalypse
Shall rend the veil of Heaven's eclipse,
This germ of Christ's own charity,
Shall blossom fair in the realm to be.

April 2, 1866.

TO THE LADIES OF BALTIMORE.

BY MRS. BETTIE C. LOCKE.

For those so fair, and kind and true, who felt for others'
    grief,
We of the south would now entwine fame's bright un-
    dying wreath!
In gratitude we still are rich; 'tis no mite of prayers and
    tears,
Is daily poured forth to Him, who in heaven kindly hears,

For blessings on the hearts and hands of those who knew
    our needs,
Yet not in words their comfort sent, but in glowing acts
    and deeds;
To renew our faith in human love, make drear homes
    bright once more,
Bring back a smile to grief-worn cheeks, hope to the
    cottage door.

Like rays of sunshine in the storm, shine out these deeds of
    love,
Touched with a sense of kindliness, e'en grim despair will
    move,
The widow mourning for her stay, who fell 'mid deeds of
    glory,
More thrilling than heroic deeds e'er penned in ancient
    story;
The mother, fair and young and sad, who gathers to her side
Her little ones, to tell of him who bravely fought and died;
And though born to gentler things, bitter want is at the
    door,
And they must face the world, with the rude, unpolished
    poor.

Maimed manhood sits and sighs beside the ashes of his
    home,
Where only stands the chimney-stack, to tell him all is
    gone;
The loving wife and gentle child—each dear tree, shrub
    and flower,
The trellis and the grape-vine that formed the garden
    bower.
No house dog bounds to meet his steps, the birds no
    longer sing,
Rank weeds are growing in the path, no willow shades the
    spring;
Rude soldiery have revelled, and left their traces there—
He turns away, unconquered, a stoic in despair.

But woman dear, inspired with love and pity for such
  grief,
Now bids the widow's heart rejoice and gives her sure
  relief.
The soldier's orphans and his wife are made to smile again,
And proud hearts cease their throbbing—such charity's
  no pain.
The homestead now is reared again o'er the ashes of the
  past,
And deeds of love have conquered the victory at last.
Southern hearts and southern homes will ever own the
  sway,
Of loving acts and kindly deeds, be the future what it
  may.

We had bright dreams, and cherished, but they have sadly
  fled,
And naught is left to cheer us, but our honor and our
  dead,
All this dreary hopelessness, and hearts that still are
  aching,
But the earth's green sod will soon, soon cover up their
  breaking ;
And when the flowers brightly bloom o'er all our desolation,
Where grew, and bloomed, and died, thy hopes, O !
  fallen Southern nation,
Fame will proudly point to all, that Charity whose
  power,
Has done so much to heal our woes and soothe our
  darkest hour.

SHENANDOAH VALLEY, *May*, 1866.

THE BLESSED HAND.

RESPECTFULLY DEDICATED TO THE LADIES OF THE SOUTHERN RELIEF FAIR.

BY S. T. WALLIS.

There is a legend of an English Monk, who died at the Monastery of Arem-
berg, where he had copied and illuminated many books, hoping to be
rewarded in Heaven. Long after his death his tomb was opened, and
nothing could be seen of his remains but the right hand, with which he
had done his pious work, and which had been miraculously preserved
from decay.

For you and me, who love the light
   Of God's uncloistered day,
It were, indeed, a dreary lot,
   To shut ourselves away
From every glad and sunny thing
   And pleasant sight and sound,
And pass, from out a silent cell,
   Into the silent ground.

Not so the good monk, Anselm, thought,
   For, in his cloister's shade,
The cheerful faith that lit his heart
   Its own sweet sunshine made;
And in its glow he prayed and wrote,
   From matin-song 'till even,
And trusted, in the Book of Life,
   To read his name in Heaven.

What holy books his gentle art
   Filled full of saintly lore!
What pages, brightened by his hand,
   The splendid missals bore!
What blossoms, almost fragrant, twined
   Around each blessed name,
And how his Saviour's cross and crown
   Shone out, from cloud and flame!

But, unto clerk as unto clown,
  Qne summons comes, alway,
And Brother Anselm heard the call,
  At vesper-chime, one day.
His busy pen was in his hand,
  His parchment by his side—
He bent him o'er the half-writ prayer,
  Kissed Jesu's name, and died!

They laid him where a window's blaze
  Flashed o'er the graven stone,
And seemed to touch his simple name,
  With pencil like his own;
And there he slept, and one by one,
  His brothers died, the while,
And trooping years went by, and trod
  His name from off the aisle.

And lifting up the pavement, then,
  An Abbot's couch to spread,
They let the jewelled sunlight in
  Where once lay Anselm's head.
No crumbling bone was there, no trace
  Of human dust that told,
But, all alone, a warm right hand
  Lay, fresh upon the mould.

It was not stiff, as dead men's are,
  But, with a tender clasp,
It seemed to hold an unseen hand
  Within its living grasp,
And ere the trembling monks could turn
  To hide their dazzled eyes,
It rose, as with a sound of wings,
  Right up into the skies!

Oh, loving, open hands, that give;
  Soft hands, the tear that dry;
Oh, patient hands, that toil to bless;
  How can ye, ever, die!

Ten thousand vows, from yearning hearts,
　To Heaven's own gates shall soar,
And bear you up, as Anselm's hand
　Those unseen angels bore !

Kind hands ! oh, never near to you
　May come the woes ye heal !
Oh, never may the hearts ye guard
　The griefs ye comfort feel !
May He, in whose sweet name ye build,
　So crown the work ye rear,
That ye may never clasped be,
　In one unanswered prayer !

BALTIMORE, *April* 8, 1866.

THE BLESSED HEART.

Suggested by "The Blessed Hand."

GRATEFULLY DEDICATED TO THE LADIES OF THE SOUTHERN RELIEF FAIR OF BALTIMORE,

BY MRS. M. M.

I sing not of "The Blessed Hand,"
　That has so well been sung,
Nor of the mercy-winged feet,
　Nor of the love-touched tongue ;
Each one being but the instrument —
　Mechanical — at best
A servant, though obedient
　Unto the *heart's* behest.

But that, that with my heart of hearts
　I now would try to sing,
Gives life to all, to all imparts
　An energizing spring.
It is — oh, how its very name
　The torpid feelings start ! —
To virtuous deeds, and noble acts,
　It is — The Blessed Heart !

What else inspired tongue, foot, and hand,
    Unto their work of love
For our poor ruined southern land!
    What might such mercy move,
But that blest influence divine!
    God's spirit doth impart,
When hand, and foot, and tongue obey
    Thy teachings, Blessed Heart.

I know a heart—a Blessed Heart—
    'Twill never, never die!
In numbing death it hath no part,
    Nor cold mortality.
In cold obstruction's apathy,
    Though buried 'neath the sod,
That Blessed Heart can never lie,
    Whose life is hid with God.

That heart has fired the faltering tongue,
    Bestirred the laggard feet,
The palsied hand has nerved, and sprung
    With vitalizing heat;
Each impulse for the right, the true,
    Has energized. Such part,
Ensures thee immortality,
    Thou ever Blessed Heart!

The Blessed Heart whose life is love—
    Not legendary lore,
But Christian faith instructeth us,
    Shall live forevermore—
Live, when the gross material all
    Hath vanished as a dream,
Live, when time's flowers have floated down
    Oblivion's silent stream.

Oh, living, loving hearts that move
    The hands to deeds sublime,
Whose boundless charity and love
    Are bounded by no clime!

Oh, may the blessings you have shower'd
  On this dear land of ours,
Reflexly on yourselves return
  In rich and copious showers!

Oh, may those hearts, those noble hearts
  That liberal things devise,
That in sweet mercy's works abound,
  And find blest exercise
In deeds of piety and love,
  Be bless'd as they have bless'd,
And find, in Heaven's approving smile,
  Their sure reward and best!

Oh, may their prayers and tears for us,
  Their gifts on us bestow'd,
As their memorial, go up
  Before the throne of God!
Oh, may we meet before that throne,
  Meet, never more to part,
The ones that here on earth have shown
  Thy fruits, oh, Blessed Heart!

Columbia, S. C.

TO MISS ——, OF VA.

BY " STELLA."

Hail gentle patron of our stricken land!
  Thrice welcome to our ever grateful shore;
When God hath chastened, should not woman's hand
  Leap kindly forth, the healing balm to pour?
"Vengeance is mine," proclaims the Thunderer's voice—
"But thine to bid the smitten one rejoice,
To cool the brow, the fevered wound to dress,
To wipe the tear from sorrow's eye, and soothe the heart's
  distress."

When late, Wars' trump had called to civil strife,
And our sunny land, with hate and rancor rife,
　　Had drunk the blood by hostile brother shed;
　　When the proud victor, with triumphant tread
　　Had trampled o'er the vanquished's gory bed,
When the gushing tide of ebbing life,
　　Had from the unconscious martyr fled,
Thy form was seen, amid the battle's din,
Like angel visiting our fallen world of sin.

Resume thy mission, gentle one; thy task.
Is but begun — our sons no more may ask
　　The guerdon of thy life-restoring hand —
　　The daughters of our suffering southern land
Demand thine aid. When th' exhausted flask
Of material good is emptied to the dregs,
　　And the stern spikes and clamps secure the gold
　　By which the stores of mental wealth are sold,
Who shall unlock the mind's rich ore, for which the nation
　　begs?

Virginia asks thine aid. Her desolated homes,
Her prostrate altars, and her ruined domes,
All bid thee aid to spread fair science' light,
And roll aloof the clouds of gothic night.
And Carolina begs, her mental soil
Dark ignorance may not her heritage despoil.
　　Mioja's cavern echoes Georgia's strain,
While mountain gorge, and copse, and glen,
　　In wild mirsule, respond the notes again.
And over all, the adamantine hills roll back the loud Amen!

Hark! from the orange-groves, o'er the coral strand,
　　Mingled with perfume and wild melody,
A voice comes bounding from the flowery land —
　　Fair Florida prefers her prayer to thee,
In tones as soft as streamlets' murmuring wave,
Or syren's minstrelsy in ocean's cave.
Now Alabama adds her welcome here,
Adorned with all the glow of gratitude's bright tear.

Lo ! Mississippi droops her suppliant head,
  And from Magnolia's chalice, pledges thee
  Her golden coffers, so thou set her Davis free.
Vain offering !   Rather say, her heart's best incense shed
Is poor return for one so rich a boon.
Oh, kind one ! help to free the captive soon,
Ere the lurid light of the prison's gloom
Be changed for the night of the silent tomb !

  ALABAMA, *August* 1, 1866.

THE WASTE OF WAR.

Give me the gold that war had cost,
  Before this peace-expanding day,
The wasted skill, the labor lost,
  The mental treasure thrown away,
And I will buy each rood of soil
  In every yet discovered land,
Where hunters roam, where peasants toil,
  Where many peopled cities stand.

I'll clothe each shivering wretch on earth,
  In needful, aye, in brave attire —
Vesture befitting banquet mirth,
  Which kings might envy and admire.
In every vale, on every plain,
  A school shall glad the gazer's sight,
Where every poor man's child may gain
  Pure knowledge, free as air and light.

I'll build asylums for the poor,
  By age or ailment made forlorn ;
And none shall thrust them from the door,
  Or sting with looks or words of scorn.

I'll link each alien hemisphere,
  Help honest men to conquer wrong,
Art, science, labor, nerve and cheer,
  Reward the poet for his song.

In every free and peopled clime,
  A vast Walhalla-hall shall stand:
A marble edifice sublime,
  For the illustrious of the land —
A Pantheon for the truly great,
  The wise, benificent and just —
A place of wide and lofty state,
  To honor and to hold their dust.

OUR DEAD.

BY COL. A. M. HOBBY.

"My house shall be called of all nations, the house of prayer; but ye have
made it a den of thieves."
  "Beware of false prophets which come to you in sheep's clothing; but in-
wardly, they are ravening wolves."
  "It was the worst work that Satan and sin undertook in this world; and
they that suffered in it, were not martyrs in a good cause, but convicts in a
bad one. 'Who shall comfort them that sit by dishonored graves?'"—*Sermon of Henry Ward Beecher.*

Vile, brutal man! and darest thou
  In God's annointed place to preach—
With impious tongue and brazen brow—
  The lessons Hell would blush to teach?
The cruel taunt thy lips have hissed,
  Beneath Religion's holy screen,
Is false—as false Iscariot's kiss,
  Is false—as thou art vile and mean.

Are these the lessons which He taught?
  And was his mission here in vain?
Peace and good will seem words of naught—
  Hell rules the earth with hate again!

And thou! its chosen instrument,
  Hyena-like, with heartless tread,
Hast dared invade, with blood-hound scent,
  The sacred precincts of the dead.

Not such from those, dear brave old South,
  Who met thee in thine hour of might!
But from the coarse, polluted mouth
  Of coward cur who feared to fight.
Dear loved old South! Contemn the curse
  That those who hate shall heap on you;
You've wept behind War's bloody hearse,
  That bore away your brave and true!

Their precious blood, though vainly shed!
  Long as thy shore old Ocean laves,
We'll bow with reverence o'er our dead,
  And bless the turf that wraps their graves.
From Mexico to Maryland,
  Those graves are strewn like autumn leaves—
What though no mother's tender hand
  Upon their tomb a chaplet weaves;

Nor wives, nor sisters bend above
  The Honored Soldiér's unmarked mound—
They are objects of eternal love
  In consecrated Southern ground.
It recks not where their bodies lie—
  By bloody hill-side, plain or river—
Their names are bright on Fame's proud sky,
  Their deeds of valor live forever.

The song-birds of the South shall sing
  From forests grand, and flowery stem,
And gentlest waters murmuring,
  Unite to hymn their requiem.
And Spring will deck their hallowed bed
  With types of resurrection's day;
And silent tears the Night hath shed,
  The Morning's beam will kiss away.

Those heroes rest in solemn fame
  On every field where Freedom bled;
And shall we let the touch of shame
  Fall like a blight upon our dead?
No! wretch! we scorn thy hatred now,
  And hiss thy shame from pole to pole;
The brutes are better far than thou,
  A beast might blush to own thy soul.

"Dishonored graves?" take back the lie
  That's breathed by more than human hate,
Lest, Ananias like, you die,
  Not less deserving of his fate.
Our Spartan women bow in dust,
  Around their country's broken shrine,
True—as their souls are noble—just,
  Pure—as their deeds have been divine;

Their Angel hands the wounded cheered—
  Did all that woman ever dares—
When wealth and homes had disappeared,
  They gave us tears, and smiles, and prayers.
They proudly gave their jewels up—
  For all they loved—as worthless toys;
Drank to the dregs Want's bitter cup
  To feed our sick and starving boys.

Their glorious flag on high no more
  Is borne by that unconquered band;
'Tis furled upon the "silent shore"—
  Its heroes around it stand.
No more beneath its folds shall meet
  The armies of immortal LEE;
The rolling of their drums last beat
  Is echoing in eternity!

Galveston News, Texas, Jan., 1866.

THE CONFEDERATE DEAD.

BY LATIENNE.

From the broad and calm Potomac,
    To the Rio Grande's waves,
Have the brave and noble fallen—
    And the earth is strewn with graves,
In the vale and on the hill side,
    Through the wood and by the stream,
Has the martial pageant faded,
    Like the vision of a dream.

Where the reveille resounded,
    And the stirring call "to arms,"
Nod the downy heads of clover
    To the wind's mesmeric charms;
Where the heels of trampling squadrons
    Beat to dust the mountain pass,
Hang the dew-drops fragile crystals
    From the slender stems of grass.

Where the shocks of meeting armies
    Roused the air in raging waves,
And with sad and hollow groanings,
    Echoed earth's deep-hidden caves;
Where the cries of crushed and dying
    Pierced the elemental strife,
Where lay Death in sick'ning horror
    'Neath the maddened rush of life;

Quiet now reigns, sweet and pensive,
    All is hushed in dreamless rest,
And the pitying arms of Nature
    Holds our heroes on her breast;

Shield them well, oh tender mother,
　While the winds in tender breath
Whisper us, the sad survivors,
　Of their victory in death.

What though no stately column,
　Their cherished names may raise,
To dim the eye and move the lip
　With gratitude and praise.
The blue sky, hung with bannered clouds,
　Their solemn dome shall be,
All Heaven's choiring winds shall chant
　The anthem of the free.

The Spring with vine-clad arms shall clasp,
　Their hillocked resting places,
And summer roses droop above
　With flushed and dewy faces;
Fair daises, rayed and crowned, shall spring
　Like stars from out their dust,
And look to kindred stars on high
　With eyes of patient trust.

And vainly shall the witling's lips
　Assail with envious dart
The fame of our heroic dead,
　Whose stronghold is the heart—
The nation's heart—not wholly crushed,
　Though each throb be in pain;
For Life and Hope will still survive,　　　—
　Where Love and Faith remain.

EUFAULA, ALA., *June.*　　　　　　　　　　*From the Macon Journal.*

SONG.

Air—"Faintly flow thy falling river."

Here we bring a fragrant tribute,
　To the bed where valor sleeps,
Though they missed the victor's triumph,
　O'er their tomb a nation weeps.
Honor through all time be rendered,
　To their proud, heroic names,
Fondly be their mem'ry cherished,
　Bright their never dying fame.

Glowing in young manhood's beauty,
　Sprang they at their country's call,
Made before the foeman's legions,
　'Round our homes a living wall.
By disease's foul breath withered,
　Ere had dawned the battle day,
On the fever couch of anguish,
　Thousands passed from earth away.

Thousands, after deeds whose daring
　With their glory filled the land,
Fell before the flying foeman,
　On the fields won by their hand.
Mourning o'er the fruitless struggle,
　Bowed beneath the hand of God,
Come we weeping and yet proudly,
　Now to deck this sacred sod.

21

LINES

Read at the Celebration of the Memorial Association of Richmond, at Holly-
wood Cemetery, May 10th, 1866.

No nobler cause than this of thine,
   May woman's heart engage,
She needs no prouder place to win
   On Fame's immortal page:
Go seek them in their graves unknown;
   And by the genial powers,
Bid on each spot in beauty spring
   A sisterhood of flowers.

No marble slab, or graven stone,
   Their gallant deeds to tell;
No monument to mark the spot
   Where they with glory fell:
Their names shall yet a herald find
   In every tongue of fame,
When valley, stream, and minstrel voice,
   Shall ring with their acclaim.

Plant flowers above their lonely graves,
   The ivy let entwine
Its tendrils there, and there be set
   The myrtle and the vine;
Memorials of your love shall mark
   Each consecrated place,
And angels wandering down from Heaven,
   Will love the spot to trace.

All o'er the land like autumn leaves,
   Borne on the wailing blast,
They lie with no mementoes raised,
   To link them with the past.
Then bid the sculptured stone renew
   The story of their fame—
Some monument to after-time,
   Their glory to proclaim.

Bring flowers to deck each patriot grave,
   And bless the vernal sod,
Where sleep those fallen ones, whose deeds
   Are written with their God;
Place the white stone above each head—
   The sacred spot enclose—
That no invading step may break
   The calm of their repose.

LINES.

These lines, dedicated by Florence Anderson to the memory of the Confederate dead in Bourbon county, Ky., were read upon the occasion of a floral tribute paid by the ladies of the county. Two crosses were placed on each grave, one of fading flowers, the other of evergreen.

They fell on the march, while Hope was bright,
Before the clouds of Disaster's Night
   Had shut out each lingering star,
They heard the pæans of Victory sound,
As they passed through the "dark and bloody ground,"
   In all the power of war.

Fair ladies smiled, and with delicate hands
Greeted the march of their gallant bands,
    Fresh from the bloody fight!
As the music from red lips rang cheerily out,
The soldiers answered with song and shout,
    In token of their delight.

Onward they moved in a living stream,
(We recall it now as a strange, wild dream,)
    That brave and toil-worn throng;
We see the flutter of banners old,
Whose tales of glory will yet be told
    In poet's proudest song.

Riddled with bullets, these flags wave high —
Radiant with names that will never die,
    While men are alive to fame!
At Belmont and Shiloh, on Richmond's field,
Where five-times his numbers to Cleburne yield,
    Had they won a deathless name!

Not long our hearts to their music beat;
Not long each road and thronged street
    Echoed beneath their tread;
Then glad, bright eyes with sorrow wept,
As the gallant army backward swept,
    Leaving its honored dead.

Calmly through storms of the past four years —
Through all the anguish of blood and tears —
    These have slept in each lowly tomb;
The War is o'er, and the Cause not won,
For which such glorious deeds were done,
    And sad is our people's doom!

But the legacy left we will not forget,
Though the day is o'er, and our sun has set,
    And the people are not free —
To gather the dust of the martyr-dead,
Lying uncared for in lowliest bed,
    And under the way-side tree.

With reverent hands, from our summer bowers
We'll cull fresh wreaths of our brightest flowers,
    To grace each humble grave:
They came from the fair South's sunny lands,
With true, brave hearts, and with ready hands,
    Our heritage to save!

Plant the two crosses o'er each still breast
Of those who have entered the soldier's rest —
    Who died for their native land!
One, fading emblem of our greatest loss,
A withered hope, like the Southern Cross,
    Fallen from the hero's hand!

The other of EVERGREEN, emblem of Fame,
Which will wreathe a halo about each name,
    As radiant as Glory's sun!
These "ashes of glory"—this sacred dust —
Shall be to Kentucky a holy trust,
    'Tis brave work they have done!

Rest then, in peace, beneath these green leaves,
Lulled by the sigh of the wind as it grieves,
    And shakes the magnolia's bloom!
Rest, though far from your loved southern land,
Your own blossoms, nursed by a fair stranger's hand,
    Shall fall o'er each honored tomb!

    21*

OUR CHERISHED DEAD.

What tho' no stately column,
  Their cherished names may raise,
To dim the eye, and move the lip,
  With gratitude and praise!
The blue sky, hung with bannered clouds,
  Their solemn domes shall be,
All Heaven's choiring winds shall chant
  The anthem of the free.

The Spring with vine-clad arms shall clasp
  Their humble resting places,
And Summer roses droop above,
  With flushed and dewy faces.
For daisies rayed and crowned shall spring,
  Like stars from out their dust,
And look to kindred stars on high,
  With eyes of patient trust.

And vainly shall the witling's lips,
  Assail with envious dart
The fame of our heroic dead,
  Whose stronghold is the heart;
The *Nation's* heart — not crushed,
  Tho'. each throb be in pain,
For Life and Hope must still survive,
  Where Love and Faith remain.

APRIL 26TH.

In the ceremonies at Memphis, Tenn., 26th April, " In Memory of the Confederate Dead," Dr. Ford (one of the Speakers,) improvised the following
appropriate lines.

In rank and file, in sad array,
  As tho' their watch still keeping,
Or waiting for the battle fray,
  The dead around are sleeping.
Shoulder to shoulder rests each rank
  As at their posts still standing,
Subdued, yet steadfast, as they sank
  To sleep at death's commanding.
No battle banner o'er them waves,
  No battle trump is sounded,
They've reached the citadel of graves,
  And *here* their arms are grounded!

*   *   *   *   *

Their hallowed memory ne'er shall die,
  But ever fresh and vernal,
Shall wake from flowers the soft sad sigh,
  Regrets—regrets eternal!

HOME—AFTER THE WAR.

BY M. E. H.

In the grassy lane, as the sun went down,
  He slackened his fevered and weary feet,
Behind, lay the ruined and battered town,
  Before him the country, deserted yet sweet!
Before him too, loomed the sunset sky,
Where the lurid clouds blazed brilliantly.

There were woodlands, green uplands, and rolling hills,
  Fairy-like stretches of land and mist,
Labyrinths of thickets, and silent rills,
  That threaded the meadows like amethyst;
A valley barren of aught but trees,
Whose pennons of branches swung wild in the breeze.

Like one a-dreaming, with face downcast,
  He stood, unheeding the fading day,
'Till darkness surrounding, awoke him at last,
  When, clutching his musket, he strode away,
First right, then left, 'till he crossed the wood,
Close girding the valley's solitude.

No chirp of cricket, no twitter of birds,
  Woke here the dread quiet that gathered around,
No laughter, no welcome to home-driven herds,
  No home's happy mirth in the silence profound —
Only *his* step crushed the withered grass,
Only *his* voice moaned a hapless "Alas!"

As his glance searched wildly that old, old scene,
  His sorrowful face blanched a paler hue,
No trace where loved household fires had been,
  No vestige of Home in that dusky view;
Only charred timbers, and ridges of stone,
And chimneys dismantled and overthrown.

Rank grasses waved in the roofless space,
  And dark moss crested each fallen wall,
And he turned away with a rigid face,
  For desolation enshrouded *all* ;
Such ruin *he* little had thought to see,
And his heart surged o'er with its misery.

"I fain would linger," he gloomily said,
  "But home is no longer home for me;
Here bats go circling about my head,
  And the owl is monarch of all he can see.
No wife's ear to heed my returning feet,
No children to sate me with kisses sweet.

"If I could, I would blot from my heart those years
  That have flown since last on this spot I stood:
Those terrible years of anguish-wrung tears,
  And battle-fields streaming with human blood,
Where I and legions have recklessly fought,
For the country our forefathers' lives had bought.

"Armed numbers have conquered, while I have lost
  Ev'ry dear heart-blossom that brightened life,
And all that is left me is memory, crost
  With broken visions of home and strife.
Home? No more home for the soldier's head,
Save the final one shelt'ring his slumbering dead!"

BALTIMORE.

THE VANQUISHED PATRIOT'S PRAYER.

Ruler of nations! bow thy ear—
  I cannot understand
Thy ways,—but Thou wilt heed this prayer
  For my beloved Land.

Dear for young joys and earnest toil,
　Through many a stirring year;
My kindred's blood has dyed her soil,
　And made her trebly dear.

Teach me to sorrow with my land,
　Yet not to hate her foe,
To bow submissive to thy hand,
　Which dealt the chastening blow.

Withholden by thy sovereign will,
　What pain I would implore,
Give us some blessing richer still,
　From out Thy boundless store.

Though now denied our blood-bought right,
　Yet grant us, Lord, to be
In Thine, and every nation's sight,
　Worthy of Liberty!

Pilgrims and strangers in the world—
　No land to call our home,
Our banner from its station hurled—
　Our freedom from its throne;

Let us not seek in scenes of mirth
　For surcease from our grief,
Help us to turn to Heaven from Earth—
　Find only there relief.

To suffer with a suffering race—
　Their bitter cup to share—
Look on that cross with patient face,
　Which vanquished patriots bear.

May Heaven draw us more and more,
  Earth less entrancing be—
Until we reach the shining shore,
  And once again be free.

Dear fettered land! this heart is given
  'Till death—to thine and thee;
When I forget thy wrongs—may Heaven
  Cease to remember me!

Amen! Amen!

HEAVEN.

Beyond these chilling winds and gloomy skies,
  Beyond death's cloudy portal,
There is a land where beauty never dies,
  And love becomes immortal.

A land whose light is never dimmed by shade,
  Whose fields are ever vernal,
Where nothing beautiful can ever fade,
  But blooms for aye — eternal.

We may not know how sweet its balmy air,
  How bright and fair its flowers;
We may not hear the songs that echo there,
  Through those enchanted bowers.

The city's shining towers we may not see,
  With our dim earthly vision,
For death, the silent warder, keeps the key,
  That opes those gates Elysian.

But sometimes, when adown the western sky,
  The fiery sunset lingers,
Its golden gates swing inward, noiselessly,
  Unlocked by unseen fingers.

And while they stand a moment half ajar,
  Gleams from the inner glory
Stream brightly through the azure vault afar,
  And half reveal the story.

Oh, land unknown! Oh, land of the divine!
  Father, All-Wise, Eternal,
Guide, guide these wandering, wayworn feet of mine
  Into those pastures vernal!

LAW AND MISCELLANEOUS BOOKS, &c.

Published by MURPHY & CO., Baltimore.

A Digest of the Decisions, Construing the Statutes of Maryland, of which the Code of Public General Laws is Composed; with Specifications of the Acts of Assembly. By LEWIS MAYER, of the Baltimore Bar. 1 vol., 8o., uniform with the Maryland Code, price...$8 00

This Work comprises a Digest of all the Decisions of the Courts of Maryland, contained in the volumes of Reports, viz.:

Harris & McHenry, 4 vols.	Gill & Johnson, 12 vols.
Harris & Johnson, 7 vols.	Md. Chancery Decisions, 4 vols.
Bland's Chancery Rep., 3 vols.	Gill, 9 vols.
Harris & Gill, 2 vols.	Md., 20 vols.

And of the Decisions of the Supreme Court of the United States, from Dallas to Wallace, construing or explaining the Acts of Assembly, which compose the Maryland Code of Public General Laws.

The Work is prefaced with two Lists of the Acts of Assembly composing the Code of Public General Laws; in one, the Title of each Article is given, and References to the Acts composing the Sections of each Article placed opposite the corresponding Sections, and, in the other, the Acts are arranged chronologically with References to the Articles and Sections where they are found.

It embodies, also, all the modifications of the Code by Legislatures subsequent to its adoption, to the end of the January Session of 1866.

The Digest of Decisions is arranged into Articles, and Sections corresponding to the divisions of the Code. All the Decisions on the Acts of Assembly, composing each Section of the Articles of the Code, are placed under such Section, headed by an Index of the Contents of the Section and a Specification of the Acts of which it is composed. A copious Index is given.

The Maryland Code, Containing all the Public General and Public Local Laws now in Force in the *State of Maryland,* compiled by OTHO SCOTT and HIRAM McCULLOUGH, Commissioners; adopted by the Legislature of Maryland, January Session, 1860, the Acts of that Session being therewith incorporated; with an Index to each Article and Section. By HENRY C. MACKALL, of the Maryland Bar. Second Edition. 2 vols., 8o., law sheep,..........$8 00

This Great Work, the preparation of which has cost the State upwards of $50,-000, is universally conceded to be a complete and perfect Compendium of our State Law, from the Provincial period, to the close of the January Session of 1860, made accessible by an elaborate and well digested Index, should be secured by every member of the Legal Profession, every Law Officer, Merchant, Manufacturer, Farmer, Mechanic, and every Citizen.

1st Supplement to the Maryland Code, Containing the Acts of the General Assembly passed at the Extra Sessions of 1861, and the Regular Session of 1862, divided into "Public General and Public Local Laws," and arranged in Articles and Sections to correspond with the Code. Also, an APPENDIX, containing the Private Acts and the Resolutions of the Extra Sessions of 1861, and the Regular Session of 1862, in Alphabetical and Numerical Order. By H. C. MACKALL, Esq. To which is added, the CONSTITUTION OF MARYLAND, with References to the Decisions of the Court of Appeals, and the CONSTITUTION OF THE UNITED STATES, with Notes and References to the Decisions of the Supreme Court. The whole carefully and accurately Indexed. By E. OTIS HINKLEY, of the Baltimore Bar. In 1 vol., 8o., uniform with the Code, price...$4 00

2d Supplement to the Maryland Code, Containing all the General and Local Laws passed by the Legislature at the January Session, 1864, arranged under their proper Titles, to correspond with the Code, accompanied with accurate TABLES, showing at a glance the Articles and Sections of the Code Repealed or Amended, with References to the Chapter and Section by which Amended or Repealed; to which is added, in an APPENDIX, References to the Private Acts and Resolutions. The whole carefully Indexed. By LEWIS MAYER, of the Baltimore Bar. To which is added the NEW CONSTITUTION OF MARYLAND, with Marginal Notes, References, &c. By EDWARD OTIS HINKLEY, of the Baltimore Bar. In 1 vol., 8o., uniform with the Code, price................$4 00

3d Supplement to the Maryland Code, Containing all the General and Local Laws passed by the Legislature, at the January Session, 1865. Uniform with the other volumes..$3 00

☞ **The Code and Supplements,** complete in 5 vols...**$18 00**

MURPHY & Co. *Publishers and Booksellers, Baltimore.*

www.ingramcontent.com/pod-product-compliance
Lightning Source LLC
Chambersburg PA
CBHW022014110726
47901CB00006B/1524